BORIS THE BEAR-HUNTER

BY FRED WHISHAW

LONDON, EDINBURGH,
AND NEW YORK
THOMAS NELSON
AND SONS

CONTENTS

I.	The Hunter Hunted
II.	Boris Finds a New Friend
III.	Boris Changes Masters
IV.	Boris Goes A-sailing
V.	How Peter the Great was knocked over
VI.	A Taste of the Knout
VII.	A Race for Life
VIII.	Boris and his Fellow-Officers
IX.	One Sword against Five
X.	A Night Ambush
XI.	A Battle against Odds
XII.	A Perilous Slide
XIII.	Boris Goes on the War-path

XIV.	Taken Prisoner
XV.	An Exciting Escape
XVI.	Home Again
XVII.	Off to England
XVIII.	How Boris threw a Big Dutchman Overboard
XIX.	Bad News from Moscow
XX.	Boris in Disgrace
XXI.	Nancy and the Big Bear
XXII.	A Wolf Maiden
XXIII.	A Notable Day among the Wolves
XXIV.	With the Tsar Again
XXV.	Boris has a Narrow Escape
XXVI.	How Boris Outwitted the Swedish Admiral
XXVII.	Small Beginnings of a Great City

XXVIII.	How the Swedes Erected a Gibbet for Boris
XXIX.	Mazeppa
XXX.	Russia's Great Day
XXXI.	Peace at Last
Biography	Frederick James Whishaw

LIST OF ILLUSTRATIONS

"The huge brute was in full pursuit of his young wife"

"That moment saved the Thar's life"

"Slashing at the wolves which swarmed about him"

"In an instant the two were upon him"

"Out sprang Boris, and alighted with terrific force upon Menshikoff's back"

"Boris lifted his kicking legs and slid them over the bulwark"

"Bringing up his clenched fists together against the fellow's chin"

BORIS THE BEAR-HUNTER.

CHAPTER I.

THE HUNTER HUNTED.

The moment at which I propose to introduce my readers to Boris the Bear-Hunter came very near, as it happened, to being the last which my hero was destined to spend upon this earth. Great hunter as Boris was, there is no doubt about it that on this particular occasion he met his match, and came within measurable distance of defeat at the hands—or rather paws—of one of the very creatures whose overthrow was at once his profession and his glory.

It happened many a year ago—about two hundred, in fact; and the scene of Boris's adventure was an exceedingly remote one, far away in the north of Europe, close to Archangel.

Boris Ivanitch was a peasant whose home was an outlying village near the large town just mentioned. He was a serf, of course, as were all his fellows at that time; but in consequence of his wonderful strength and courage, and of his aptitude for pursuing and killing every kind of wild beast and game, he was exempt, by favour of his lord, both from taxation and from the manual labour which the owner of the soil could have exacted from him. In a word, Boris was employed to keep the country clear, or as clear as possible, of bears and wolves, which, when left to themselves, were at that time the cause of much danger and loss to the inhabitants of that portion of the Russian empire.

Boris performed his duties well. There was no man, young or old, for hundreds of miles around who could compare with this young giant in any of those sports or competitions in which the palm went to the strongest. Tall and muscular beyond his years—for he was but nineteen at this time—lithe as a willow, straight as a poplar, Boris excelled in anything which called into play the qualities of activity and strength. Had he lived in our day and attended an English public school, he would undoubtedly have come to the front, whether on the cricket or the football field, on the running path or on the river. But being debarred from the privileges of English schoolboys, Boris was obliged to expend his energies in those exercises which were open to him, and which alone were familiar to the people of his country—snow-shoeing, hunting, swimming, and similar sports natural to the livers of a wild, outdoor life in a scarcely civilized land.

It was early summer-time, and the woods, or rather forests, about Archangel were in their fullest heyday of life and beauty. Hundreds of square miles of pine trees were the principal feature of the landscape, dotted here and there by a patch of cultivated land, or watched over by a tumble-down village nestling beneath the shadow of the forest. Oats and wheat, now fast ripening, waved in the soft air of June, and told of peace and plenty for those who took the trouble to till the generous soil for a living. The prospects of the crops around Dubinka, Boris's village, appeared at first sight to be promising enough—the rye was tall and nearly ripe, and the oats were doing capitally; but had you asked the peasants, the owners of the crops, they would have told you, with the lamentations common to the Russian peasant, that God had certainly been very good to them and sent them a fine harvest, but that the devil had spoiled all the good work by sending two large bears to eat up and trample down the fruits of the field, and to ruin the poor peasants. Ivan's field was half eaten up already, they would have said, and Andrey's would go next. And Boris couldn't find the bears, or he would soon give them "something in their stomachs better for them than the peasants' oats;" but there was no snow, and Boris could not track them without it, though he had been after the brutes for a fortnight and more.

This was all true enough—indeed, Boris was "after them" at the present moment, though to look at him you would scarcely have thought it; for the hunter was busily engaged strolling lazily through the forest, picking and enjoying the beautiful wild strawberries which covered the ground in profusion. He had propped his bear-spear against a tree, and was at the moment some distance from the weapon—tempted away from it against his usual habit by the peculiar lusciousness of the fruit, which was warm from the sun, and very delicious.

Even strawberry eating palls at length upon the satiated palate, and Boris began to think that he had had enough. He would now resume, he thought, his search for those marauding bears who had broken into the village corn-fields and destroyed the peace of the poor peasants. So he picked one more handful of the strawberries, crammed them into his mouth, sighed, glanced regretfully at the delicious fruit at his feet, and finally raised his head to look for his bear-spear. As he did so, he became aware of a huge form standing close at hand, some ten yards away, showing its teeth, and quietly watching his movements. It was a bear!

Boris's first feeling was one of great joy at meeting his enemy at last; his second was one of dismay as he realized the want of his trusty spear.

It must not for a moment be supposed that Boris was alarmed by the situation. If any one had told him that he was in a situation of peril, he would have laughed aloud at the very idea of such a thing. His regret was caused solely by the fear that, being unarmed, he might lose the opportunity of doing business with that bear upon this particular occasion, and would probably have to find him again before settling accounts.

Hoping to catch sight of his spear, and to reach it before the bear could make off, Boris backed slowly towards the place where he thought he had left the weapon. Bruin did not, as he had expected, give a loud roar to show his enemy that he was an awful fellow if he liked, and then straightway turn and run. On the contrary, the brute advanced towards the hunter, growling and showing certain very large and business-like teeth. Then Boris felt that it would be well to find that spear of his as quickly as possible, for he had no other weapon about him, and the bear appeared to be very much in earnest. So the hunter turned and ran, with the bear at his heels.

At first Boris rather enjoyed the chase. It would be an amusing story to tell at the village when he arrived there with the bear's skin. How the peasants would all laugh, and how they would sing and make merry in the evening over the downfall of their enemy! Boris could afford to tell a good story about himself and a bear, even though the laugh had been on the bear's side to begin with, if he produced the skin of the bear at the same time.

Yes, *if*. But the growling of the brute sounded rather close at his ear, and Boris was forced to dodge in and out between the tree trunks in order to avoid capture.

As the moments passed, and he grew more and more out of breath, Boris longed eagerly for the welcome sight of his bear-spear. Once or twice the bear had so nearly collared him that he bethought him that he must devise some plan by which to gain a little breath. A roar and a rush from behind at this moment, together with the loss of a considerable portion of the tail of his shirt, which, being worn outside the trousers, Russian fashion, had fluttered in the breeze, made it plain that there was no time to be lost. He must take to a tree and gain time. So Boris pulled himself together, put on a mighty spurt, and was five feet up the stem of a pine tree just as Bruin reached the foot of it, and rose on his hind legs to follow him aloft.

Up went Boris and up went Bruin, both fine climbers, and both scrambling and puffing as though their very lives depended upon their agility, as indeed was the case so far as concerned one at least of them. Quick as he was, Boris was nearly caught. He had barely time to climb along a branch and let himself fall to the earth, when the bear was already upon the same bough and looking down after him, meditating as to whether he too should drop to the ground or adopt the slower and safer course of climbing down again by the trunk, as he had come up. Luckily for Boris the discretion of that bear prevailed over his desire to save time, and he decided upon the slower method of descent. This decision gave Boris a moment or two of breathing time, which he sadly required.

He sat down to rest, and looked around frantically in every direction in hopes of catching sight of his spear. That action nearly cost him his life. The bear, impatient as bears are when irritated, could not tolerate the slow process of descending which it had chosen, and when half-way down the stem of the pine had dropped the rest of the way in order to gain time. Boris was barely able to rise and slip away when the heavy brute dropped upon the very spot where he had been sitting. Away went Boris, slightly refreshed, and with his "second wind" coming on, and after him flew Bruin, furious and determined. Again Boris dodged and ran, and ran and dodged, and again he felt the hot breath and heard the loud pants and growls at his ear; again his breath began to fail him, and his heart as well, when, just as he was nearly spent, his eye fell upon that which was to him at that moment the fairest sight that ever his eye beheld—his beloved spear leaning against a tree-trunk one hundred yards away.

CHAPTER II.

BORIS FINDS A NEW FRIEND.

Boris was so exhausted with the long chase that he had hardly sufficient strength to reach the weapon and turn it against his furious pursuer. To do this he must gain ground upon the bear, which was at the instant so close behind that he could have kicked it with his heel. Summoning therefore all the energy of which he was still master, the hunted hunter filled his lungs to the full, and started to run the fastest hundred yards that he had ever covered. So swiftly did he fly over the ground that he was some twenty-five good paces in front of the bear when his hands closed upon his faithful spear, and he knew that, for the moment at least, he was saved, and that if only his strength did not fail him he should now hold his own and perhaps a little more when Bruin came to close quarters.

Twisting round with the rapidity of a spindle, Boris felt for a steady foothold for both of his feet, found it, poised his long steel-tipped wooden spear, took a long, deep breath, set his teeth, and in a moment the struggle had commenced. The bear, slightly rising on his hind legs to seize and hug his foe, threw himself with a loud roar of rage upon Boris, impaling himself as he did so upon the cruel point of the spear. This was a critical moment. Strong as he was, and firmly as he had taken his stand, the shock of the huge brute's rush all but knocked poor weary Boris off his legs and nearly tore his muscular arms from their sockets. The bear, mad with pain and rage, pressed in its fury upon the stout spear, and bit and tore at the good oak until the splinters flew and the whole spear shook and trembled in the hunter's grasp.

Breathless and weary as he was, Boris nevertheless held his own, and for some time budged not an inch.

There is a limit, however, to the powers of the hardest muscles and of the stoutest hearts, and the present tension was more than the bravest and the strongest could support for any length of time. Boris was evidently tiring. Had he been fresh when this great wrestling match began, he would long since have made an irresistible rush, pushed the monster over backwards, and despatched him with repeated digs of the spear, as he had many a time treated bears before. But Boris was weary with his long struggle. He could not hold on much longer, but in desperation he still clung to his quivering spear, and pushed with all his might and determination against his giant enemy.

And now his head began to swim, and his eyes grew hot and dimmed, and there was a sound in his ears as of waters that rushed in and overwhelmed him. Still his senses did not desert him, nor his nerve. As he became conscious that his strength was failing him he became the more determined to hold out, and with a hoarse shout of defiance he pulled himself together for one supreme effort. His failing grasp clutched tighter at the shaft; his stiff and aching feet planted themselves yet more firmly in their grip of the foothold from which they had not budged by a hair's-breadth; his tightened muscles tightened themselves yet more as he bore upon the shaft, and forced it by sheer strength of will a couple of inches further towards victory. The bear tottered, his eyes rolled and his tongue showed between his teeth, and for a moment it seemed that Boris had won the battle. Now it is anybody's game! For an instant and another neither bear nor man has the advantage. Then the bear rallies. Growling, sputtering, roaring, the monster slowly recovers his lost ground, then gains an inch, and another. Boris feels faint and dizzy; his strength is failing, his grasp relaxing. Still he fights on; but it is useless now. His brave feet, that have held their own so long, give way; his muscles too, they have made a good fight, but they cannot hold out longer—they are relaxing; his fingers are loosening their hold upon the shaft; his eyes are so dim now that they cannot see the monster who is falling upon him to slay him; he is vanquished, he is giving ground rapidly; in another instant he will fall, and die. The bear will die too, of course; that thought will be his dying consolation.

A shout of encouragement behind him, and the sound of rushing feet! "Hold tight there just one minute more!" somebody cries; and automatically the stiffened fingers tighten themselves, and the feet grip the ground. Then a fresh hand grasps the shaft; two powerful feet plant themselves in the place where the failing ones have stood; and as the wearied and vanquished Boris falls fainting to the earth, the new arrival bears upon that stout staff with a force which even the mighty bear cannot withstand.

Back goes the bear by inches—now he is tottering—another shout and an irresistible rush forwards, and he is down, fighting and tearing to the last as a bold king of the forest should.

One more dig into the dying monster, a kick upon the prostrate carcass with the long, heavy Russian boot, and then the stranger turns to look after poor Boris. But first he wipes his hands upon a tuft of purple-fruited bilberry leaves, and from an inner pocket of his somewhat rich-looking *kaftan*, or tunic, he produces a silver-tipped flagon of Russian spirits. This he puts to the lips of Boris, who soon revives under the treatment, and sits up, dazed, to stare around with his hand to his eyes. First he fixes a long look upon the prostrate bear and the spear lying beside it; then he catches sight of the stranger, and stares long and fixedly at him. At last he says, "Are you St. Boris come to save me in answer to my call?"

The stranger burst into a loud, jovial guffaw.

"Bless your heart," he shouted, "I'm not a saint! Very far from it, I'm afraid. I'm only a man, like yourself."

"A man indeed!" said Boris; "and such a man as I have not seen the likeness of—well, since I last looked in the looking-glass!"

Boris made this remark in perfectly good faith, and without the slightest intention of paying himself a compliment. He knew well enough that he was by many degrees the strongest and finest-looking man in the country side, and by comparing the stranger with himself he merely offered honest testimony to the magnificent appearance of the latter. Nor was his admiration misplaced, for a finer-looking young fellow than he who now bent over Boris was rarely seen. Scarcely more than a boy—he was about the same age as Boris himself—the stranger was tall and robust, and straight as a young pine; taller than Boris, and broader too, though not more athletic-looking. His face was handsome and powerful, and his black hair curled in masses over a wide forehead and bold, rather cruel eyes. Boris gazed in admiration at this magnificent specimen of humanity—it was a new sensation to him to see any one physically superior to himself.

"You made a good fight," said the stranger, guffawing once more over the last speech of Boris; "but though you seem to have a fairly good opinion of yourself, that bear would have been lying on the top of you by this time if I had not come up in the nick of time. I watched the fight for some minutes. You have pluck, I am pleased to observe. What is your name?"

"Boris the Bear-Hunter," replied that worthy.

"Ha, ha! Boris the Bear-*Hunted*, you mean," laughed the stranger. "Well, I should like to know more of you, if you will. Come and see me to-morrow morning at Archangel, and we'll have a chat."

"Very well, *barin*" (gentleman), said Boris, feeling, in spite of his own usually defiant independence of spirit, that here was one who must of necessity command and be obeyed; "for I see you are a barin by your kaftan. What are you called, and where shall I seek you?"

"Petka, and sometimes Petrushka, is my name," said the big

youth; "and you may ask for me at the burgomaster's house in the town. You will hear of me there till eleven to-morrow; after that I take ship for a sail abroad. And now I will leave you and *mishka* yonder to take care of one another. Beware, while you skin him, that he doesn't jump up and skin *you*. He may be shamming while I am here, you see; but he has no cause to be afraid of you."

With which gentle sarcasm and another jovial laugh the tall youth departed, leaving Boris to reflect upon the extreme good fortune which had sent him the right man at the right moment to extract him from the tightest fix he had ever succeeded in getting himself into during the whole course of his nineteen summers.

FOOTNOTE:

Mishka is the familiar Russian name for a bear.

CHAPTER III.

BORIS CHANGES MASTERS.

Boris, when he returned to the village that same afternoon, enjoyed a veritable triumph at the hands of his delighted fellows. He was honest enough to confess his indebtedness to the stranger, but this did not make the slightest difference in the gratitude of the peasants; and indeed the service which Boris had rendered them, in thus ridding them of an infliction worse than the most terrible blight, was no slight one. A large bear, when so disposed, and when allowed to work his wicked will upon the corn-fields of a village, will very speedily either consume or trample into hay the entire grain wealth of the community; so that the gratitude of the peasants was proportionate to their clear gain in the death of one of the two monster pests which had come, like a scourge upon the village, to devour the fatness thereof.

Boris was carried shoulder-high through the one street of the place; while the carcass of the dead robber, slung by his four legs to a pole, was borne behind, escorted by a booing, yelling crowd of women and children. A bonfire was lighted at night in honour of the hunter and his achievement, when portions of the bear were cooked and eaten, more as an expression of contempt for the late owner of the flesh than for love of the food. Most of the carcass was given to the dogs, however, and they, at least, were delighted with the feast.

Boris was well feasted with *vodka* and with other delicacies equally bad for him; but being a sensible youth and steady withal, he did not retire at night in the degraded condition of most of his fellow-villagers. He was elated, no doubt, not by the fumes of the spirits, however, but by the sense of triumph; yet the more he pondered over his fight and victory, the more clearly did he realize his indebtedness to the timely aid of the strong young giant who had come to his assistance. As he lay and dozed, half conscious, through the hot hours of the summer night, Boris weaved the adventure of the day into a thousand fantastic shapes, in all of which, however, the stranger played an important part: sometimes he was his own patron saint; then he was a benevolent *lieshui*, or wood-spirit, a class of beings fully believed in by the peasants, but, according to popular tradition, more likely to take the part of the bear than of Boris in a fight between the two. In a word, the stranger assumed so many various shapes in the hunter's overwrought brain at night, that when day came Boris was by no means certain whether the stranger had in reality existed at all, and was inclined to fancy that the whole thing had been a dream as he lay and slept after the death of the bear, which he had slain single-handed.

Half hoping that this might prove to be the case—for the idea that he had almost been worsted by a bear, however huge, was an unwelcome thought to so renowned a hunter—Boris determined, nevertheless, that he would at least journey as far as the town, which was but a mile or two distant, in order to learn for himself whether there indeed existed a young giant of the name of Petka.

Boris set out at the appointed hour for Archangel and the house of the burgomaster. The house was easily found, for it was the principal building of the place, and was so grand, indeed, to look upon that Boris scarcely liked his mission. What if the whole thing should have been a dream? Why, what a fool he would appear, coming to this grand place and inquiring for some one who did not exist; all these serfs and dressed-up people about the front door would laugh at him, and tell him to go home and drink less vodka the next time he killed a bear. However, Boris reflected, if any one should laugh at him, laughers were easily knocked down. He was as good a man, and perhaps a trifle better, than any of these embroidered chaps. Let them laugh if they liked; their mirth might cost them a little of their embroidery! So Boris pulled himself together, and marched up to the porch of the big wooden structure which had been pointed out to him as the house of the burgomaster. A stately doorkeeper, dressed, in spite of the warmth of the season, in a gold-laced kaftan and a high fur cap, listened to the young peasant's inquiry with some bewilderment. Was there any one living there of the name of Petka? Boris had asked,—a young fellow about his own age? Boris believed he was a barin, but could not be sure; he gave this address.

"Petka?" repeated the astonished porter. "What do you mean? Petka who? What's his family name?"

"I only know he called himself Petka; he said sometimes he was known as Petrushka," said Boris, beginning to feel assured that he was the victim of a dream. "He was a tall, well-set-up sort of a fellow," he continued, "as big as I am, or bigger. Come now; is he here, or is he not? I warn you I am not a man to annoy; I am Boris the Bear-Hunter."

It was not meant as an idle boast. Had the doorkeeper been a native of the town he would have known well enough who the bearer of this name was; but it so happened that this man was a new arrival from Moscow, whence he had come with the retinue of his master the Tsar, and therefore the title meant nothing to him, but savoured only of boasting and the conceit of local celebrity.

"Well," he said, "you can go home again and hunt your bears at leisure; there's no Petka, nor yet Petrushka, here. As for annoying you, I know nothing about that, but you are going the right way to get yourself a taste of the knout, my friend; and if you don't clear out of this street in double quick time, I shall summon those who are very well able to make you cry, though you may be the best bear-sticker that ever walked. Now then, off you go!"

The fellow laid his hand upon the hunter's arm, as though to put his threat of violence into execution; but in doing so he made a great mistake. Boris was fearless and independent; he was unaccustomed to threats and interference. As a rule people were afraid of him, and showed him deference: what right had this man to browbeat and threaten him? Boris's hot blood resented the insult, and in a moment the man lay sprawling at his feet, bellowing loudly for help, crying and swearing in a breath, in a manner which is natural to the Russian peasant. His cries instantly brought around the pair a host of serfs and servants, who quickly hustled Boris within the passage, and made as though they would lay hold of him. But this the high-spirited hunter of bears would not submit to, and, with his back to the wall, he hit out right and left with so good effect that the number of his assailants was considerably reduced in very quick time indeed.

This was a row quite after Boris's own heart, and he was thoroughly enjoying himself among the noisy crowd of shouting and whining serving-men, when a loud voice broke in above the noise—a voice that Boris seemed to recognize, and at the sound of which every other voice in that noisy hall died away into instant silence. The fallen assailants of Boris uprose from the earth and ranged themselves in line, prepared to denounce the foe or to excuse themselves according as occasion arose. But the new arrival exacted no explanations.

"Why," he cried, "it's my friend the bear-eater! Come along this way, Bear-eater, and tell me all about this disturbance. Have you killed so few bears of late that you must needs work off your spare energies at the expense of my poor servants? Well, well, if you were to rid me of a score or two of the thieving rogues, I should do well enough without them, I daresay. But what is it all about?"

"The man with the embroidery wanted to give me the knout because I asked for you by the name of Petka," said Boris, feeling that there was more in all this than he had quite understood. This must be something like a barin, who could talk in so airy a way of a "score or two" of his servants. "You said your name was Petka, didn't you?"

"Assuredly," said the other, leading the way into a private chamber; "Petka or Petrushka, sometimes Peter—I answer to all these names. But come now, to business. I like the look of you, Boris. I want Russians with strong bodies and brave hearts; I shall have work for them. Do you feel inclined to enter my service? I will pay you well if you serve me well. Now, then, no wasting words, for I am due down at the harbour—is it yes or no?"

"But I am not my own master," said the astonished Boris. "I am the property of my barin, who employs me to hunt the bears and wolves. I cannot say I will leave him and serve you, though I like the look of you well enough. Besides, what do you want me for—to kill bears?"

"You shall hunt the bears to your heart's content," said the barin; "and as for your master, I will see that he does not object to your transfer to my service. Is it agreed? come, yes or no."

"Yes, then," said Boris, who both spoke and acted as in a dream. The mastery of this young giant over him seemed so complete that he could not have answered otherwise than in the affirmative even if he had wished to do so. He was drawn by a power stronger than himself.

"Very well," said the other, writing rapidly, "excellently well; shake hands upon it. Take this to your master, and come to this place to enter upon your service to-morrow morning. You may ask for Piotr [Peter] Alexeyevitch, and I shall be ready to receive you. Now I must go sailing with Meinheer de Kuyper. Stay; your hand-grip now. Good! that's more like a grip than any I have felt for some time. I shall like you, I think; only serve me faithfully."

Peter Alexeyevitch, as he had called himself, left the room with these words. But Boris preserved somewhat painful reminiscences of his new friend and master for several hours, for the return hand-grip had been such that the bones of his hand had ground together in the mighty clasp.

CHAPTER IV.

BORIS GOES A-SAILING.

It was all very well for Boris to tell his new friend that he would enter his service; but when, away from the glamour of his presence, he considered the matter in cold blood, it appeared to him to be a somewhat audacious proceeding on his part to coolly bring to his master a note from some one else, whom he could only describe as a tall and masterful young barin of the name of Peter Alexeyevitch, stating that somebody proposed to deprive his lawful lord of the services of his paid serf and servant, the bear-hunter! Why, after all, should his lord consent to so audacious a proposal from a total stranger? There was no reason that Boris knew why he should do so; in all probability he would refuse, and perhaps punish Boris besides for his impertinence and disloyalty in proposing such a thing, or at least being a consenting party to such a proposal. Hence Boris entered the barin's house at Dubinka in some trepidation, and gave his letter into the master's own hands, quite expecting an angry reception.

"Well, Boris, so you killed one of the two bears, I'm told," began the barin. "You've come for your 'tea-money,' I suppose? Well, you have deserved it this time, and I shall pay it with pleasure. What's this?—a letter? from whom?"

"That's what I can't tell your Mercifulness," said Boris. "Petka, he calls himself, but I don't know who he is, excepting that he is a gentleman like yourself, and very big and strong—like me."

The barin took the letter and glanced at it; then he flushed, and uttered an exclamation of surprise. Then he laughed, and patted Boris kindly on the back.

"Bravo, Boris!" he said, "you have made a useful friend. Do you know whom this letter is from?"

"From Petka, of course!" said blunt Boris.

"Your friend is the Tsar of all the Russias, my son; and, moreover, he has requested me to transfer you to his service. You are a lucky boy, Boris, and I hope you may do your new master credit. Serve him well. He is Peter, the Hope of the Nation; all Russia looks to him, for he promises much. You are a lucky fellow, Boris, and you may be a great man yet."

Astonishment and wonder had caused the bear-hunter to collapse into a chair, a liberty he would never have thought of taking except under extraordinary circumstances. The Tsar! it was actually the Tsar himself who had stepped forward to save his humble life. Boris pinched his leg to see whether he was awake or asleep: it was all right, he was not dreaming. And he had called him "Petka," and the Tsar had not promptly cut off his head for the impertinence! Perhaps he would to-morrow when he went to the burgomaster's house in the morning. And those were the Tsar's servants with whose whining forms he had carpeted the floor of the entrance hall! Assuredly he would pay for all this with his head.

In a dazed condition Boris left the barin's presence, and walked home to his father's cottage, wondering whether it would not be wiser, on the whole, to disappear into the depths of the forest until such time as the Tsar should have left Archangel and returned to Moscow? But worthier thoughts quickly succeeded these promptings of cowardice. Boris recalled the Tsar's kind words—he had taken a fancy to the bear-hunter, he said; and again, "Russia had need of strong arms and brave hearts!" If this was so, and he could please the magnificent young Tsar by doing it, he should unreservedly place his life and his service at Peter's disposal.

The next morning found Boris once again at the house of the burgomaster. This time the embroidered functionary in charge of the front entrance, mindful of his experience of the preceding day, was careful to keep his conversation void of offence, and to preserve a respectful demeanour to the owner of two such powerful fists. Acting perhaps on orders received, he ushered the young bear-hunter directly into the presence of his new master.

Peter sat at a table, busily employed in manipulating a model sailing-vessel, explaining the uses of the various sails and other portions of the ship's furniture to a stolidly attentive companion, who sat and listened and smoked, and occasionally bowed his head in assent to the propositions laid down by his handsome young companion. There could not well be a greater contrast between any two men than existed between these two—the one, a short, thick-set, squat-figured, Dutch-built caricature of a man;

the other, tall, far beyond the ordinary height of man, straight as any one of all the millions of pines that stood sentinel over his vast dominions, noble and majestic, the very incarnate spirit of majesty.

Peter paused in his lesson to greet the new-comer.

"De Kuyper," he said, "look here! This is a fellow who calls himself a bear-hunter, and I saw him the other day running away from a bear for dear life, like a hare from a hound—it was grand! If I had not interfered, the bear would have deprived me of the services of an excellent soldier, or sailor, or keeper, or whatever I may decide to make of him—eh, Boris?"

"I will serve your Majesty with my life blood in whatever manner you may be pleased to use me," said Boris, kneeling before the young Tsar and touching the ground with his forehead; "and I entreat you to forgive my ignorance yesterday, and my impertinence in treating you as little better than my equal——"

"Nonsense," said Peter; "get up. I hate cringing and all foolery. You shall show me what you are good for; I shall see that you have ample opportunity. Meanwhile let's have no talk about equality or inferiority. You will find that they who serve me well are my equals in all but the name. For the present you are my special body-servant, to attend me wherever I go. And first you shall attend me on board De Kuyper's ship, and we shall see what prospect there is of making a sailor of you.—Come on, De Kuyper, the wind is getting up. We shall have a glorious sail.—Come on you too, Boris."

De Kuyper was the fortunate skipper of the first foreign vessel which had entered the port of Archangel during the present season, after the disappearance of the ice had left the harbour open to arrivals from abroad. Peter had instantly boarded the *Drei Gebrüder* on its appearance, and having himself purchased the cargo, and handsomely rewarded the skipper and crew for their enterprise, carried away De Kuyper to be his guest and favourite companion until his departure from Archangel. Under the Dutch skipper's guidance, Peter was laying the foundations of that nautical experience which was so often to stand him in good stead in after life.

Boris was no sailor—indeed, he had never been fifty yards from the shore upon shipboard, though he had ventured very much further in swimming. His sensations, therefore, as the lumbering old vessel plunged through the waves, were the reverse of enviable. Peter himself handled the rudder, and gave all the necessary orders for managing the sails, insisting upon Boris doing his share of the work in spite of the misery of sea-sickness which sat heavily upon the poor landsman.

It was a splendid day—hot on shore, but delightfully cool and pleasant out at sea. The wind blew freshly from the north and east, and Peter crowded on all the sail he could. The clumsy old vessel, squat-built and broad in the beam like her master, strained and groaned beneath the weight of canvas, but sped along at a rate which filled the young Tsar's soul with the wildest delight. As usual, when particularly happy, he was boisterous and very noisy, poking fun at De Kuyper, Boris, and the sailors, and from time to time singing snatches of his favourite songs.

It so happened that a small boat which was attached by a short length of tow-rope to the stern of the *Drei Gebrüder* presently broke adrift, in consequence of the strain, and floated away astern. The young Tsar was annoyed. He loved a good boat, and disliked to see one needlessly lost before his eyes.

"De Kuyper," he shouted, "have you a swimmer on board? Send one of your Dutchmen after it! Come, look sharp about it! They're not afraid surely? Why, I'll go myself; see here!"

Before the horrified skipper could prevent him, the rash young Tsar had thrown away his kaftan and boots, and was in the act of mounting the bulwark, when a strong hand seized his shoulder and pulled him back. The Tsar flushed with anger, and raised his big right hand to strike the man who had presumed to take so great a liberty; but Boris pushed back the lifted arm with a sweep of his own, leaped upon a hen-coop near at hand, so to the bulwark of the vessel, and in an instant was overboard, battling with the waves, and making good progress towards the fast-disappearing boat, now far astern. The Tsar's face was all beaming with delight in a moment.

"De Kuyper!" he cried, "look at the lad—a Russian lad, mind you, skipper; none of your Dutchmen! Would your Dutchmen swim those waves? I think not. I tell you, skipper, that bear-hunter is a man after my own heart. Did you observe him push me aside—glorious!—as though I had been the cabin-boy? Oh, for ten thousand such Russians!"

De Kuyper grunted and took the rudder, which Peter in his excitement had neglected.

"Your bear-hunter had better look sharp and get into that boat," he muttered, "for the sky looks squally, and we shall have a knock-about before we reach Archangel. The sooner we get him and the boat aboard the better I shall be pleased!"

Boris meanwhile was fast gaining upon the lost boat. Soon he had reached it and was hauling himself over the side. The oars were safe, so that he had little difficulty in propelling the small craft towards the larger vessel, which had put about, and was now coming round as quickly as possible, in order to take up the recovered boat and its occupant.

With some considerable difficulty, owing to the roughness of the sea, this was at last effected; and Boris felt that he was amply repaid for the risk he had run by the few words of the Tsar, and his mighty grip of the hand.

"Bear-eater," he had said, "you are my brother; let that be understood between us."

After this episode neither sea-sickness nor the discomfort of sitting in wet clothes could divert the mind of Boris from the thought of his exceeding great joy. He had been called "brother" by the young Tsar—the god-like Peter, who had been hailed almost from his cradle as the hope of Russia; of whom even the unlettered Boris in far-off Archangel had heard distant and indistinct rumours, as of some prince of fairyland, come from no one knew where, to work wonders for his empire, and astonish the world by his power and magnificence! Now he had seen this wonder of the age with his own eyes—he had spoken with him—was his servant—had received his approbation, nay, had been called "brother" by him.

Boris, musing thus on his great good fortune, suddenly became aware of a commotion on board. A squall had violently struck the vessel, and she was heeling over till her rail lay deep in the surging sea, and her deck sloped like the side of one of his beloved snow-hills. Peter, at the helm, was shouting orders to the seamen, with his eyes fixed upon the sails, while the vessel plunged and lay over till the seas washed her fore and aft.

De Kuyper rushed to the rudder.

"Steady her—steady, Tsar!" he shouted, "or we shall founder in a minute!"

Peter, wanting experience and unused to squalls and emergencies, was thinking only of the splendid excitement of rushing through the big waves as fast as the ship could be made to go; the danger of the moment was nothing to him. Perhaps he did not realize it; he certainly did not heed it.

"Steady her, I tell you!" shrieked the skipper once more. "Here; let me come! I won't go to the bottom for a hundred Russian kings. Let go, I say!"

Peter's face flushed angrily.

"Keep away, De Kuyper, keep away," he cried; "don't anger me. This is glorious!"

But De Kuyper knew that this was no time for the politeness of courts and the deference due to princes. He seized Peter by the shoulders and forced him from the tiller.

"I'm skipper of this vessel," he shouted, "and I intend to be obeyed while aboard of her. You shall command when we get ashore, if we ever do!"

Peter let go his hold of the clumsy tiller-shaft, looking for a moment like a thunder-cloud. During that moment he revolved in his mind whether or not he should take up that squat little Dutch skipper in his great arms and throw him overboard; but better impulses prevailed. The vessel quickly righted under De Kuyper's experienced guidance, and flew through the water actually quicker than before, and upon a more even keel. In a moment Peter had recovered his equanimity. He burst into a roar of laughter, and brought his big hand with a whack upon the little Dutchman's shoulder.

"Skipper," he cried, in his hearty loud tones of approval, "forgive me! You are a better sailor than I am, and a plucky fellow to boot. I love a man who stands up to me. You Dutchmen are a fine race, and good sailors."

De Kuyper, the excitement over and the danger past, was much upset by the recollection of his rudeness to one who, though his inferior in the art of sailing, was so immeasurably his superior in position and importance. He apologized profusely and humbly, and on his knees begged to be forgiven.

"Get up," said Peter, "and don't be a fool, skipper. I liked you far better when you forced me away from the tiller. I was a fool, and you told me so; that is what I like in a man."

CHAPTER V.

HOW PETER THE GREAT WAS KNOCKED OVER.

Before Boris had been very long in the service of the Tsar he had become quite an expert sailor; indeed, he and his young master were scarcely ever absent from shipboard of one kind or another. Archangel was at this time Russia's one outlet to the sea. St. Petersburg was not yet built, nor Cronstadt thought of; the Baltic ports had still to be wrested from their proprietors; only the little northern port at the mouth of the Dwina was open to receive the ships and commerce of the world. Consequently, as the season proceeded, vessels of all nationalities, including English, appeared with their merchandise at this distant market; and Peter passed many weeks in the most congenial occupation of studying each vessel that entered the port, sailing about in them, making friends with their captains, and learning everything he could gather of the history and circumstances of the people to which each belonged. Boris, too, learned many marvels concerning this planet of ours and its inhabitants, undreamed of hitherto. The young hunter was constantly in attendance on Peter—waited upon him at dinner, slept at his door at night, sailed with him, walked abroad with him, and was, in a word, his inseparable companion.

The villagers at Dubinka greatly deplored the departure of Boris from among them; for what were they going to do without him when the winter-time came round, and the wolves began to be both numerous and assertive? Who was to keep them in check now that the great Boris was gone? Even now they had the best of reasons for acutely deploring the hunter's absence. It will be remembered that whereas there had been two bears engaged in the plundering of the peasants' corn-fields, only one of these had been accounted for by Boris before his departure. The second bear had disappeared for some little time after the death of its liege lord; but the days of her mourning being now accomplished, she had reappeared, and with appetite largely improved by her period of abstinence. Her depredations became so serious at last that it was resolved by the council of the peasants to send into the town a request to Boris to devote his earliest leisure to a personal interview with the widow of his late antagonist.

Boris received the message of the good folks of Dubinka with delight. The very mention of a bear aroused all his old sporting instincts, and he went straight to the Tsar to obtain his permission to absent himself for a day.

"Ho, ho!" laughed Peter. "So you want to be eaten up again, do you? I doubt whether I can spare you; you have made yourself too useful to me. Had you not better stay? It is safer here."

Boris blushed. "The bear isn't born yet, sire," he said, "that will make me run again. The bear you killed had caught me napping. I shall never leave my spear again, to eat strawberries."

"Well, well," said Peter, "you shall go on one condition—that I go with you to see you safely through with the adventure."

And so it came about that Boris and his master walked out very early one summer morning to relieve the peasants of Dubinka of their unwelcome visitor. The two young giants called first at the house of the *starost*, or principal peasant of the place, whom they aroused from his slumbers and carried off with them into the fields at the edge of the forest, to show them the exact spot at which the robber had concluded her supper on the previous evening; for it was probable that she would recommence her plundering at or about the same spot. The starost brought the hunters to the place they sought, approaching it in abject terror, and scudding home again like a hare, lest the bear should pursue him back over the fields.

Boris was the Tsar's master in their present occupation, and thoroughly understood what he was about. The pair concealed themselves in a dense clump of cover at the edge of the wood. Just in front of their ambush lay the oat-field last honoured by the attentions of the bear. A large portion of it looked as though a battle had been fought on it, so downtrodden and crushed were the tall, delicate stalks. It was arranged that Peter should hold the spear, while Boris was to be content with the hunting-knife, one which the Tsar had brought with him, a long and business-like blade, both tough and sharp, as a blade needs to be to be driven through the thick hide of a bear. The young monarch was anxious to try his "'prentice hand" with the spear, for he had never handled one excepting on that memorable occasion when he gave the final push to the huge brute which had first winded and then overpowered poor Boris. The hunter very carefully explained the exact way in which Peter must poise his body, how he must grip the spear-shaft, and how he must plant his feet so as to balance his body conveniently and at the same time obtain a purchase with his heel which should enable him to support any, even the greatest, strain. Then the two men waited in silence for the arrival of the widow of the late lamented Mr. Bruin.

It was still very early, about four o'clock. There was no sound to break the repose of the young day, save the boisterous song which now and again some little bird set up for a moment, and as suddenly broke off, finding itself to be the only singer. The pines swayed solemnly in the faint morning breeze, sending down showers of bright dewdrops far and wide. A hare was playing quietly in the oat-field, quite unconscious of the presence of its natural enemy, man; and presently a proudly-clucking grouse walked out with her brood into the oat-strown space beyond the wood, and there demonstrated to her young hopefuls how easily a breakfast could be picked up by people who knew where to look for it. In the far distance a family of cranes could be heard at intervals, exchanging confidences upon the adventures of the past night and the delights of a hearty breakfast of frog.

Suddenly, and without apparent reason, the hare raised its head, sniffed the air, and in a moment was scuttling full speed across the field, heading for the village, as though it had remembered a message for the starost which it had omitted to deliver while he was on the spot. The careful grouse at the same moment rose from the earth with a loud cluck, and darted away, followed by her little brood. Over the tops of the pines they went, far away into the heart of the forest.

In another moment the reason for this abrupt departure of bird and beast became apparent. Shuffling awkwardly along, and mumbling in a querulous way as she went, as though complaining that she had been called up to breakfast earlier than was necessary, came the wicked old widow-bear, marching straight for the standing oats, as though everything in the district belonged to her. She was a huge creature, a fitting helpmate for the gigantic old warrior whom Peter had slain. Slowly she picked her way along, swinging her heavy body and half-turning her great head at each step, looking alternately to right and to left in a perfunctory manner, as though making a concession to the principle of precaution, while declining to believe in the possibility of misadventure.

Boris's finger was at his lip, enjoining patience and prudence, for the impulsive young Tsar was excited, and quite capable of ruining the chances of a successful hunt by doing something rash and ill-timed. Boris touched the Tsar's arm and whispered. Peter was to creep cautiously along and place himself in the very spot at which the bear had issued from the forest. When there, he was to hold his spear ready for action and await events. Boris himself would walk out into the oat-field, in full view of the bear, who would probably not charge him. Most likely she would hurry back to the cover, entering the wood where she had left it; and if Boris could influence her course, he would encourage her to choose that particular direction. Then the Tsar must suddenly step out from his ambush and receive the bear upon his spear; and if matters went smoothly, the impetus of her flight would bring her down upon him, whether she liked it or not.

The plan of attack thus settled, Peter withdrew under cover of the bushes and pine trunks to take up the position assigned him, while Boris boldly stepped forth from his ambush, and made for a point beyond the place where the bear was now busy gobbling the grain greedily, and emitting grunts of satisfaction and high content. So well occupied was she, indeed, that she took no notice of the hunter's approach until Boris was nearly level with her. Then she raised her head with a grunt, and expressed her surprise and displeasure in a loud roar. For a moment it appeared likely that she would charge Boris, who, having nothing but a hunting-knife wherewith to defend himself, might in that event have fared badly; for he would have died rather than turn his back upon her and run, since Peter was at hand to see. But timid counsels prevailed, and Mrs. Bruin quickly determined to take the safer course. She twisted her bulky body round, and made off, as Boris had foretold, straight for the spot at which she had left the forest. Boris ran after her, shouting, in hopes of accelerating her speed; and in this he was entirely successful. Straight down for the Tsar's ambush she raced, and close at her heels went Boris, shouting instructions to Peter as he sped. The result of all this speed and excitement was that by the time the great creature had reached the spot where Peter awaited her, the impetus of her flight was so great that she was upon him, as he stepped out to meet her, ere she had time to swerve sufficiently to avoid him.

The Tsar had stepped forth at precisely the right moment, and was ready with poised spear to receive the rush. His feet had gripped the earth as tightly as in the somewhat slippery condition of the ground was practicable. With a roar the monster hurled herself upon the spear-point, uttering a second and very bitter cry as she felt the steel enter into her vitals.

The shock of her rush was terrific. Peter, strong as he was and firmly as he had planted himself, was knocked off his feet in an instant, and ere Boris could realize the full horror of the situation, the most valuable life in all Russia lay at the mercy of an enraged and maddened she-bear. Peter fell backwards; but as the huge brute precipitated herself upon the top of him, the good spear-shaft of seasoned wood caught in the ground, and for a moment held her suspended, so that she could reach her enemy with neither teeth nor claws.

That moment saved the Tsar's life. Boris was but a few yards behind, and it was the work of an instant for him to cast himself headlong upon the carcass of the roaring, blood-stained brute, and with an accurately placed thrust of the knife in her throat put an end in the nick of time to her cravings for vengeance. With his additional weight thrown suddenly into the scale the good spear-shaft snapped in two, and bear and hunter together toppled over upon the prostrate figure of Russia's Tsar.

"That moment saved the Tsar's life."

"Thank you, Brother Boris," said the Tsar quietly, rising from the ground and wiping the bear's blood from his clothes. "It was well done; we are quits. When you see me over-proud, my son, you shall remind me of this morning, and how an old she-bear sent me head over heels. Now let's get home to breakfast."

CHAPTER VI.

A TASTE OF THE KNOUT.

Thus were laid and cemented the foundations of a friendship destined to last for many a long, history-making year. Boris was a man after Peter's own heart, and from those early Archangel days until the end of their lives the two were rarely parted for long, excepting when the exigencies of public affairs necessitated the departure of one of them for distant portions of the realm.

The summer in Archangel is a short one, and by the end of August autumn is in full progress, with icy warnings of winter at night-time. Peter the Tsar had, besides, many important duties which called for his presence at the capital, Moscow; and towards the end of July it became necessary to bring his delightful seaside holiday to an end, and return to sterner duties at home. Peter decided to travel in a three-horse *tarantass*, a springless carriage slung upon a pole instead of springs—comfortable enough on soft country roads, but desperately jolting on stony ones.

Boris had begged to be allowed to accompany his beloved patron and friend, in order that he might instruct the Tsar in the art of "calling" wolves and perhaps lynxes, and thus while away a few of the tedious hours of the long journey. Peter was delighted to acquiesce in this arrangement; for if there was one thing in the world that this most energetic of sovereigns could not tolerate, it was to sit idle with no possibility of finding food for observation for his eyes or new facts and new ideas for assimilation in his ever active and receptive brain. So the two posted on in front of the long procession of servants and luggage, comfortably housed in a covered tarantass, drawn by three horses abreast, and driven by a notable driver renowned for his skill in persuading that erratic animal, the Russian pony, to move along faster than had been its intention when it started. Ivan arrived at this happy result by a judicious mixture of coaxing and abuse, calling the ponies every pet name in the Russian vocabulary at one moment, and sounding the very depths and shoals of the language of the slums at the next. Ivan was never silent for a moment, but spoke to his ponies incessantly; and these latter generously decided as a rule that they must do their best for such an orator.

Through the tumble-down villages of northern Russia the tarantass flew, while the inhabitants stared round-eyed as it passed, not dreaming for a moment that it was their Tsar who glided by, but taking him for one of the many traders who posted between the seaport and the capital in tarantasses crammed with merchandise of every description. Peter was well armed with matchlock and pistols, for there was the possibility of a *rencontre* with wolves or robbers, and it was well to be prepared for every contingency.

The two young men frequently stopped at some village *traktir*, or inn, as they passed, to refresh themselves with a meal of peasant fare and a chat with the village people, whose opinions about his august self Peter loved to learn. Since they had not the slightest idea of the identity of their questioner, the Tsar gathered much information of great value to himself in indicating which way, to use a familiar expression, "the cat jumped" with regard to popular opinion upon some of the important questions of the day.

Most peasants, Peter found, were convinced that the Tsar was more than human. Exaggerated versions of his intelligence and vigour as child and boy had reached them, and it was a common belief that the young prince had been specially sent by Providence to right the wrongs of the Russian people, and to make life for the peasantry a sweet dream of marrow and fatness and exemption from work.

The priests, on the other hand, had widely different ideas upon the subject. The young Tsar, they said, mournfully shaking their heads, was a fine young fellow, no doubt, but his character was full of danger for Holy Russia. He was too liberal and progressive. Progress was the enemy of Russia and of the Holy Church. Russia required no western civilization imported within her peaceful borders. She was not a secular country, but the specially favoured of the church, and foreigners and foreign manners and so-called civilization would be the curse of the country, and Peter threatened to introduce both. He was all for progress, and the priests did not believe in progress.

Occasionally discussion waxed warm at the traktirs visited by the two young men, and once or twice blows were exchanged.

Once a party of drunken peasants uproariously declared that the Tsar Peter was a mere usurper, and that if he had had his deserts he would have been "put away" long since in some monastery or castle, never more to be heard of. Peter flushed when he heard this, for the question of his right to the throne of Russia was always to him a sore point; whereupon Boris, seeing that his master was annoyed, sprang up and knocked the speaker down. The landlord then rushed in, and finding that two strangers had set a company of his regular customers by the ears, bade them depart from his house that instant.

Peter laughed good-naturedly, but on the landlord becoming abusive he seized the man by the neck and trousers and pitched him upon the top of the stove. Then Boris and the Tsar took the rest of the company, who fought with drunken desperation, and pitched them up, one after the other, to join the landlord, until there were nine men in all huddled together on the wide top of the stove, whining and afraid to come down again.

Peter was perfectly good-humoured throughout, and enjoyed the fun; but the landlord was naturally furious, and when his two tall guests, having paid their reckoning, left the house, he took the opportunity of scrambling down from his prison and going for the village policeman, whom he despatched at full speed after the travellers. The policeman, being well mounted, overtook the tarantass, and explained his mission, when Peter immediately gave orders to the driver to turn the horses' heads and return to the village.

There the pair, to their great amusement and delight, were placed in the village lock-up, pending inquiries by the village council of peasants; and there they still were when, with bells jingling, and horses galloping, and dust flying, and with much shouting and pomp, the Tsar's retinue drove into the place, and pulled up at the traktir.

It so happened that the whole of Peter's late antagonists, including, of course, the landlord, were still present, having all by this time climbed down from the stove. They were discussing, in the highest good-humour and with much self-satisfaction, the promptitude with which the landlord had avenged the insult to his customers, and discussing also what punishment would be suitable for the delinquents now confined in the village lock-up. The arrival of the Tsar's retinue broke up the deliberations, however, and the peasants retired to the far end of the room in order to make way for the crowd of kaftaned and uniformed servants of the Tsar, who quickly monopolized all the tables and chairs, and settled themselves for a quarter of an hour's rest and refreshment.

The visitors were noisy, and took to ill-using the peasants and chaffing the irate landlord. One of them threw a glass of vodka in his face, and asked him if that was the only sort of stuff he had to offer to gentlemen of quality? The landlord sputtered and raged, and, in the pride of his late successful capture of two travellers, threatened. His threats largely increased the merriment of his guests, who thumped him on the back and roared with laughter. One seized him by the nose in order to cause his mouth to open wide, when he dashed down his throat the contents of a huge tumblerful of *kvass*, a kind of beer very nauseous to any palate save that of a Russian peasant. The poor landlord choked and sputtered and abused, but succeeded in escaping out of the room, returning, however, in a few minutes armed with authority in the shape of the *ooriadnik*, or village policeman, whom he requested instantly to "arrest these men."

The little policeman glanced at the uproarious company in a bewildered way. He was not a coward, and he relied much upon the power of the law—of which he was the embodiment—to overawe the minds of all good Russians. Besides, had he not, a few minutes since, successfully arrested and locked up two giants, in comparison with whom these noisy people were mere puppets? He therefore pulled himself together, and tentatively laid his hand upon the arm of one who seemed to be quieter than the rest of the party; he was smaller, anyhow, and would therefore do very well to practise upon first. But the man shook him off and warned him.

"Don't be a fool," he said; "get out of this and let us alone. Don't you see we could strangle you and the whole villageful of peasants if we pleased? Go home while you can walk on two legs, and let us alone!"

But the plucky little ooriadnik was not so easily discouraged.

"You may threaten as much as you please," he said, "but you will find I am not afraid of a party of tipsy cowards like you. Why, it isn't half-an-hour since I arrested, all by myself, a couple of fellows three times your size. Didn't they fight, too!"

The Tsar's servants interchanged glances.

"Where are the two men you speak of?" some one asked.—"What were they driving in, and where were they coming from?" said another.

"They're in the village lock-up at this moment," said the

ooriadnik; "and that's where you'll be in another minute or two."

Some of the party looked serious, some burst into roars of laughter, others started up excitedly.

"You must show us this lock-up first," said the small person whose arrest was half accomplished; "we can't submit to be huddled into a little hole of a place incapable of holding more than the two you have there already!"

"Oh, there's plenty of room for you, never fear!" said the brave ooriadnik. "Come along, by all means, and see for yourself!"

The policeman foresaw an easy way to effect the arrest of at least one or two of those present, and they would serve as hostages for the rest. He would push them in as they stood at the door of the lock-up, and fasten the bolt upon them!

So the whole party adjourned to the lock-up. The door was opened, and there, to the horror of his frightened servants, sat the Tsar of all the Russias, unconcernedly playing cards with Boris the Bear-Hunter.

One official instantly seized the ooriadnik by the throat and pinned him to the wall; another performed the same service on the landlord. Others threw themselves upon the floor at Peter's feet and whined out incoherent reproaches that their beloved sovereign should have trusted himself to travel so far in advance of his faithful servants and guards, and thus lay himself open to outrage of this description.

"What is the matter?" asked Peter; "what's all the disturbance about? Let those men go. Get up, all you fools there, and stop whining; there's no harm done.—Listen, Mr. Landlord. You have had me arrested; very well, here I am. I am the Tsar; but what of that? If I have done wrong, I desire to be treated just as any other delinquent would be treated. Call your village council together, and let's have the inquiry over as quickly as possible. We must push on!"

The landlord, followed by the ooriadnik, both in tears and with loud lamentations, threw themselves at Peter's feet, asking his pardon and pleading ignorance of his identity with their beloved Tsar. But Peter insisted upon being treated exactly as any other offender, and the *moujiks* of the community were convened as quickly as possible to the village court. All these, including the persons whose upheaval upon the stove had been the original cause of all the disturbance, came in terror for their lives—most of them loudly weeping—for there was not one but made sure that the lives of every moujik in the village must of necessity be forfeit, since so terrible an outrage and insult had been inflicted upon the Tsar.

Peter bade the landlord state his case, and instructed the starost, or elder of the community, to question both accuser and accused according to the usual procedure of the village court. But it appeared that both landlord and starost were far too frightened to find their tongues. Then the Tsar took upon himself to state the case. He and his body-servant, he explained, had violently assaulted the landlord of the inn, together with certain of his customers. There had been provocation, but nevertheless the assault was undoubtedly committed. What was the penalty for assault?

The starost, to whom the Tsar addressed this remark, burst into tears and knelt with his forehead tapping the floor at Peter's feet. All the moujiks followed suit, and for some minutes there was naught to be heard save groanings and whinings and bits of the litany in use in the Russo-Greek Church. But neither the starost nor any of his peers of the community offered a reply.

"Speak up, man!" said the Tsar angrily, and then immediately bursting into one of his loud guffaws. "What's the penalty for assault? Speak! I am determined to be told, and by yourself."

Once more the entire company of peasants made as though they would throw themselves upon the ground and whine and pray as they had done before; but when Peter angrily stamped upon the floor, they all, with one accord, renounced the intention and stood quaking in their places.

"Come, come," said Peter impatiently; "don't be a fool, man. You are here to state the law, and you shall state it! What is the penalty for assault?"

The wretched starost strove to speak, but his lips would not open. He essayed once again, and this time succeeded in whispering,—

"Your High Mercifulness—pardon—it is ten cuts of the knout."

Then his legs failed him once more, and he fell, together with his moujiks, upon the floor, weeping and wailing, and calling upon the Tsar and upon Heaven for mercy. When the hubbub had in part subsided, Peter spoke again.

"Very well," he said. "Ooriadnik, do your duty. Don't be afraid; I prefer to see duty fearlessly done. Take your knout and lay on!"

The unfortunate ooriadnik was sufficiently master of himself to comprehend that it was useless to resist when the Tsar's will had once been expressed. He took his knout in his nerveless hand, and with white face and haggard expression tapped the Tsar's back the necessary number of times, inflicting strokes which would hardly have caused a fly, had one of these insects happened to settle upon Peter's broad back, to raise its head and inquire what the matter was. Then he threw down his knout and grovelled at the Tsar's feet, begging forgiveness.

"Nonsense, man," said Peter, but kindly; "finish your work first, and then we can talk of other matters.—Now, Boris, your turn.—Lay on, ooriadnik, and put a little more muscle into it; this fellow's skin is as hard as leather!"

The ooriadnik, intensely relieved by the Tsar's evident good-humour, laid on with some vigour, and flogged poor Boris in a manner not entirely agreeable to the hunter's feelings, who, nevertheless, did not flinch, though he felt that the young Tsar's manner of amusing himself was somewhat expensive to his friends. Boris lived to learn that this was so indeed. Nothing ever pleased Peter more than to enjoy a hearty laugh at the expense of his familiar companions.

But the ooriadnik's duties were not yet concluded. The Tsar patted him kindly on the back. "Bravo, ooriadnik!" he cried; "you are improving.—Now, then, you gentlemen who threw vodka and kvass at the landlord of the traktir, step out.—Lay on again, ooriadnik, and teach these persons not to waste good vodka!"

Then those servants found that they had committed an error in having assaulted the landlord; for the ooriadnik, having warmed to his work, and remembering the laughter and contempt with which his authority had been treated by these men at the inn, laid on his blows with such good will that the unfortunate culprits howled for mercy, to the huge delight of the Tsar.

After which object-lesson upon the impartiality of true justice, and the duty of respect towards the powers that be, Peter and his retinue resumed their journey.

CHAPTER VII.

A RACE FOR LIFE.

It has been already mentioned that Boris had promised to instruct his master in the art of calling various animals. In this art Boris was marvellously expert, and could imitate the cry of the wolf, lynx, and other creatures so exactly that if any member of the particular family whose language he was imitating chanced to be within hearing, it would invariably respond to his call—sometimes to its destruction, if it did not find out in time that it had been made the victim of a gross deception. The practice of this art was a source of unfailing delight and amusement to the Tsar during that weary drive of hundreds of miles through the plains and forests of northern and central Russia; for most of the journey was performed by land, though the Dwina offered a good water-way for a considerable distance.

The aptitude of Boris for imitation extended to the calling of birds as well as beasts, and many were the tree-partridges that were lured by him to their doom, and subsequently eaten by the monarch with much enjoyment as a welcome change from the sour cabbage-soup and black bread and salt, which were for the most part all that the party could get to subsist upon.

It was rarely, indeed, that wolf or lynx ventured to approach close enough to the carriage of the Tsar to permit of a successful shot with his old matchlock; but these animals, wolves especially, were frequently seen at a distance, appearing for an instant amid the gloom of the dense pines, but rapidly disappearing as soon as they had ascertained that they had been deceived. But once, when within two or three days' journey of Moscow, this now favourite pastime of the Tsar came near to involving himself and Boris in a fate which would have saved the present writer the trouble of following any further the fortunes of Boris, and would have caused the history of Russia, and indeed that of Europe, to be written in an altogether different manner, for the stirring pages of the life and work of Peter the Great would never have been penned at all.

Boris, as usual, was reclining easily in the front seat of the travelling carriage, idly smoking and chatting, and now and again, at the bidding of Peter, who occupied the back seat, sending out loud invitations in wolf language, in the hope that some wandering member of the family might happen to be within call and respond to his advances. Of a sudden Boris's cries were answered; a melancholy howl was distinctly heard by both men to proceed from within the heart of the dense forest through which the road lay. The howl appeared to proceed from a distance of half-a-mile, and was instantly followed by a second a little further away. The Tsar quickly sat up, gun in hand, while Boris excitedly reiterated his cries, producing tones so pathetically melancholy that the wolf would be hard-hearted indeed that could resist so touching an appeal for companionship. To his surprise, however, there came not one reply but several; half-a-dozen wolves, seemingly, had heard the invitation, and were hastening to respond to it. This was splendid. The young Tsar was now extremely excited.

"Howl away, Boris," he whispered; "there are several of them. We are sure of a shot this time!"

Nothing loath, Boris continued his howlings, and at each repetition the number of wolves that took part in the responding calls appeared to increase, until some twenty distinct voices could be made out, each coming from a slightly different quarter.

Ivan the driver turned half round and crossed himself; then he spat on the ground—a sure sign of discontent in a Russian; then he addressed the young Tsar with the easy familiarity of an old Russian servant.

"Stop it, Peter, the son of Alexis," he said; "there are too many wolves here! My horses will lose their heads if they see them.—Don't howl any more, Boris Ivanitch, if you love your life!"

Boris himself was looking somewhat grave, for he was well aware of the truth of old Ivan's remark that there were too many wolves—it was a pack, not a doubt of it; and the character of wolves when in a pack is as different from that of the same animals when alone or in pairs as is the harmless malevolence of a skulking beggar in the streets compared with the mischief-making capacity of an armed and howling mob of roughs and blackguards. But the Tsar had never seen a pack of wolves, and knew little of the dangers of which both Boris and Ivan were well aware; therefore he directed the former to continue his calls, bidding Ivan, at the same time, keep a proper hold upon his horses if he was afraid of them.

Old Ivan crossed himself once more and spat a second time, but he gathered up the reins as the Tsar commanded. As for Boris, he looked graver than ever, and howled in a half-hearted manner.

In a very few moments the vanguard of the wolf-host made its appearance. First one gaunt, gray-pointed snout appeared amid the pines on the right of the road, then another; almost at the same instant three cantering forms hove into view close behind; and two more were seen taking a survey in front of the horses' heads.

Peter was in a high state of excitement; he thought nothing of the danger of the moment—it is doubtful whether he realized it. His gun-barrel was raised and pointed now at one gray form, now at another, as each in turn appeared to offer a better chance of a successful shot. Just as he fired, however, the horses had caught sight of the leaders of the pack, but a few paces from their noses, and the sudden apparition so startled them that all three shied with one accord, bringing the wheel of the tarantass into a gigantic rut, and so nearly upsetting the carriage that the gun flew out of Peter's hands as he clutched at the side of the vehicle to save himself from being pitched out.

The next instant the horses, entirely beyond the control of poor Ivan, were dashing along the road at full gallop, the wolves accelerating their easy canter in order to keep up. It now became apparent that there were many more of these grim-looking creatures present than had at first seemed to be the case; indeed, the wood on either side of the roadway appeared to swarm with their gaunt figures, while numbers followed behind, and a few headed the carriage. Even Peter, now that his gun was lost to him, began to feel that the position was not so agreeable as he had thought; while Boris said little, but watched gravely the slightest movement of the leaders of the wolf-mob, loosening the knife at his side the while and bidding Peter do the same.

"How far to the next post-station, Ivan?" the Tsar shouted presently.

"Twelve versts," Ivan shouted back, without turning his head.

It was all the old man could do to keep the horses' heads straight; so mad were they with terror that they would have rushed wildly into the forest at the side of the road if permitted to do so.

Twelve versts are eight English miles, and Boris was well aware that the wolves would be unlikely to content themselves with passively following or accompanying the carriage for so great a distance; they would, he knew, attack the horses before very long, for their excitement would carry them away into what wolves with cool heads would consider an indiscretion. Occasionally a wolf would push ahead of its fellows, impelled by the desire to have the first taste of blood, advancing its gray nose so close to the side of the carriage that Boris or his master was able to aim a vicious dig at it, and once or twice a howl of pain attested to the fact that the blow had reached and either scratched or gashed the indiscreet assailant.

And so, for several miles, matters remained. Boris began to take heart, for half the journey had been accomplished, and if nothing more serious were attempted by the wolves than had been ventured by them up till now, there was no reason to fear any evil consequences. The wolves would pursue them thus up to within a few yards of the village, and then slink back into the woods to reflect upon what might have been had they been more enterprising.

Peter clearly shared the favourable view of Boris; no gloomy fears oppressed his sturdy mind. He laughed as he gashed at the trespassers, calling them all the bad names in the Russian vocabulary, including "cholera," which is a favourite term of abuse in that country, for sufficiently apparent reasons, and "Pharaoh," which, with less obvious point, is to a Russian the most irritating and offensive of all the bad names you can call him.

But while the two young men were thus busily engaged in the hinder portion of the carriage, a cry from old Ivan on the box caused them to desist from their exciting occupation and to look ahead. Not a moment too soon had the old driver uttered his warning note. Three huge wolves had pushed in front of their fellows and had commenced their attack upon the horses, just as Boris had feared would be the case. The fierce brutes were leaping up on either side, attempting to seize the horses by the throat, but making their springs as yet in a half-hearted way, as though they had not quite worked themselves up to the necessary point of audacity. The poor horses, however, at each spring of their assailants, jerked up their heads in terror, losing their step, and thus causing a new danger, for at the present rate of speed a stumble from any of the three might have had fatal results to the occupants of the carriage.

Boris realized the danger in a moment. Quickly directing his companion to remain where he was and attend to the attack from the rear, he sprang upon the coach-box, and thence upon the back of the shaft-horse. The other two horses were attached to the carriage by pieces of rope only, fastened to leather collars about their necks; and it was these two outsiders against whose flanks and throats the wolves were now directing their attacks. Boris with difficulty obtained a position upon the back of one of them, lying along its spine and hitching his feet into the rope at either side, while he clasped the leather collar with one hand and held his long sharp knife in the other. In this awkward and insecure position he managed to slash at the wolves, two of which were now making determined springs, as though resolved at all hazards to pull the unfortunate horse down and put an end to this prolonged chase.

It was a good fight. Boris aimed his blows well, and before a couple of hundred yards had been covered one of the rash assailants, leaping rather higher than before, received a dig from the big knife that sent him yelping and somersaulting among his fellows, and a detachment of them quickly fell behind to eat him up. This did not affect the rest, however, and Boris found that he had about as much as he could do to beat off the constantly increasing number of assailants.

Meanwhile another warning from old Ivan caused Boris to look up for a moment, when he became aware that the second outsider was in need of instant assistance. A large wolf had succeeded in effecting for a moment a hold upon the throat of the poor brute, which had, however, either shaken or kicked it off again with its galloping front legs. Peter was fully occupied in beating off the increasingly audacious attacks of the rearguard, while Ivan could, of course, give him no assistance. Boris quickly made up his mind that something must be done, and that instantly, or one of the horses must inevitably be pulled down, with fatal results to all parties. Thereupon Boris slashed with his knife the rope which attached the left-hand horse; and as the animal, feeling itself free, darted towards the forest, he was pleased to see that it was immediately followed by a dozen gray pursuers, which were thus drawn away from the main body. Horse and assailants quickly disappeared among the trees, whither the historian is unable to follow them, and the last tragedy of that steed, and its escape or death, was played out far away in the heart of the pine forest.

And now recommenced that fierce fight between Boris and his numerous antagonists which had been interrupted for a moment by the last recorded incident. Deftly as Boris fought, the wolves were so aggressive and numerous that it soon became apparent to the hunter that they were gaining ground upon him, and that in all probability they would succeed before long in pulling down one of the two remaining horses, which he was striving so determinedly to defend. Boris was accustomed to make up his mind quickly in cases of emergency. He shouted back to the Tsar to hand up to Ivan the long bear-spear which was strapped to the side of the tarantass. With this weapon he directed Ivan to prod at those wolves which attacked the shaft-horse, while he himself confined his attention to those whose springs were aimed at the remaining outsider. Old Ivan rose to the occasion; he gathered the reins in one hand, and with the other struck manfully at the brutes which ever swarmed at flank and throat of the poor shafter. Some of his blows grazed the horse's shoulder and neck, causing it to rush on with even greater speed. The post-village was now but a mile away, and if only Boris could keep off the swarming brutes for a few minutes longer the Tsar would be safe.

"Slashing at the wolves which swarmed about him."

On flew the horses, and on hacked Boris; while Peter, in the carriage, slashed at the hindmost wolves, and old Ivan prodded bravely and shouted loudly at those in front. If things were to go wrong, and he should be unable to keep the leaders at bay until the Tsar was in safety, Boris knew what he would do.

Meanwhile the chase went on for another half-mile. Then the outside horse, harassed beyond endurance by the ever-increasing number of his assailants, stumbled repeatedly. In an instant Boris had slashed in two the cords which attached him to the vehicle, and freed from the incubus of the carriage, the poor animal darted forward and turned aside into the forest, Boris himself still lying full length upon its back, but assuming as quickly as he could a sitting posture. In this position, still slashing at the wolves which swarmed about him, and waving adieu to the Tsar with his left hand, he disappeared from sight; and in the distance the horrified Peter heard the clatter of his horse's hoofs as the devoted hunter was borne away from him to his doom.

For one wild moment Peter was for bidding Ivan direct the carriage in pursuit; but the absurdity of such a course was apparent on the face of it, and the Tsar was obliged, with grief and reluctance, to leave his faithful servant and friend to his fate. At least half the wolves or more had followed Boris into the depths of the forest, and Peter and Ivan together succeeded in keeping the rest at bay long enough to allow the panting shafter to drag the carriage in safety to within sight of the village, when, with a gasp of despair, the poor creature stumbled and fell, causing the carriage to stop suddenly with a jolt that almost unseated the driver. Peter, with that personal courage in which he has never been surpassed, leaped out to cut the traces and allow the gallant animal which had served him so well to gallop for life. Seeing him on foot, the wolves, unable even now to overcome altogether their natural terror of man, drew off for a moment, and in that moment Peter freed the horse, which dashed madly away into the woods like its fellows, followed by all the wolves with the exception of two or three which preferred to hang about the two men as they walked on towards the village, but not daring to approach within striking distance of spear or knife. When within a few yards of the first dwelling-house of the village, these disappeared into the forest also, looking round once or twice ere they finally retreated, and licking their lips, as though their imagination dwelt upon the delights of a feast that might have been.

The Tsar was morose and silent; and his attendants, who arrived within an hour after himself, and who declared that they had met neither wolves nor Boris, left the young monarch to his supper, avowing to one another that they had never yet seen the Tsar so terrible to look upon.

CHAPTER VIII.

BORIS AND HIS FELLOW-OFFICERS.

The young Tsar was himself surprised, as he sat alone at his evening meal, to find how very heavily the loss of poor Boris weighed upon him. He had scarcely realized how closely the young hunter had wound himself already around his heart—a heart which, in spite of its hardness and waywardness, was capable of forming the warmest attachments. Peter was all through his life on the look-out for men who were after his own ideal, and upon whom he could rely for assistance in carrying out the vast schemes and plans for the good of his people, and the development and aggrandizement of his country, with which his brain was filled from the first. Such a man Peter thought he had found in Boris—one upon whose absolute faithfulness he could rely, and whose courage, as he had seen already more than once, was equal to any emergency. He felt that he could have trained Boris to be the ideal man for his purposes, to be employed far or near with equal confidence, and in any capacity that seemed good to his employer; and instead, here was the poor fellow gone already, a martyr to his devotion to himself! "Why are there not more of my poor Russians like this one?" thought the young Tsar; "and where am I to lay my hand upon such another—even *one*?" It certainly was most unfortunate and deplorable; so no wonder the Tsar's servants found their master in his most dangerous mood, and left him, as soon as might be, to himself.

Peter ate his cabbage-soup, and sighed as he ate. Why had he not anticipated the sudden action of Boris, and sternly forbidden him to sacrifice himself—ah, why indeed? Peter was not accustomed to personal devotion of this sort. He had not come across a Boris before this one, or he might have guessed what the brave fellow would do, and could have pulled him back into the carriage at the last moment. He would rather have fed those thrice-accursed gray brutes upon the whole of his retinue than that they should have feasted upon that brave heart. Poor Bear-Hunter! he had killed his last bear. What a fight there must have been at the very last before he permitted the skulking brutes to crowd around and pull him down!

Wrapped in these sad reflections, Peter sat before his neglected bowl of soup, when of a sudden the door opened, and the apparition of the very subject of his dismal reflections stood before him. Bootless, dishevelled, and with his clothes, what was left of them, blood-stained and in rags, was it the ghost of Boris as he had appeared at his last moment on earth? Peter was not superstitious, wonderfully little so for a Russian, but for a full minute he gazed in doubt and uncertainty upon the apparition before him. Then he burst into one of his very loudest guffaws.

"Boris!" he cried. "Yes! it is certainly Boris. Come here, my brother. I was already mourning you for dead. How did you escape those accursed gray brutes? Here is a hunter indeed! Come here, my brother." Peter kissed his friend upon both cheeks; then administered a pat on the back which might have felled an ox, laughed aloud once more, and poured into a tumbler an immense draught of strong vodka. "There," he said, "sit down and drink that, my tsar of hunters, and tell me all about it."

"There's little to tell your Majesty," said Boris, taking a big sip at the spirits. "God was very merciful to me; and as the wolves rushed in and dragged the poor horse down, which they did almost immediately after I left you, I grabbed at the branch of a pine and hauled myself up out of their reach just in time—not quite in time to save my boots, in fact; for two active fellows jumped up and pulled them both off my legs. I hope they choked the brutes! Afterwards I settled myself comfortably in the branches of the tree, and threw fir-cones at them while they pulled poor Vaiska the horse to pieces and fought over his carcass. In five minutes there was not as much of Vaiska left as would make a meal for a sparrow. When they had eaten Vaiska, they sat around my tree, watching me and hoping that I should soon let go and fall into their jaws. I howled at them in their own language instead, and they howled back at me. What I said seemed greatly to excite them, for they ran round the tree, and jumped up at me, and licked their lips. I climbed down to a point just above that which they could reach by leaping, and there I reclined at my ease and slashed at them with my knife as long as they were inclined for the game. When they grew tired of it, they sat round the tree licking their chops and looking up at me, and we exchanged complimentary remarks at intervals in their language.

"After a while the rumble and jingle of the carriages of your Majesty's retinue was heard approaching. The wolves pricked up their ears to listen. They made as though they would go back to the road at first, in the hope of picking up more horse-flesh—greedy brutes! as if Vaiska was not enough for them—but thought better of it, there was so much noise and rattle; and as the carriages came nearer and nearer, they grew more and more anxious, until at length, with a final chorus of abuse levelled at me as I sat up in my perch, they one after the other retired into the wood. Then I came down and ran for the village; and here I am, alive to serve your Majesty for many a long year, I trust."

"Glad am I to see you, my prince of hunters," said the Tsar earnestly. "But what of your wounds—is there anything serious? You look as though you had been half-way down their throats; you must have had a nasty gash somewhere to have got all that blood on you. Call the surgeon and let him see to it. I can't afford to lose so much of your good blood, my Boris; Russia has not too much of the right quality."

Boris laughed, and glanced at his saturated shirt and waistcoat. "It's all wolf's blood," he said, "and I wish there were more of it; I haven't a scratch." And this was the simple truth.

So ended happily an adventure which came near to depriving Russia of her greatest son and me of a hero.

Two days after this the Tsar with his following reached the capital, and Boris was given a commission in one of the Streltsi regiments, while retaining his place at the side of his master as body-attendant. In the ranks of the Streltsi our hunter soon learned the simple drill which the soldiers of the Russia of that day had to acquire. The Streltsi were at this time practically the only regular regiments of the country, though they were not destined to remain so long under the progressive rule of their present enlightened Tsar. Being the one armed power in the state, and having on several occasions successfully taken advantage of their position, the Streltsi had been loaded with privileges wrung from rulers and statesmen who were afraid of them, and their present position was most enviable. The men were allowed to marry, and to live at their private homes; to carry on any business or trade they pleased by way of adding to the substantial incomes which they already enjoyed at the expense of the state; and, in a word, to do very much as they liked as long as they attended the easy drills and parades which the regulations enjoined. Hence Boris had plenty of time to spare from his military duties to devote to attendance upon his beloved master.

Peter had a double object in placing Boris in a Streltsi regiment.

He was anxious that the hunter should learn all that there was to be learned in so poor a military school of the life and duties of the soldier; but chiefly because he had good reason to mistrust the Streltsi as a body, and it suited his purpose to distribute a few of his more enlightened and devoted adherents among the various regiments, in order that he might rest assured that in case of disaffection among the troops he would hear of it at the first whisper. Peter had not forgotten a certain horrible scene of violence enacted before his eyes by these very regiments in the days of his early childhood, when the entire corps had revolted, and, in presence of himself and his young co-Tsar, had massacred their chiefs and others in the square of the palace of the Kremlin. It is probable that, young as he had been at that time, Peter never forgave the Streltsi for that terrible experience, and that his distrust of them as a danger to the state dated from that day. Growing as time went on, his hatred of them culminated in the horrors attending their ultimate extermination, to which brief reference will be made at a later stage of this narrative.

Meanwhile Boris hastened to acquire all that he could pick up of military knowledge. He did not like this city life, accustomed as he was to the free and healthy open-air existence of the old Dubinka days, neither did he like his fellows in the Streltsi regiment to which he had been appointed; but it was enough for our faithful hunter to know that it was the Tsar's desire that he should associate with these men: so long as he could render service to his beloved master, Boris was content. Nor, in truth, was Boris popular with his comrades. It was well known that the new-comer was the *protégé* and favourite of the Tsar, and he was distrusted on this account; for the conscience of the regiment was not altogether void of offence towards the young head of the realm, and it was more than suspected that Peter had on that very account placed Boris as a kind of spy upon their inner counsels.

The reason for the dislike entertained by the Streltsi for their Tsar was this:—The elder brother of Peter, Ivan, was still alive and physically in good health; but, as is well known, though he had acted at one time as co-Tsar with Peter, Ivan was quite incapable, by reason of the weakness of his intellect, of taking any real part in the government of the country, and Peter, by his own brother's earnest wish, as well as by the expressed desire of the nation, had assumed the sole authority over the destinies of the country. The Streltsi, full of their own importance as the actual backbone of the state, and on this account "busy-bodies" to a man, were never perfectly satisfied with this state of affairs, and evinced at all times a nervous anxiety as to their duty in the matter. Ivan, they considered, was the real Tsar or Cæsar, successor to the Byzantine and Roman Cæsars, and therefore the lord, by divine right, of Holy Russia. It mattered little that he was incompetent and unwilling to govern; that was regrettable, no doubt, but it did not justify another, either Peter or any one else, sitting in his place and holding a sceptre which did not belong to him. The Streltsi were probably perfectly honest in their opinions. They had nothing to gain by a revolution; their position was assured, and a very good position it was. It was the feeling of responsibility which weighed upon them, and filled them with a restless sense that they ought by rights to interfere.

Peter, acute as he was, undoubtedly realized the exact state of affairs, and was well aware that a constant danger of trouble with his Streltsi regiments stood in the way of the many reforms and projects with which his active brain teemed at all times; and it is probable that he was on the look-out even now for a plausible excuse to rid himself of an incubus which he felt was inconsistent with his own ideas of the fitness of things and with the spirit of the times. Boris was therefore, more or less, that very thing which the regiment believed him to be—namely, a spy upon their actions and intentions.

The hunter was far too simple-minded to comprehend that this was his position. As a matter of fact, unlettered peasant as he was, he knew little of the history of the last few years. He was aware, indeed, of the existence of Ivan, but he had no suspicion whatever of the good faith of his companions towards the Tsar; all of which became, moreover, so apparent to his fellow Streltsi, that they soon learned to look indulgently upon "simple Boris," as he was called, as one who was too much a fool to be a dangerous spy. Hence, though never openly airing their views before their latest recruit, the young officers of the regiment gradually began to disregard the presence of Boris, and to indulge in hints and innuendoes referring to the matter which they had at heart, even though Boris was in the room and sharing in the conversation.

Now Boris, as is the case with many others, was by no means such a fool as he looked. He heard references to matters which he did not understand, and which he knew he was not intended to understand. He observed frequently that parties of officers seated dining at the eating-houses frequented by the regiment would glance at him as he entered the room and moderate their loud tones to a whisper. He overheard such sentences as—"The priests count for much, and they are with us!" or again, "Who is to persuade the Grand Duke that his brother is a mere usurper?" And once Boris thought he caught the Tsar's name, as he entered the room, received with groans, and striding to the table with flushed face, asked whose name the company had received with these manifestations of dislike; whereupon the Streltsi officers had laughed aloud, and replied that they had spoken of a dog which had stolen a bone that didn't belong to it.

The simple-minded Boris laughed also, and said, "What dog?"

Whereat the company roared with laughter, and the major replied with streaming eyes,—

"Oh, a big dog I saw up at the Kremlin, that found a little dog with a nice bone, and bow-wowed at him till the little dog thought he had better let it go with a good grace. We all thought this so mean of the big dog that we hooted him and drank his health backwards!"

Afterwards Boris recalled this and other curious sayings of his companions, and revolved them in his mind as he lay at the Tsar's door at night.

CHAPTER IX.

ONE SWORD AGAINST FIVE.

The result of Boris's reflections was that he became suspicious and unhappy. He felt that his position was a delicate and difficult one, and that it would be impossible for him to maintain it under present conditions. Putting two and two together, he had concluded that there was something existing in the minds of his brother officers to which he was no party, and which he feared—though he hesitated to believe it—might be treason against his beloved master. If this should prove to be the case, he reflected, what course ought he to pursue? Should he inform the Tsar, and thus be the means of terrible trouble to the regiment of which he was a member, or allow matters to take their course in the hope that either his suspicions would prove unfounded, or that his companions might shortly see the iniquity of their ways, and return to full loyalty, as behoved true officers of the Tsar? After all, it was merely a suspicion; all that talk about big dogs and little dogs might be the purest nonsense. What right had he to take serious action upon so feeble a suspicion? Boris finally decided that he would do nothing rash and ill-considered; for the generous Tsar would be the first to laugh at him for jumping at ill-based conclusions, and Boris was very sensitive to derision, especially at Peter's mouth.

Very soon after the discussion on canine iniquity recorded above, Boris had the decision as to his duty in these trying circumstances taken out of his hands by the workings of destiny. Sitting over his dinner at the restaurant patronized by the officers of the Streltsi, he found himself listening in spite of himself to the conversation of a group of his companions dining at a table close to his own. The vodka had flowed pretty freely, it appeared, and tongues were growing looser and slipping the leash which restraint and discretion usually put upon them in the presence of Boris. The major, Platonof, was the noisiest speaker—he of the dog story; and Boris several times recognized his somewhat strident voice raised above that of his fellows, who, however, generally hushed him down before his words became distinctly audible. Once Boris overheard his own name spoken by one of the younger officers, whereupon the major said aloud,—

"What! simple Boris—our Bear-hunter? Why, he's a capital fellow is our Boris—he's one of us—we needn't be afraid of Boris.—Need we, Boris?" he continued, looking tipsily over his shoulder at the hunter. "You'll fight for the lord of Russia, won't you, Boris, in case of need?"

"I'll fight for the Tsar with my last drop of blood, if that's what you mean," said Boris, flushing.

"Say the Tsar that should be—the friend of the church and of the priests—in fact, the lord of Russia!" continued Platonof.

"Certainly the lord of Russia," said Boris, "but why the Tsar that 'should be'?"

"Because," hiccoughed the major solemnly, "while Peter remains upon the throne, the lord of Russia reigns only in our hearts. When the Streltsi have ousted the big dog from the little dog's kennel—Peter being the big dog—and given the little dog back his bone—that's Ivan—then—"

Platonof never finished that sentence. Boris had sprung to his feet, and drawing his sword, dashed from the major's hand the tumbler which he tipsily waved before his face as he spoke these significant words. The vodka which the glass contained bespattered half the company as they, too, rose excitedly to their feet.

"Traitors!" cried Boris, "so this is the meaning of your whisperings and secrecy; and but for yonder drunken fool I might have remained in ignorance of your treachery. Out with your swords and defend yourselves if you are men. I am on Peter's side!"

The party consisted of the major and four others. All drew their swords, including Platonof, who was somewhat unsteady, though partly sobered by the turn events had taken. The rest were pale and determined, for they realized the fact that the tipsy major had plunged them into a serious dilemma. Either they must kill this favourite of the Tsar, and incur Peter's wrath on that account, or else he must be allowed to escape alive, but with the certainty that all he had heard would be repeated for Peter's private benefit. And then—well, the young Tsar's character was already sufficiently understood by his subjects to leave no doubt in the minds of these Streltsi officers that he would make a terrible example of them. Under the circumstances there was practically no choice for them: it was Boris's life or theirs; Boris must not leave the room alive.

One of the younger officers sprang to the door and locked it, placing the key in his pocket. Meanwhile Boris had crossed swords with Platonof, but finding that the major was too unsteady to make a fight of it, he pushed him out of the way. Platonof tumbled over the table, dragging the glasses and bottles with him. This was fortunate for Boris, for it placed the table between himself and his adversaries, and prevented overcrowding.

Then the four men fiercely attacked the one, hacking savagely but unscientifically at him, each retreating as he thrust back. Boris had the advantage of a long reach, and before many blows had been exchanged he had put one of his assailants *hors de combat* with a straight thrust which penetrated his sword-arm. Boris knew, as yet, little swordsmanship, but he had a good natural idea of thrusting straight and quickly, acquired in his bear-hunting days. He had, besides, the advantages of great strength and agility, in both of which qualities he far excelled any of the five men opposed to him, of whom but three were now left to carry on the battle. These three now separated, one presently advancing from either side, while the third endeavoured to get behind him in order to take him in the rear. Boris backed towards the wall, hoping to frustrate his intention, while the others pressed him hard in the endeavour to entice him to follow one of them up. But Boris, waiting until his third assailant was well behind him, suddenly swept round with so terrible a backhander that the unfortunate officer's arm was cut through and half of his body besides. The man dropped where he stood and never moved again.

Then Boris made so savage an attack upon his two remaining opponents that they fled, and were pursued by him twice round the room, fighting as they ran, until Boris, tripping over the sleeping major, fell among the bottles and glasses. During the moment or two which expired before the redoubtable bear-hunter could recover his footing, the two fugitive heroes succeeded in opening the door and escaping, but not before Boris, seizing a heavy wooden stool from the floor, hurled it after them with so true an aim that it struck the hindmost between the shoulders, sending him head first downstairs, to the great injury of his front teeth and the bridge of his nose.

Then Boris endeavoured to arouse Platonof, to bid him see to his wounded friends, but found this impossible. Moreover, he discovered on looking up that the young officer first wounded had taken the opportunity, during Boris's preoccupation with the tipsy major, to escape through the open door. As for the fifth man, Boris soon found that he would need no help from the major or any one else. He therefore administered a final kick to the snoring form of Platonof, and quitted the apartment which had witnessed so exciting a struggle for life.

Then only did Boris discover that he had not come through the fierce fight scathless. His hand was bleeding from a gash over the knuckles, and a pain just above the knee, and a rent in his kaftan, plainly indicated that he had received a second wound more or less severe. He was able to walk home, however, to the palace in the Kremlin, and to attend to his duties about the person of the Tsar. But there the keen glance of Peter detected at once the cut over the fingers, and this discovery was instantly followed by a demand for an explanation.

Boris had firmly resolved that even at the Tsar's bidding he would never reveal the names of his assailants, or say more than was absolutely necessary as to the treasonable words which he had overheard. When therefore the Tsar inquired what was the matter with his hand, Boris blushed and stammered, and said that he had hurt it.

"That much I see already," said Peter. "I see also that this is a sword cut, and that you have a rent in your kaftan. You have been fighting, my Bear-eater, but not with a bear this time, nor yet with a wolf, except it be a human one. Come, who is it? Don't be afraid, man—are we not sworn brothers?"

"It is true, your Majesty, I have fought," said poor Boris, and stopped.

"And pray with whom," Peter insisted, "and with what results? Come, Boris, this is interesting, and you shall tell me all about it ere we sleep to-night. I desire it. Have you killed a man? Speak up; I shall not mind if the cause is good."

"I have killed a man, your Majesty," Boris stammered, "and the cause is good. The man was an officer; he is dead, and therefore I may tell his name—Zouboff, the Streltsi Captain, of my regiment."

"Oho! Zouboff killed—and the cause good!" said the Tsar,

looking grave. "And the others of his company—Platonof, Katkoff, Zaitzoff, Shurin—what of them? Those five are never apart. Fear nothing, tell me all. I have watched them, and guessed their disaffection."

Boris was thunderstruck at the Tsar's knowledge, but he was not startled into committing himself.

"There were others, your Majesty, who took his part; but I entreat you not to bid me name them, nor to insist upon the cause of our quarrel. It was but certain drunken nonsense to which I objected. I entreat your Majesty to press me no further."

Peter strode up and down the apartment looking his blackest. For a moment or two it seemed as though the storm would burst; then his eye fell once more upon wounded Boris, and his brow cleared.

"And the rest," he asked kindly, "are they wounded too?"

"Some are wounded; one was too drunk to fight," Boris replied, his cheek flushing with martial ardour as he recalled the circumstances of the late encounter.

"Ho, ho!" laughed the Tsar; "would I had been there to see, my valiant Bear-eater. Now I will tell you what happened before the fight, and you shall narrate to me, without mentioning names, how the fight itself was conducted; that is a fair compromise. First, then, one of them—perhaps Zouboff, who is dead, or drunken Platonof, who deserves to be—made a remark about one Peter Alexeyevitch Romanof which our Boris disapproved of—no matter what he said. Then up strode Boris. 'Sir,' he said, 'you are a liar!' or words to that effect, perhaps striking the speaker with his hand or with the back of his sword. Then out flew all the swords, five traitor swords against one honest and loyal one, and then—well, then comes your part of the story; so put off that melancholy expression and speak up. I love to hear of a good fight."

Boris laughed in spite of himself, for the Tsar's acuteness delighted him and comforted him also; for, he reflected, his puny enemies could surely never triumph over this mighty, all-seeing, all-knowing young demi-god, his master. Therefore Boris made no further difficulty about the matter, but did as Peter bade him, and told the story of his fight in detail, naming no names.

Peter heard the tale with alternate rage and delight.

"Very good, my Bear-hunter," he said, when the recital was ended; "excellently good. You have done well, and for reward I shall take no notice of the individuals concerned. But for your personal intercession they should have hung in chains to-morrow morning from the four corners of their own barracks. I know their names, though you have not mentioned them. Now, good-night, Captain Bear-Eater—you are captain from to-morrow's date—and thank you."

Boris threw himself at the Tsar's feet in gratitude for the magnanimity with which he had consented to forego his just wrath against these traitors—he could have kissed those feet in his joy and in the intensity of his relief—for he felt that though he would have no compunction in slaying these men in fair fight, he could never have forgiven himself had he as informer been the means of bringing them to a disgraceful end upon the gibbet.

"But grant me one more favour, your Majesty," he pleaded. "I will not ask another until I shall have earned the right to do so; but grant me this one I entreat you: send our regiment far away from Moscow; send it to any distant garrison town, but do not let it remain here."

"And why not, my Bear-eater?" asked the Tsar, amused at the earnestness of the appeal.

"Your Majesty knows why not," said Boris; "when a bough is rotten who would lean upon it?"

"When a bough is rotten," repeated the Tsar, looking grave, "it is best cut down and burned. But I will think upon your request—perhaps you are right—though, my Bear-eater, you too would go with them in that case, which would be regrettable. Meanwhile you take care of your own skin, for the Streltsi officers hold together. Keep that good sword loose when you approach the dark corners of the city. I will think of what you have said. Good-night!"

CHAPTER X.

A NIGHT AMBUSH.

Contrary to his expectations, Boris found that his position in the regiment after the *fracas* described in the foregoing chapter was in no respect more unpleasant than it had been before; indeed, it appeared to him that his fellow-officers now treated him with greater consideration. No reference whatever was made to the death of Zouboff, or indeed to any circumstance in connection with the fight at the restaurant. In those days the taking of life was little thought of, and if an officer chose to brawl with others of his regiment, and lose his life in the struggle, that was considered his own look-out, and so much the worse for him. As for punishing those at whose hands he met his death, no one thought of such a thing. Hence matters in the regiment remained very much as they were before; the officers taking care, however, to keep a discreet tongue in the presence of Boris, and to maintain outwardly an appearance of respect for that dangerously formidable young man. As for his late opponents, these glared at him whenever they met on parade or elsewhere, and exchanged no word with their late antagonist; but Boris was not anxious to enter into friendly intercourse with men whom he had, as he considered, actually convicted of treason to the Tsar, and he was glad enough of their coldness towards him. Platonof, having no recollection of the circumstances of that fatal afternoon, was not without a feeling of gratified surprise, when informed of his indiscretion and its results, that he had been permitted to depart alive and in peace, and was inclined to make friendly advances towards the magnanimous young man who had neither dug him between the ribs with a sword thrust—as he undoubtedly might have done—nor delivered him alive and guilty into the hands of an enraged Tsar. But Boris showed no disposition to respond to his advances, and treated him with the same disregard which he showed towards the rest of the party of avowed traitors to his master.

Meanwhile the Tsar had not as yet acceded to the urgent request of Boris that the regiment might be sent out of the capital. Peter was unwilling to make any concession to a feeling of unworthy anxiety for his personal safety; but, at the same time, he now only awaited an opportunity to banish the regiment upon some plausible pretext, for reflection had quite convinced him that the presence of disaffected Streltsi in Moscow was a needless standing danger to the peace of the realm.

The opportunity he sought came in the course of a few months. It became necessary to send troops into the south of Russia in preparation for the contemplated siege of Azof, a fortress of the Mohammedans, and one of the last still held in the country by the once all-conquering Mussulman hosts. The Streltsi of Boris's regiment were ordered to proceed to the Ukraine, where they were to hold themselves at the disposal of the Cossack chieftain or hetman Mazeppa, who had begged of the Tsar some support in order to enable him to maintain and strengthen his lately-acquired position at the head of the warlike tribes he had been called to govern. Peter at all times showed the most loyal regard for this Mazeppa, who was destined in after years to ill repay him for his generosity; and it was in his desire to accede to the Cossacks request for temporary assistance, and at the same time to push on his preparations for the intended Azof campaign, that the Tsar now found an excellent opportunity for ridding Moscow of a dangerous element by despatching this disaffected body of men far away from the seat of government and out of the reach of any ill-advised interference on their part.

The order for their departure—exile, as they termed it—was received with a storm of rage and indignation by all ranks in the regiment. The men had never before been called upon to leave Moscow for prolonged service, though many others of the Streltsi regiments had not been so fortunate. Many of them were married men with large families, and were engaged in various profitable trades and professions, without the exercise of which, they declared, they would be unable to support those dependent upon them. Besides this, each man and officer had a thousand ties and interests which bound him to the capital, and would bear it ill to have these suddenly torn away and himself cast adrift into unknown places and among strange people, and submitted to dangers and discomforts to which he had not been trained, and which he feared to encounter.

All sorts of reasons for the Tsar's sudden *ookaz*, or edict, were suggested and considered by men and officers. Had he discovered the disaffection of the regiment? If so, how? The affair of Boris and Platonof and his party had not become generally known, at the urgent request of Platonof, who was naturally anxious that his tipsy indiscretion should not be spoken of. Those who were acquainted with the details of the affair, however, had no doubt whatever of the cause which had brought the displeasure of the Tsar upon the regiment: Boris had revealed the whole story. But in that case why had the Tsar's vengeance not been—as the vengeance of Peter was wont to be—immediate and terrible? Why, in other words, were not Platonof and his three friends dangling aloft far above the heads of the crowd, upon improvised gibbets, as a warning to the treasonable and the conspiring? Probably, these men concluded, because the Tsar was somewhat afraid of the Streltsi, and was therefore unwilling to risk giving provocation which might lead to a sudden rising.

Anyhow, it was not the fault of Boris that worse things had not happened than this sufficiently annoying ookaz from the Tsar; and if opportunity arose during the three days remaining to the regiment in Moscow, Boris should be made to regret his position as spy and tale-bearer-in-ordinary to the Tsar. So vowed Platonof and his friends, and with them a few other choice spirits who were acquainted with the state of affairs, and were not averse to a little night work at street corners, provided the dangerous element was eliminated as far as possible!

"Boris, my trusty one, eater of bears and render of wolves," said the Tsar, on the second evening after the issue of the ookaz dismissing the Streltsi from Moscow, "I feel inclined for an evening out. What say you to a visit to Lefort and a taste of his French wine, and perhaps a game or two at cards, to-night? If Lefort is asleep, so much the better; we'll pull him out of bed, and bid him send for Gordon and the rest, and we can order supper while he's dressing."

Lefort, one of Peter's prime favourites, as he well deserved to be when his services to Russia and the Tsar are taken into consideration, was the third of the trio selected by the monarch as his constant companions and advisers, the remaining members of this trinity of favour being Menshikoff and Patrick Gordon, once a Scotsman, and related to some of the best and oldest Scottish families, now a naturalized Russian and the ablest of Peter's generals, as well as his most faithful and honoured servant. Menshikoff had not as yet come into prominence; but Gordon and Lefort—the latter a Russianized foreigner as Gordon was—were already the chosen advisers and friends of the Tsar, both men after his own heart—capable, brave, hard workers, ready at an instant's notice either to drink and fool with their master, to command his armies or direct his fleets, to wrestle with him and engage in any kind of athletic competition, to build boats with him, to make love with him, or, in a word, share with the Tsar in any and every occupation or duty which Peter might call upon them to perform.

It was no uncommon event for the young monarch to suddenly descend thus upon his friends at any hour of the day or night, and General (Patrick) Gordon has left it on record that occasionally these visits were made at the dinner-hour, upon short notice, and sometimes with a retinue of a hundred companions. Thus it was necessary for the friends of the Tsar to keep in the house a constant stock of wine for the consumption of Peter and his following, which might consist of one or two persons, or, as I have said, of a hundred men.

"We will go incognito," Peter added. "Muffle yourself in this cloak, and I will do the same; it is better not to be seen. I love to go among my people in the streets and hear what they say about me."

Nothing loath, Boris took the Tsar's spare cloak, which was much too big for him in spite of his seventy odd inches of bone and muscle, and followed his master from the Kremlin. Through the streets of the old city went the tall pair, pausing here and there in the darker corners in order to listen to the conversation of the townsfolk as they passed. This was a favourite pastime of Peter's, who loved to gather at first-hand the opinions and wishes of his poorer subjects, with whom he was ever the popular hero as well as the beloved sovereign, and from whose lips there was therefore little risk of hearing anything about himself which would sound unpleasant in his ears. On this occasion he heard little of interest. A few remarks were made about the impending departure of the Streltsi, which the people appeared to regret but little. Presently, however, two young Streltsi officers came walking down the street talking confidentially. Peter and Boris withdrew deeper into the shadow and listened.

"Consequently," said one, "there's no doubt whatever about it—we have to thank him and him only for the ookaz."

"What! do you suppose he told the Tsar about what that fool Platonof said, and all that?" said the second officer, who apparently had just been informed by his companion of the encounter between Boris and his assailants.

"Undoubtedly he did, confound him!" said the first; "and that's why we are all off the day after to-morrow."

"Well, why don't we get hold of the spying rascal and"—the officer made a gesture as of a knife at his throat. The other laughed.

"That's just what's going on now, I hope," he said; "for Zaitzoff and a few others have sworn to have him before we go. They watched all last night; and to-night they are keeping guard at the corner of the Uspensky, where he goes for his supper. I hope they kill him—hateful spy!"

Peter almost danced with delight as the footsteps of the men died away in the distance. "Bear-eater, my son, we are in luck!" he whispered excitedly. "Come along quickly. Got your sword?"

Boris rattled his weapon for answer, but he looked grave and preoccupied. "Go home, your Majesty, I entreat you," he said; "don't run into needless danger. I can settle accounts with these men alone."

For a moment the Tsar looked as black as thunder. "*What!*" he cried; "go home, and miss the play? Don't be a fool, man. Am I to be afraid of my own officers? No, my Bear-eater. You may cut and run from an old bear if you like, but not I from a Streletz, or any number of Streltsi. Come on!" The Tsar ended with one of his loud laughs, and dragged after him poor Boris, whose cheek was red by reason of Peter's allusion to his escapade with the bear.

Through the wretchedly lighted streets they sped until they reached the Uspensky, where, in the distance, they soon espied a group of figures standing at the corner as though awaiting an arrival.

The two tall men, shrouded in their mantles as they were, approached close up to the group of officers before they were recognized.

"It's the Tsar!" some one whispered at length. "Round the corner all, and away—quick!"

Off went the party, scudding down the road like a pack of frightened sheep; but the Tsar's loud voice of authority soon recalled them. They crept back in a huddled, scared group.

"Good evening, Zaitzoff," said Peter. "How are you, Shurin? What, Ulanof, is that you? Good evening, gentlemen all. You are waiting for the pleasure of seeing my friend Boris Ivanitch, I believe. Well, here he is."

No one spoke a word. The Tsar laughed. "Is it not so? Zaitzoff, speak!"

"It is true, your Majesty," said Zaitzoff at length. "We came to meet the gentleman you name, with whom we have a quarrel."

"Oh, indeed!" said the Tsar, in affected surprise; "what, all of you? Do you *all* desire to quarrel with my friend? It is most flattering, upon my word, gentlemen. And do you still wish to quarrel with Boris Ivanitch, now he is here? Positively I was under the impression that I observed you all racing down the road there, as though anxious to get out of his way!"

"Our quarrel is a private one, your Majesty," said Ulanof; "and if your Majesty will withdraw, we shall proceed with it."

"What!—withdraw? I, his second? No, my good Ulanof, that is impossible; the quarrel must proceed. Boris Ivanitch is here to give you every satisfaction, and I shall act as his second. Now then, gentlemen, who is to lay on first? One would suppose that you had contemplated a combined assault in the—ha! ha!—in the dark, were we not acquainted with the strictly honourable traditions of the Streltsi officers. Come, Zaitzoff, you seem to be the leader of the party; you shall have the first opportunity of depriving the rest of their prey.—Come, Boris, draw!"

CHAPTER XI.

A BATTLE AGAINST ODDS.

The experience of two months ago, when he had last been called upon to defend his life against some of these very men, had not been lost upon Boris. He had then realized that he was but a poor swordsman, and that he was indebted more to his superior agility and strength than to his skill for his safety on that occasion. True, his antagonists had shown that their knowledge of the science was not greater than his own; but nevertheless Boris had made a mental note of his incapacity, and had registered at the same time a vow to make the science of the sword his principal study until he should have gained at least a fair degree of proficiency. He had not failed to put this good resolution into practice, and had assiduously worked at his fencing daily with an exponent of the art, a German named Schmidt, under whose skilful tuition, and with his natural aptitude for every kind of manly exercise, Boris had quickly acquired no little skill in the use of his somewhat clumsy but formidable Russian weapon.

At the first onset, the Tsar was surprised and delighted to observe that Boris was more than a match for his opponent. Before the swords had been crossed for two minutes, Zaitzoff was disabled and disarmed.

The Tsar bade him give up his sword and retire to the opposite wall, where he might watch the fun with as much comfort as was possible with a hole through his sword-arm and a deepish cut in the shoulder as well. Then Ulanof came to take his place.

Ulanof was a big and heavy man, determined and very powerful, but lacking skill. He made so furious an onslaught upon his antagonist, cutting and slashing and thrusting at him with extreme rapidity though quite without method, that for some moments Boris was fully occupied in defending his own person without attempting to carry the fight into the enemy's camp—in fact he actually lost ground, being surprised into stepping backwards by the unexpectedly furious character of Ulanof's attack upon him. But as soon as the Tsar whispered encouragingly, "Steady, my Bear-eater!" Boris quickly recovered his position, and pulling himself together delivered an equally furious but a more scientific counter-attack upon Ulanof, whose exertions had already deprived him of much breath.

Still fiercely battling, and contesting every inch of ground, Ulanof was now driven backwards yard by yard until he stood at bay with his back to the wall of the house opposite. To that wall Boris speedily spitted him, his sword passing through Ulanof's body and into the wooden side of the house, whence Boris with difficulty drew it forth. As he did so, Ulanof fell with a gasp at his feet, and the officers' list of the Streltsi regiment was shorter by one name.

"Bravo, bravo, my good Boris!" cried the Tsar; "it was well and scientifically done, and after the German method, I perceive. We shall see you sticking bears in the Prussian fashion on our next trip.—Now, gentlemen, how many more of you? Four, is it not? —Now, what say you, Boris, to taking them two at a time? This single process grows tedious. I shall see fair play—is it agreed?"

"With all my heart, your Majesty, if you desire it," said Boris, eying his still untried foes as though to estimate his chances against them, two swords to one.

After a short whispered consultation, these officers, however, stepped forward and informed the Tsar that their honour was satisfied—there was no need for the fight to continue.

But the Tsar would not hear of it. The matter rested with Boris Ivanitch, he declared; and, if Boris so desired it, every one of them should meet him until *his* honour had obtained ample satisfaction. "As for *your* honour, gentlemen, you left it at home when you sallied forth this evening like common midnight assassins to fall upon him unawares and murder him. No, officers of the Streltsi, you are here to fight, and fight you shall. If any man shirks, I too have a sword, and with my sword I shall write 'coward' on his body for all men to see!"

Then the two, Katkoff and Shurin, fell upon the one, and the fight recommenced; and a good fight it was. Katkoff was a good swordsman, Shurin was strong and active, and the battle was at first sight unequal. The Tsar would not suffer the pair to separate. If either attempted to edge to one side and take Boris in the flank, the Tsar angrily bade him return to line. The battle was to be fought fair, this much was plainly evident; it behoved Shurin and his partner, therefore, to be careful and watch, and to take the first advantage that offered.

Boris fought like a lion, or like one of his own bears at bay. In vain Katkoff slashed and Shurin thrust; his sword was always there to intercept, and even to aim an answering blow before the pair were able to repeat the attack. Once a thrust from Shurin touched his cheek and made the blood spirt. Shurin cheered, and redoubled his exertions, well backed up by Katkoff. Then Boris, like an enraged tiger, fell upon the pair so fiercely, raining his blows upon them like hailstones in June, that they gave ground both together. Pursuing his advantage quickly Boris drove them round by the wall, the two whole men and the wounded one moving out of their way as they went, Peter close at their heels to see fair play. One tripped over dead Ulanof and nearly fell, but recovered himself and fought on. Then Boris in his turn tripped and fell on his knee. In an instant the two were upon him, and

Shurin's thrust pierced through his left arm, while he just saved his head from the downward blow of Katkoff's weapon. But before Shurin could withdraw his sword, Boris aimed a cut at the arm that held it with such terrible force that it was severed at the wrist. Shurin caught at the kaftan of Boris to pull him over; while Katkoff, seeing that now, if ever, he must make his effort and end this struggle, rained his blows from above. Then Boris, in guarding his shoulder, nevertheless contrived at the same time to administer to Shurin a backhander which laid him flat beside Ulanof, and rising from his kneeling position he so furiously fell upon Katkoff that in a moment the latter was disarmed, his sword flying through the air with a whistle, and alighting point-down upon the low wooden roof of an adjoining house, where it stuck, vibrating with the force of its flight.

"In an instant the two were upon him."

But this was Boris's final effort—tired nature could do no more. He turned, as though to return to Peter's side, but slipped and fell fainting into the Tsar's strong embrace.

Peter looked darkly around at the remains of the party which had been so roughly handled by Boris. "Go!" he said, "get you gone, you that can walk. Leave your swords. You shall hear of me to-morrow. Meanwhile, you that have escaped, be thankful that I am not tempted myself to finish what Boris Ivanitch has left undone. I should know well how to treat midnight assassins. Leave your swords, I say. Now go!"

As the party of discomfited warriors limped and slunk away in the darkness, leaving Shurin and Ulanof behind them, the Tsar tenderly picked up the still unconscious Boris in his great arms, and carried him like a child to the nearest house. Thither he sent his own doctor, a Scotsman of much skill, under whose care Boris very quickly came round, and, his arm being carefully bandaged and treated, he was able to return on foot to the palace, to the delight of his master.

But though Boris was able to make his own way home, he was not destined to come through this matter quite so easily as he had at first believed. His wound proved somewhat obstinate, and the poor hunter tossed for many days upon his plain camp-bed, racked with pain and fever, during which time he longed incessantly for the fresh air, and the forest, and the delights of his old open-air life. All that could be done to relieve his pain and hasten his recovery was done by Macintyre, the Tsar's own doctor, who tended him assiduously, having taken a great liking to this fine specimen of a Russian peasant.

The Tsar himself frequently stole an hour from his various pressing duties in order to sit by his favourite servant and chat over what had been and what was yet to be—fighting over again their battles with bear and wolf, which, to the joy of Boris, Peter solemnly promised should be repeated at the earliest opportunity; and discussing many projects at that time in the brain of the Tsar—such as the development of a standing army, which idea was already beginning to take practical form; the organization of a navy; the building of a capital which should be a seaport; the necessity for recommencing that which Ivan the Terrible had so nearly accomplished, but in which that monarch had eventually failed—namely, the wresting from their lieges of those ports in the Baltic which were absolutely necessary for the development of the empire; and, lastly, Eastern conquest—overland trade with India, and many other dazzling projects upon which the heart of Peter was set.

From the Tsar, also, Boris learned that the banishment of the Streltsi regiment to which the wounded hunter was attached was now an accomplished fact. After the disgraceful conduct of the officers at the corner of the Uspensky, Peter had determined that the regiment should not remain another hour in the capital, but be marched out of it as early as possible on the following morning. The Tsar therefore himself attended the early parade of the regiment, when he read aloud a revised list of officers, in

which the names of the six midnight assailants of Boris had no place. In their stead were substituted those of six privates, men who had shown aptitude for military service, and whose good conduct had entitled them to recognition. Then Peter read the names of six officers who, he said, in consequence of conduct which disqualified them for ever from associating with men of their own position in the service, were degraded to the ranks. These men were directed to step out in order to be deprived of their insignia of officer's rank, when Peter himself tore from their shoulders the epaulets of their order. It was observed that but four men appeared instead of six, and that one of these wore his arm in a sling, while another limped as he walked.

After this ceremony, the Tsar bade the commanding officer pass the regiment in review, when Peter himself uttered several words of command; finally in stentorian tones giving the order,—

"Gentlemen of the Streltsi, form in marching order! Right about face! Quick march! to the Ukraine!"

As the Tsar uttered these words, the consternation and surprise of the regiment, men and officers, was indescribable. None had expected this sudden change of date; no one was ready; final arrangements for the winding up or transfer of business had been left by many to the last moment, and were still in abeyance; farewells to families and lovers were still unsaid; many of the men were but half dressed, their long kaftans serving to conceal the shortcomings of the unseen portion of their costume. But none dared disobey the personal ookaz of the masterful young giant whose stern lips had uttered it.

Sobbing and whining the regiment marched slowly through the streets of Moscow, followed by troops of women and children, who sobbed and whined also. The officers strode along looking pale and gloomy, many with tears streaming down their faces. The word had soon passed from street to street, and from house to house, and as the woful procession approached the gates of the city the ranks of the weeping crowd of friends and relatives became largely increased, until, when the regiment had reached the open country, the colonel, who doubtless had matters of his own to attend to, called a halt in order that the unfortunate men might at least take a last farewell of their wives and families ere they marched out into an exile the duration of which none could foretell.

Then ensued a remarkable scene. Most of the men were married, and most of the wives and a great host of children of all ages had heard the news of the sudden departure of their lords, and had hastened after them to get a last glimpse of them, and if possible a last word. No sooner had the ranks obeyed the order to halt, than the lines were instantly invaded by swarms of sobbing women and children, each seeking her own, and calling his name aloud. The confusion became indescribable, the din deafening. Frantic women, unable to find their husbands or lovers, rushed shrieking from line to line, imploring sergeants and soldiers to tell them where to seek their lords. Others, having found their belongings, clung about their necks, while the children clasped the knees of their fathers and cried aloud. For a full hour the scene of woe and noise was prolonged, and then at last the word was given to resume the march, the women and children being forbidden to follow further. Many young wives and girls, however, refused to obey the colonel's command, and followed or accompanied the troops for many miles, wailing and crying and shouting last words of love and farewell to their friends in the ranks.

Thus did Peter rid himself, in a characteristic manner, of a regiment which he knew to be rotten at the core. And thus it happened that Boris remained behind while the rest went into exile.

CHAPTER XII.

A PERILOUS SLIDE.

To Boris the news that the Streltsi had gone away without him was the best and most acceptable news in the world. To his simple, honest mind the atmosphere of disloyalty and disaffection in which he had been forced to live, as well as the unrest and actual physical danger which were the unavoidable consequence of the unpopularity in which he was held by his fellows, as one outside their own circle and therefore dangerous—all this was intolerable. Boris was not a quarrelsome man, yet he had been forced into several fights already; and if he had proceeded to the Ukraine with the rest he would undoubtedly have been drawn into many other quarrels as soon as the repressive influence of the Tsar's presence had ceased to work upon the minds of his comrades. The departure of the Streltsi, therefore, acted like a tonic upon his system, and his recovery was speedy from this day onwards. Within a week after the scene on the parade-ground Boris was up and about attending once more upon his master, the Tsar, and learning with astonishment the remarkable phases and contrasts of Peter's character—a character which must ever puzzle students and analysts in the inconsistencies and contradictions which it revealed from day to day.

Peter was particularly busy just at this time enrolling soldiers for certain new regiments of Guards which he designed should take the place of the erratic Streltsi. Lefort, of whom mention has already been made, was most energetic in this work, and proved himself a most successful recruiting officer. Foreigners—Englishmen, Germans, and others—were engaged as far as possible to officer these new troops; but Boris, to his great joy, was permitted to exchange from his Streltsi regiment, which he hated, into one of the newly-organized corps.

The Tsar was radiant and happy over the congenial work upon which he was engaged, and worked night and day in order to accomplish the task he had set before himself. Yet, in spite of his activity and energy, and of the amazing amount of work he managed to get through during the day, this remarkable young monarch found time for boisterous carousals almost every evening. At these Boris was expected to attend the Tsar, and did so; but he was never a lover of indoor amusements, and did not take to card-playing and heavy drinking with the zeal infused into the pursuit of such joys by his betters, including Peter himself.

At the court, too, Boris was out of his element. The big bear-hunter was not used to the society of ladies; and though the manners of Peter's court were far from being characterized by all that we in our day understand when we speak of refinement and breeding, yet the measure of their civilization was naturally far beyond that reached by the good folks at Dubinka, or even at Archangel.

The ladies of the court, including the empress, were one and all attracted by the handsome young hunter, now officer, and some made no secret of their admiration. The empress was kind and condescending, and occasionally preached Boris a little sermon on the iniquity of making friends of foreigners, warning him to beware of familiarity with those alien officers who had lately been imported into Russia. These men, the Tsaritsa declared, would be the ruin—they and the foreign institutions and vices which they foreshadowed—of holy Russia and her exclusiveness. The church, she said, and all her dignitaries looked with horror upon the many un-Russian innovations which were the ruling spirit of the day.

Boris thought that the empress ought to know all about the church and her opinions, if anybody did, for the palace, or her own portion of it, was always full of priests and confessors; but he thought it a curious circumstance, nevertheless, that the wife should speak thus of the work upon which the husband was engaged. To his frank and simple mind it appeared unnatural and wrong that the very person in all the world who should have been the first to encourage and help the Tsar in his work of reformation and progress should have neglected no opportunity of hindering and crying it down.

In short, the ladies of the court had for Boris but little attraction; he had not been used to the society of ladies, and did not understand them and their mysterious ways. He was glad when Peter avoided his wife's portion of the palace for days together; and though he did not particularly enjoy the carouses with Lefort and Gordon, and other kindred spirits of the Tsar, yet he preferred these noisy and rowdy gatherings to the society of the ladies. In a word, Boris was not a lady's man, although there were many fair damsels at court and out of it who would fain it had been otherwise.

But Boris had a little adventure early in this first winter in Moscow which laid the foundation of a great and momentous friendship, the greatest and most important of any formed by him throughout his life, even though we include that which united him with his beloved Tsar. The circumstances were romantic, and may be given with propriety in this place.

It has been mentioned that many foreigners were at this time being attracted into Russia by the liberal offers made to them of lucrative employment in the service of the Tsar. Among the officers thus engaged by Peter to train and command his newly-levied troops of the Guard was a certain Englishman of the name of Drury, who, with his wife and little daughter aged twelve, had but lately arrived in the great northern city. Boris had seen and made the acquaintance of the English officer at Peter's palace, and had moreover met the wife and child at the court of the Tsaritsa, where he had admired the little, bright-eyed, flaxen-haired English maiden, and had even played ball with her, and taught her the use of the Russian swing in the courtyard.

Nancy Drury, as she was called, possessed all the love for outdoor amusements and exercise which is the heritage of the British race; and, consequently, no sooner did the early northern winter bring enough frost to cover the narrow Moscow river with a thin layer of ice, than Miss Nancy determined to make the most of the advantages of living "up north," by enjoying an hour's sliding at the very first opportunity. Thus, on the second day after the appearance of the ice, though no Russian would have thought of stepping upon it for at least another week, the child walked fearlessly out to the centre of the stream and commenced her sliding.

The ice was smooth and very elastic, and Nancy found the sliding excellent; but, as might have been expected, at the third or fourth slide the ice gave way beneath even her light feet, and in went Nancy, sprawling forwards as her footing played her false, and thus breaking up a large hole for herself to splash into. Luckily Nancy was a brave child, and did not struggle and choke and go straight to the bottom, or under the ice. She supported herself as best she could upon the sound ice which surrounded the hole she had made, and shouted for assistance.

The streets were full of people; but that circumstance was of little comfort to poor Nancy, had she known it. For if she had found herself in this fix on ninety-nine out of a hundred occasions, she would have received no doubt the deepest sympathy from those on shore, evidenced by much weeping and wailing from the women, and running about and shouting of conflicting instructions and advice on the part of the men; but as for solid assistance, she would have gone to the bottom long before the one man in a hundred or a thousand who could render it to her had arrived upon the scene. Luckily again for Nancy, however, that one man chanced to pass by on this occasion, in the shape of our brave bear-hunter, and in the very nick of time.

Boris grasped the situation at a glance, though without as yet recognizing the child. Kicking off his heavy Russian boots, he ran nimbly over the intervening ice, which lay in broken, floating pieces behind him as he crushed it beneath his feet at each quick step, and reached the child in a twinkling, seizing her in his arms and floating with her for a moment as he reflected upon the best way to get back.

During that moment Nancy recognized her preserver and clung to him, shivering and crying a little, but with an assurance of safety in his strong arms which she did her best to express by burying her face in his breast and half drowning him with her clinging arms about his neck.

A wonderfully tender spirit fell over the rough hunter as he felt the confiding hugs of this little English girl, and he realized that she must be saved at all hazards. But it was exceedingly difficult to swim with her in his arms, as those who have tried it will know, especially as his course was impeded by floating ice of sufficient strength and thickness to offer an awkward obstacle to a burdened swimmer. Boris was aware that little Nancy had picked up but little Russian as yet; nevertheless he succeeded in conveying to her that she must not clasp his neck so tightly, or both would presently go to the bottom; also that he intended to help her to climb back upon the ice, but that he would be near if it should break again and let her through. Then, finding a sound edge which looked strong enough for his purpose, with an effort he raised the child sufficiently high to slide her out upon unbroken ice, where Nancy quickly regained her feet and ran lightly to the shore. As for Boris, relieved of his burden, he easily swam to shore, where he found his little friend awaiting him.

To the immense amusement of the onlookers, of whom there was a considerable gathering, Nancy, having first with her little hand helped him out of the water, sprang up into the arms of her big preserver and covered his wet face with kisses. Then the tall hunter and his little English friend walked off together, amid the admiring comments of the crowd, who were unanimous in their opinion that the officer was a *molodyets*, or, as a British schoolboy would call it, "a rare good chap;" and that the little *Anglichanka* was very sweet to look upon, and wore very nice clothes.

From this day commenced a firm friendship between these two persons, which strengthened and ripened from week to week and from month to month. They were in some respects an oddly-assorted couple; and yet there was much in common between them, as for instance the intense love which both bore towards the open air and all that appertains to life in the country. Nancy had lived, while still in her English home, far away from the town; her sympathies were all for the fields, the woods, birds, and rabbits, and wild fowl, and the sights and sounds of the country.

Neither Drury nor his wife had the slightest objection to the great friendship existing between their little daughter and this fine young officer of the Tsar; as indeed why should they? On the contrary, they were glad enough to intrust her to one who could be so thoroughly trusted to take good care of her under any and every circumstance and emergency which could arise, whether in the forest or in the streets of the city. Consequently the two were often together; and Boris loved nothing better than to set his little friend in a *kibitka*, or covered sledge drawn by two horses, and drive out with her into the country, far away beyond the smoke and din of Moscow.

There he would spend a few happy hours in teaching the child the art of tracking and trapping hares, foxes, and larger game, an art in which Nancy proved an apt pupil; while his skill in calling birds and beasts to him proved a source of unfailing delight and amusement to her. Concealed in a tiny conical hut made of fir boughs, and built to represent as far as possible a snow-laden pine tree, the pair would sit for an hour or two and watch the effects of Boris's skilful imitation of the various voices of the forest. Many a time did Nancy enjoy the excitement of hearing and even occasionally of seeing a wolf, as he came inquisitively peering and listening close up to the hut, wondering where in the world his talkative friend had hidden himself, and evidently half beginning to fear that he had been the victim of a hoax. On such occasions a loud report from Boris's old-fashioned matchlock quickly assured the poor wolf that he had indeed been deluded to his destruction, and that this hoax was the very last he should live to be the victim of.

Rare, indeed, was the day when the hunter and his little English friend returned to Moscow without something to show as the result of their drive out into the forest. Whether it was a hare, or a brace of tree-partridges, or the pretty red overcoat of a fox, or the gray hide of a wolf—something was sure to accompany little Nancy when she returned to her father's apartments; for Boris was a hunter whose skill never failed.

Thus the winter passed and the summer came, and another winter, and the Tsar was ever busy with his recruiting, and his drilling, and his revellings, and his designing of ships and fleets. And Boris was busy also with his duty and his pleasure—his duty with his regiment and with his Tsar, and his chief pleasure in the company of the little English girl who had found for herself a place so close to his heart. And Boris was happy both in his pleasure and in his duties, as should be the case with every right-minded person, and is, I trust, with every reader of these lines.

CHAPTER XIII.

BORIS GOES ON THE WAR-PATH.

One day the Tsar asked Boris whether he would like to be one of the electors of the College of Bacchus, and take part in the election of a new president.

The College of Bacchus was one of the products of those all too frequent uproarious moods of the Tsar, when he and his friends would meet to drink and make a noise, to gamble, wrestle, play with the *kegels*, or skittles, and, in short, pass a day or a night in those festivities which Peter found necessary in order to work off some of the superabundant energy with which nature had dowered him. The college was, as its name implies, a mere drinking institution, wherein the hardest drinker was king, or pope, or president; and the last president of this society having lately died, it became necessary to elect a successor.

When the Tsar proposed to Boris, however, that the latter should form one of the electors, he doubtless offered the suggestion more by way of banter than in sober seriousness; for none knew better than Peter that such a thing as an election at the College of Bacchus was not at all in Boris's line. It is distinctly to the credit of the many-sided Tsar that he thought none the worse of his faithful hunter because the latter had not proved so good a boon companion as others of his favourites of the day. He was fully conscious of Boris's many excellent qualities, and easily forgave him his shortcomings as a reveller in consideration of his humble birth and upbringing, as well as of his pre-eminence in other directions. Hence when Peter made the suggestion, he was not offended, but only amused, when Boris said, with a grimace, that he thought his Majesty must probably possess many subjects better qualified than a poor bear-hunter for so exalted an office. Peter, with a laugh, agreed that this might be so; but added that he was not so certain that he could find any one better qualified than Boris to act as judge or referee at the election, since it would be the duty of that functionary to keep the peace and to restrain the ardour, if necessary, of the electors, who would be likely to prove an awkward body to manage, and would require both a strong hand and a cool head to keep in order during the excitement of the election.

Since Peter appeared anxious that Boris should act in the capacity last suggested—that of referee—the hunter did not refuse to comply with his request. The experience was of service to him because it gave him once for all so great a horror of the vice of drinking that he never afterwards, to his dying day, took spirits of any kind excepting on special occasions when he considered the stuff to be required medicinally, and then in small quantities.

It was no wonder that a sober-minded man like Boris should have refused to act as one of the electors, as my readers will agree when I explain the function in use at the elections of the College of Bacchus. The body of twelve electors were locked up together in a room which contained a large table in the centre of which was a wine cask, upon which one of them sat astride, representing Bacchus. On either side of this emblematical figure were a stuffed bear and a live monkey.

The hour at which those chosen to elect the new president were locked up was about seven in the evening, from which time until the following morning, when the door was thrown open once more, each elector was obliged to swallow at regular intervals a large glassful of vodka, a spirit nearly, though not quite, so strong as whisky. He whose head proved best able to support this trying ordeal was the chosen president for the following year, or series of years.

The function to which Boris had been called was to see that each elector was supplied with his proper allowance of vodka at the stipulated times, and to prevent any quarrelling between them.

The hunter found that the office of judge and peacemaker was no sinecure, and a thousand times during the night did poor Boris bitterly repent his compliance with the Tsar's wishes in this matter, and long for the arrival of morning to put an end to the scene of which he was a thoroughly disgusted and sickened spectator.

This was one of the peculiar ways in which the greatest and by far the ablest and most enlightened monarch that Russia had ever seen amused himself, the sovereign but for whom Russia would have lagged hundreds of years behind in the race of civilization and progress, but for whose foresight and sagacity, too, Russia might never have occupied the position she now holds in the councils of Europe and of the world. This was Peter at his lowest and meanest; and if we shall see him in these pages at his cruelest and most brutal, we shall also have the opportunity, I trust, of viewing this many-sided and truly remarkable man at his highest and noblest—and none was ever nobler and more self-sacrificing and devoted than he when occasion arose for the display of his best qualities, for the truth of which statement let the manner of his death testify.

It must not be supposed that the Tsar himself took part in the degrading ceremony I have just described. Beyond locking and sealing the door upon the electors, and again unlocking it at morning, Peter took no personal part in the proceedings, thus exercising a wise discretion.

Boris came forth from that room feeling that he could never again attend the Tsar at one of his drinking bouts at Lefort's or at Gordon's, or elsewhere; he had seen enough drinking and drunkenness to make him hate the very sight of a vodka bottle. When he told Peter of this, and of his intense desire to be exempted from the duty of attending any further carousals, the Tsar slapped him on the back and laughed in his loud way.

"I am glad, my Bear-eater," he said, "that I have at least one friend who is not afraid of being great when I am little! There are plenty left to drink with me. You shall be a total abstainer, and then I am sure of some one to steady me when I return at nights less master of myself than of Russia. I am glad of your decision, my good Boris; you shall be as sober as you please, so long as I need not follow your example." With that Peter laughed again, louder than ever, and gave Boris a great push by the shoulders, which sent him flying backwards against the wall, and proved conclusively that whatever the Tsar might be "when he returned late at night," he was master of himself, at all events, at this particular moment.

Thus it came about that Boris gradually became practically a teetotaller—which is a *rara avis* in Russia, and was still more so in those old days when drunkenness was thought little of, and was even habitually indulged in by the honoured head of the realm.

Boris had many friends now, chiefly among the officers of his regiment, with whom, in spite of his humble origin, he was extremely popular. By this time he excelled in all those arts which were the peculiar property of the military—in swordsmanship, in drill, and even in gunnery, upon the practice of which the Tsar laid great stress. Competitions were held among the officers; and here Boris soon displayed a marked superiority over his fellows, his accurate eye and steady hand enabling him to do far better work with the big clumsy ordnance than his fellows, many of whom could rarely boast of a steady hand at any time of day. It was a peculiarity of the Tsar himself, however, who indeed was an exception to all rules, that however deep his potations might have been, either on the previous evening or on the very day of the competition, his hand was always steady and his eye true—in fact, he was at all times the chief rival of Boris for first gunnery honours.

Such was the life in Moscow during the two or three years which our friend passed in the capital at this stage of his career—years which were of incalculable benefit to him as a period of education and experience; years also which were passed very happily, and during which the friendship between the young guardsman and Nancy Drury ever ripened and matured. From Nancy, Boris gradually picked up more than a smattering of the English language, and by the time he had known her for two full years the pair were able to converse in English—a circumstance greatly applauded by Peter, who meditated a visit to our country, and declared that the hunter should go with him and do the talking for him.

But before the plans for a trip to England and the Continent had taken definite shape, events occurred to postpone the journey for a while. The regiment of Guards to which Boris was attached was ordered to proceed to the south of Russia, where the Streltsi were already gathered before the walls of the city of Azof in preparation for a siege. Boris took an affectionate farewell of his beloved master, who bade him God-speed and a quick return home. "Don't get into trouble with your old enemies of the Streltsi," were the Tsar's parting words. "See if you can be the first man into Azof—I expect it of you—and be home as quickly as possible; for what am I to do without my faithful old Sobersides Bear-eater to keep me in order and take care of me?"

Boris laughed at the allusion to his old acquaintances the Streltsi; he had quite grown out of his dislike and horror for those poor misguided men, and was inclined to recall their treatment of him with indulgence and pity rather than with indignation. "I am sure to be back soon, your Majesty," he said, "if the Tartars don't pick me off. We'll soon pepper them out of Azof. And, besides, I have attractions here besides your Majesty's person."

"Ah, the fair Nancy! I had forgotten," said Peter, laughing. "Well, well, my Bear-eater, happy is he who is beloved by a child; their love is better than woman's love, and wears better, too. Now go and bid farewell to your Nancy. Tell her Peter will look after her right well in your absence!"

Boris went straight from the Tsar to the house of the Drurys, where he was ever a welcome guest.

Poor Nancy was very miserable at the prospect of parting with her friend, for she felt that there would be no more long sledge drives for her over the crisp snow roads, no more pleasant days in mid-forest watching for bird and beast, nor jolly skating expeditions along the smooth surface of the river when the wind or thaws had cleared it of its deep snow-mantle, nor happy half-hours spent in laughing over the hunter's attempts to master the pronunciation of her own difficult language. Life would be very dull and miserable for her now, and the colonel informed Boris that Nancy had even spoken of persuading him, Boris, to take her with him to the south. "In fact, Boris Ivanitch," added Drury, "my wife and I both complain that you have quite stolen the child's heart from us; and, if we know anything of Nancy, we shall have our hands full to manage her while you are away."

Nancy had disappeared out of the room, for her feelings had proved too much for her, and Boris regretfully felt obliged to depart at length without seeing the child again. But as he groped his way out of the dark, badly-lighted passage to the front door, he was surprised by a small, light figure bouncing suddenly into his arms, and a flaxen head burying itself in his bosom, while hot tears were freely shed and hot kisses rained over his face and neck and wherever the two soft lips could plant them. With difficulty Boris unclasped the fond arms, and detached the pretty head from his shoulder, and tenderly placed the little feet upon the ground. Then Nancy quickly ran away, and disappeared without a word, though Boris heard a great sob as the dainty figure passed out of sight in the dusky distance of the passage. When the young guardsman, mighty hunter and redoubtable soldier as he was, left the house and strode down the familiar street for the last time, there was a tear in his eye that would not be denied, but rolled deliberately down his cheek till it was dashed away.

On the following morning Boris marched out of Moscow with his regiment, bound for the seat of war, far away in the south, on the Sea of Azof.

FOOTNOTE:

Peter the Great contracted his last illness through a chill caught while saving a boat's crew from drowning, which he did at the risk of his life and unaided, rescuing nearly thirty men one by one.

CHAPTER XIV.

TAKEN PRISONER.

The fortress of Azof, upon the sea of that name, was principally used by the Turks and Tartars, who at this time occupied it, as a centre for their plundering and marauding expeditions inland. Some sixty-five years before this, in 1627, the city had been surprised and captured by the enterprising Don Cossacks, who found that it lay too close to their own hunting-grounds to be an altogether acceptable neighbour. Having possessed themselves of the city, the Don Cossacks offered it as a free gift to their liege lord, the then Tsar of Muscovy, Michael, Peter's grandfather.

The Tsar sent down officers and experts, before accepting the gift, to report upon the place; but these announced that the fortress was rotten and indefensible, and not worth having. The Cossacks were therefore directed to evacuate the city; which they did, but not before they had razed every building to the ground, so that not one stone stood upon another.

But now, at the date of my story, the young Tsar Peter was full of schemes for aggrandizement by land and sea; his mind was intent upon fleet-building as well as upon army-organizing. But the difficulty was, as one of his intimates pointed out to the Tsar, "What was the use of building a large number of ships with no ports for them to go to?" for, besides Archangel—which was a terribly long way off—Russia had at this time no windows looking out to the sea. The Baltic was in the hands of Sweden, the Black Sea was held by the Turk, the Caspian by Persia. In one of these directions Russia must look for new outlets to the ocean highroads. Peter's reply was characteristic. He said, "My ships shall make ports for themselves"—a boast indeed, but, as events showed, not an idle one.

But the question arose, which foreign power should be first attacked and made to disgorge that without which the development of Russia was hampered and impracticable? The Caspian was, after all, but an inland sea; that could wait. The Baltic was well enough, but Peter knew that he was as yet quite unprepared to tackle Sweden, either by land or sea; that must wait also. There remained the Black Sea. And here Peter would fulfil a double purpose in attacking the dominions of the Turk. He would secure a much-needed port to begin with—that was reason sufficient in itself for the contemplated onslaught; but besides this, he would be dealing a blow for Christianity by smiting Islamism in its stronghold, and chasing from their lair the enemies of Christ.

So Peter decided upon the siege of Azof as a first step towards greater ends. In 1694 he sent down from Moscow several regiments of his new troops, the Preobrajensk, of which the Tsar was himself a member, having entered the regiment at the very lowest grade, and enjoying at this time the rank of "bombardier;" Lefort's regiment of twelve thousand men, mostly foreigners; the Semenofski, and the Batusitski. Besides these were our old friends the Streltsi; and the entire army, numbering one hundred thousand men, was led by Golovnin, Schéin, Gordon, and Lefort. Accompanying this force went, as we have seen, Boris, late bear-hunter, now captain in the Preobrajensk regiment. Though our friend had bidden farewell to the Tsar at Moscow, Peter nevertheless changed his mind and followed the expedition in person, joining the troops beneath the walls of Azof, still as "Bombardier Peter Alexeyevitch," which character he kept up throughout the subsequent proceedings, being determined, as an example to his people, to pass through every grade of both the military and the naval services.

Boris greatly enjoyed the march southwards. He welcomed with all his heart the change from the close, stuffy life in the Moscow drawing-rooms and barracks to his beloved woods and moors and open air at night and day. He was the life of the regiment throughout the long march, entertaining the officers with exhibitions of his animal-calling talent, and teaching them the arts of the forest at every opportunity. Big game naturally kept out of the way of the great host of men, and never came within a mile of the road, though answering calls from wolves might frequently be heard in the distance; but the officers' mess was indebted daily to Boris and his knowledge of woodcraft for constant supplies of toothsome partridge, or delicious willow-grouse, with sometimes a fine blackcock, or even a lordly capercailzie. There was no more popular officer of the Preobrajensk than Boris, whose position was thus very different from that he had held in his late Streltsi regiment, where every officer had been at heart a revolutionist, and therefore hated him for his known devotion to the person of the Tsar.

But the long march was finished at last, and the entire force assembled beneath the walls of Azof.

And now "Bombardier Peter Alexeyevitch" realized with sorrow that without ships to support his land forces he was likely to have a tough struggle to capture the city. When, seventy years before, the Don Cossacks had surprised and taken it, Azof had been a very inferior stronghold to this which now frowned upon him but a mile or less from his outposts. The new city now possessed a high wall, strongly built, and likely to defy awhile the assault of the heavy but feeble ordnance of that time. Peter accordingly determined, in council with Lefort and the rest, that rather than lay siege to the place, it would be advisable, in the absence of ships, to attempt its capture by assault.

Arrangements were made that the artillery fire should be concentrated upon that portion of the wall which appeared to be the weakest, and that the instant a breach was made the Preobrajensk, supported by the rest, should advance to the assault and carry the town *vi et armis*. The attack was fixed for the following morning.

During that evening an unfortunate quarrel took place between the general Schéin and the principal artillery officer, a German named Jansen, familiarly known to the Russian soldiers as "Yakooshka." Schéin fixed upon one portion of the wall as that to be attacked, while Jansen was determined that another spot offered a more suitable mark for the Russian guns. Schéin insisted, and Jansen, with blunt German obstinacy, insisted also. Schéin lost his temper and abused Jansen, when Jansen grew angry also and said, no doubt, what was unbecoming in an inferior to a superior officer. Then Schéin lost control over himself, and commanded the guard to arrest poor "Yakooshka," whereupon the latter was led away and actually bastinadoed for insubordination.

That night Jansen escaped from his undignified captivity, and having first made the round of the Russian guns and spiked them all, quietly shook the dust from off his feet, turned his back upon the Russian lines, and went over to the enemy, being admitted into Azof by its Mussulman holders with joy and thanksgiving.

On the following morning, when the order was given to train the guns upon the city walls and to open fire, the treachery of Jansen was discovered. The Bombardier Peter Alexeyevitch, when this information was brought to him, was a terrible object to behold.

Great spasms of passion shook him from head to foot, while his face—black as any storm-cloud—worked in contortions and grimaces like the features of one in a terrible fit. For a few moments he said no word. Then he took his note-book and wrote therein large and prominent the name *Jansen.* After which he gave orders for the assault of Azof, guns or no guns, and in a few moments the brave Preobrajensk were in full career towards the walls of the city.

The guns opened fire upon them so soon as the guard became conscious of the surprisingly rash intentions of the Russians; but the shot flew over their heads. Boris, mindful of the Tsar's words to him while still in Moscow, that he should do his best to be the first man into Azof, led his company cheering and waving his sword. Russians have never held back when there was storming work to do, and the troops advanced quickly at the double, singing, as Russians love to do, one of their stirring military songs.

The musketry fire opened from the top of the walls as they came to close quarters, and though the shooting was very wild, still many wide gaps were made in the ranks. In a moment the foot of the wall was reached, and now came the difficult work of ascending. Scaling-ladders were placed, and knocked ever from above, and placed again. Scores of men endeavoured to climb the wall without the aid of ladders, but were easily shot down or knocked on the head if they ever succeeded in climbing within reach of the sharp swords and scimitars waving in readiness above.

The din was deafening, the cries of Christian and Mussulman outvying the roar of musketry. Now and again a squad of Russians firing from below would clear the wall, and a ladder would be placed for half-a-dozen brave fellows to rush upwards and be cut down by new defenders who came to fill the gaps of the fallen. Once a roar of applause was set up by the Russian hosts as a Russian officer, followed by half-a-dozen men, rushed up one of the ladders, and with a shout of triumph stood upon the top of the wall, waving their swords, and shouting to their companions to follow. This triumph was short-lived. First one man fell, pierced through the heart by a bullet; then another and another was knocked on the head, while those who essayed to come to their rescue were shot down in their attempt to mount the ladder. At length there remained alive the officer alone, he who had first surmounted the wall. This officer was Boris, whose superior agility had once more stood him in good stead, and enabled him to climb where the rest had failed. That same activity appeared, however, to have got him into a terrible fix. Alone he stood for a few moments, fighting bravely but hopelessly against a dozen swords, until at length, to the consternation of his friends below, he was seen to receive a blow which tumbled him off the wall upon the Azof side, and no more was seen of him.

For an hour or more the Russians fought bravely on, endeavouring to obtain a foothold upon those grim walls, but all in vain. The Tartar women brought boiling water and threw it down upon the "Christian dogs," together with every sort of filth, and large stones. Every inhabitant of the city appeared to have come out upon the walls in order to assist in beating off the infidel; and though many fell pierced by Russian bullets, they were entirely successful in their patriotic endeavours, for, with the exception of the half-dozen men who followed Boris upon the walls, no single Russian succeeded in mounting the ladders, or in any other way effecting a footing within the Mussulman stronghold.

Meanwhile the guns of the town, probably aimed by the treacherous though much provoked Jansen, rained fire and hail upon the main body of the besiegers, who, with spiked guns, were unable to retaliate. Peter the Bombardier was gloomy and black. He strode among his guns, superintending the efforts of his smiths to get them into working order; he swore at his generals right and left, in a manner ill-befitting a humble bombardier; he swore with yet more deadly wrath at Jansen, and with greater justice. But in spite of all his ferocity and fury he did not lose his discretion; and finding that his troops were doing and could do no good under present circumstances, the Tsar gave orders that the assaulting columns should retire. Thus the day, the first of many, passed without result.

As time went on, and Peter found that his attacks upon Azof made no progress, but that he lost daily large numbers of his best soldiers to no purpose, he decided reluctantly that until he should become possessed of a fleet which could blockade the city by sea, while he attacked it at the same time, and in force, by land, he must abandon all hope of capturing the place. At present, as he had now realized to his loss, the city could be reinforced and revictualled at any moment. Besides this, his mainstay in the science of artillery attack, Jansen, had basely failed him; he had no one competent to take his place. Such an officer, together with clever engineers, must be invited to enter his service as quickly as might be—an Englishman, a Frenchman, even a German again, but not a touchy and quarrelsome and treacherous one, such as Yakooshka had proved himself.

So Peter wisely, but sorrowfully, abandoned the siege of Azof for that season, promising himself a speedy return in the following summer, when he was fully determined he would possess a fleet capable of blockading the city from the sea side, as well as capable and experienced foreign officers, who should lead his brave fellows to that victory which had been snatched from them this season through no fault of their own.

Peter had still much to learn in the art of war; but, like a man of sense, he accepted defeat on this and on future occasions as object-lessons for the benefit of his own inexperience. The great Tsar had his own patient way of attaining his ends through many defeats and much discouragement. He learned from his enemies at each repulse, assimilating the experience thus gained until he was in a position, in his turn, to teach. How thorough was his method of impressing a lesson upon those who had once been his teachers, let Pultowa and Nystad testify.

Nevertheless, Peter's rebuff at Azof in 1695 was to him an exceedingly serious matter in the peculiar condition of affairs in the Russia of that day; for it gave to his enemies, and the enemies of progress, the opportunity to point the finger of scorn at his foreign soldiers and his un-Russian policy generally, and smile and say, "Ha, we told you so! these foreigners will be the ruin of Russia. The priests are right, and we shall yet see this young man, the Tsar, acknowledge the error of his ways, and turn his great energies to clearing the land of the foreigner, with his alien manners and civilization."

But these men imagined a vain thing; and the young Tsar, like a young lion, did but shake his mane and lick his wounded paw, and sally forth once again to encounter and slay the enemy who had wounded him.

CHAPTER XV.

AN EXCITING ESCAPE.

When the Tsar returned to Moscow and set himself deliberately to count up his losses, he was obliged to admit that what affected him more grievously than anything else was the disappearance of poor Boris; a disappearance which he could not but feel certain meant death, or captivity and torture, in comparison with which death would be vastly preferable. Peter missed his devoted servant and friend at every turn and at every hour of the day.

On the second day after his arrival, the Tsar was surprised to receive a request for an audience from, as his orderly informed him, "a little English fairy." Permission being given, the door opened, and in walked Nancy Drury, now nearly fifteen years old, and as sweet-looking an example of English maidenhood as any could wish to see. Nancy was very grave and hollow-eyed, and her face showed signs of many tears.

"Is it true?" said Nancy, advancing towards the Tsar, and speaking in the hollowest and most tragic of voices.

"Is what true, my dear?" asked Peter kindly, taking the child on his knee, though he thought he knew well enough what she required of him.

"Is it true that he is lost—my Boris—and perhaps dead?" Poor Nancy burst into tears as she spoke the last word, and hid her face in her hands. "Oh, what have you done with him, and why did you let the Tartars have him?" she continued, through sobs and tears.

Peter did his best to pacify the child, assuring her, against his own convictions, that Boris was certainly alive and well, and promising faithfully that at the renewed campaign next summer his troops should certainly release Boris from captivity before they did anything else.

When Nancy had extracted this promise from the Tsar, she dried her tears, and thanked him and smiled. Peter kissed the sweet English face. "If only I were not married already, Nancy," he said, laughing, "I declare I should be tempted to make an empress of you when you were old enough! Would you like to be an empress?"

Nancy blushed. "I love your Majesty very much," she said, "but I would never be empress—" She hesitated.

"And why not, my little English fairy?" said the Tsar kindly.

"I—I shouldn't like to live in a big palace all my life," faltered Nancy. "I love the woods and the fields, and—"

"But if Boris were emperor?" laughed the Tsar.

Nancy hid her face, and flushed scarlet. Then she jumped off his knee and burst into tears again, throwing herself at his feet, and sobbing, "Oh, save him from the Tartars, your Majesty—do save him! Take him away from the enemies of Christ, and God will bless you for it!"

There was not much of the man of sentiment about this practical young potentate, but Peter could not help feeling greatly touched to see the child's anxiety and sorrow. Once more he assured her that all would be well, and Nancy accepted his assurance and left the Tsar's cabinet smiling and hopeful.

But my readers will wish to know what has become of poor Boris all this time. They will think, very properly, that the fate of a single Christian falling wounded into the hands of an excited mob of the children of the Prophet must be pretty well settled before ever his feet have touched the ground. So it would be, undoubtedly, in ninety-nine cases out of a hundred; but Boris was not quite "done for" when he fell, and therefore the swords and knives which were anxiously awaiting the opportunity to dip into his Christian blood were obliged first to fight for the privilege. He had received a terrific blow, certainly, but had guarded in time, and though overbalanced and tumbled off the wall, he was still unhurt. Regaining his feet in an instant, he had placed his back against the wall, and stood to receive attack. Half-a-dozen swords soon sprang out to give him battle, and in a minute he was engaged in an encounter compared with which his fight with the Streltsi was the tamest of toy battles. Boris felt that there was little hope of his keeping his antagonists at bay until some of his friends should have mounted the wall and arrived to give him the much-needed assistance; but he was resolved, nevertheless, to keep up the game until either death or assistance came, and to exact at least twelve Mussulman lives as the price of his own!

Boris fought a good fight that day. Turk after Turk fell before his big swinging sword, and whenever one fell another took his place. Bravely he cut and thrust and guarded, and the very Turks themselves stayed their crowding upon the walls to see out this fine exhibition of skill and endurance and Muscovitish pluck. But cutting and thrusting and guarding one's body from two or three assailants at once is tiring work, and poor Boris felt his strength failing him, and his eye grew dim, so that he could scarcely see accurately where he struck, and some of his blows began to fall at random. His breath came and went in gasps, and his arms ached with weariness. In another moment one of those flashing blades would find a billet somewhere in the region of his stout heart, and the career of the brave bear-hunter would be over and done with.

But fate had decided that the readers of these records of Boris should have many more pages of his history to peruse, and just when the hunter was making up his mind that he had fought his last fight and lost it, this same fate, in the person of a Turkish pasha who had watched the fray admiringly from the beginning, strode up and knocked aside the swords of the assailants of Boris just in time to prevent them from dyeing themselves red in his blood. The pasha felt that here was a splendid slave being wasted, or perhaps a prisoner for whom a good ransom might be eventually forthcoming. So he struck away the swords, and skipping aside to avoid a savage thrust from poor dim-eyed Boris, who could not see and knew not the signification of this new assailant's interference, he rushed in and pinned the half-fainting Russian to the wall. The sword dropped from Boris's hand as the fingers of the pasha closed around his throat, a thick film came over his eyes, black fog enveloped his brain, and the shouts and cries of the battle around him receded further and further into space; his consciousness faded and failed, his senses vanished one by one like the extinguishing of candles, and Boris knew no more.

When Boris came to himself he was in a small room, whose only window was at a height of some five feet from the floor and iron-barred. He could hear a sentinel pass and repass beneath it, and from a distance came the sounds of musketry and artillery fire, which quickly recalled to his mind the events of the morning—or of yesterday, for he was without means of ascertaining how long he had remained unconscious. Food—some coarse bread and a dish of water—stood upon the floor beside the straw upon which he found himself outstretched. Boris was very hungry, and at once ravenously consumed the food, finishing the bread to the last crumb, and wishing there were more of it, coarse though it was. He felt very weary still, and though unwounded, save for a prick or two in the hand and fore-arm, quite incapable of and disinclined for thought or exertion. So Boris lay still, and presently fell asleep.

He was awakened at night by voices as of people conversing within the room, and opened his eyes to find the pasha, his captor, with another Turk and a third figure whose presence first filled him with joy, and then, as he remembered, with bitter loathing. It was Jansen, the treacherous gunner, to whose perfidy and desire for vengeance was due the repulse of Peter and his army, and, indeed, indirectly, his own present situation.

Boris was for upraising his voice in angry denunciation of the traitor, but the pasha dealt him a blow in the mouth and bade him roughly be silent. Boris felt for his sword, but found it was no longer at his side, neither was his dagger nor his big clumsy pistol; he was entirely unarmed.

Jansen and the Turks were conversing in a language unknown to Boris, the pasha asking questions and putting down Jansen's replies in a note-book. Then Jansen, addressing Boris, informed him that the pasha had spared his life in order to employ him in his own service, either to teach his soldiers the art of swordsmanship, in which, the pasha had observed, he excelled, or perhaps to help him, Jansen, in managing the big guns mounted upon the walls.

But at this point the tongue of Boris would be silent no longer, and burst into furious invective. That this man should desert his master the Tsar in his need was bad enough, but that the traitor should expect him, Boris, to employ his skill in gunnery against his own beloved sovereign and his own people passed the patience of man, and Boris was with difficulty prevented from casting himself upon the deserter and throttling him as he stood. Three swords flashing out of their scabbards at the same moment, however, reminded the captive of his helplessness, and Boris relinquished, reluctantly, the pleasure of suffocating the traitor.

Whether Jansen persuaded the pasha of the impracticability of compelling Boris to do any useful work with the guns, or whether it struck the pasha that Boris might easily do more harm than good at the walls, I know not, but the prisoner was never requested to take part in artillery practice at the Russian lines. His duties, he found, consisted chiefly in helping to carry the pasha's palanquin about the streets of the city—an occupation rendered exceedingly disagreeable by the rudeness of the population, who pushed, and jostled, and cursed, and spat upon the "Christian dog" whenever he appeared. Occasionally he was directed to practise sword exercise with chosen Mussulman swordsmen; and this he was glad enough to do, for it gave him amusement in plenty to teach these Easterns all manner of Western malpractices, tricks of swordsmanship of an obsolete and exploded nature such as would undoubtedly expose them, should they come to blows with an experienced fencer, to speedy defeat. Besides these occupations Boris was ever busy in another way—a field of activity in which his energies were employed without the sanction or the knowledge of his master, for he was labouring every day to loosen the iron bars of his prison room. By means of peeping out of his window at moments when the sentry was at a distance Boris had discovered that between him and the outer wall of the city there was but a space of thirty yards of stone pavement, up and down which paced the sentinel. Beyond this was the wall; and over the wall, not indeed the plain whereon the Russian troops had till lately been encamped, but the shining waters of that arm of the Black Sea known as the Sea of Azof.

Day by day Boris worked at his bar, choosing those moments when the sentinel was farthest from him. Once, during the sword instruction in the courtyard, a sword broke, and the broken end of the weapon, a blunt piece of steel about eight inches in length, was left on the ground. Boris found an opportunity to seize this and secrete it before leaving the spot, and the fragment proved of the utmost service to him in scraping the mortar from beneath and around the iron bars. Two months after his capture Boris saw to his delight that he could now at any moment he chose remove these bars and attempt his escape.

The opportunity arrived at last: a warm, dark night, drizzling with rain; the sentry, muffled in his *bashlik*, could see little and hear less; no one else would be about the walls in such weather and so late. The bit of sword end, by constant working, had worn to itself by this time a sharp and formidable edge; it was no longer a weapon to be despised. In Boris's wallet were stored the economized savings of many meals—food enough to keep him alive for several days. The hunter removed carefully the iron bars which had made this little room a prison-house for two long months, and clambering upon the somewhat narrow ledge, sat in the darkness and waited. Would the sentinel never pass close enough for his purpose? To and fro the man went, but he did not guess what was required of him, and passed along rather further from the window than exactly suited the designs of Boris.

Seeing that the man was evidently a person of method, and stepped time after time in his old tracks, Boris determined that he must accept the inevitable and deal with matters as they were, without waiting longer for desirable contingencies which destiny refused to bring about. Standing crouched upon the ledge, Boris waited until the sentinel was opposite, as nearly as he could guess in the darkness; then setting every muscle in his body, he sprang out as far as he could towards the spot where he judged the man to be. So vigorous was his leap, that though the soldier was upwards of five yards from the window, Boris alighted with tremendous force upon his shoulders, bearing him to the ground and himself falling over him.

The wretched sentry, conscious only that something very heavy indeed had fallen down upon him, apparently from the skies, was about to howl to his Prophet for help; but in an instant Boris had one big hand over the fellow's mouth, and with the other felt for a spot where a dig of his little weapon might serve to silence for ever the man's appeals, whether to Mohammed or to any one else. A quick struggle as they rolled together on the ground, a sharp dig, and the sentinel lay still and harmless, and Boris had accomplished his task so far.

Taking the man's outer garment and bashlik, and leaving his own, taking also the fellow's musket and pistol, Boris clambered up the outer wall and looked for a moment into the darkness beneath. That the sea was there was certain, for he could hear the sound of the wavelets lapping the wall below him; but how far down was the water—in other words, how high was the wall?

However, this was no time for anxious reflection. If Boris ever wished to see his home again, and his beloved Tsar, and, lastly, his little friend Nancy Drury, he must jump now and at once. Murmuring a prayer, then giving one somewhat trembling look down into the grim darkness beneath him, Boris took a long breath and jumped.

It must have been a high wall, for as Boris fell through the air it seemed to him as though he would never reach the water. At last he felt the cold waves close over him, and then it seemed as though he would never rise to the surface again; but when his breath was nearly exhausted, and he was well-nigh choked for want of air, his head emerged once more, and he was able to float quietly for a while, in order to obtain a fresh supply of breath, and to listen for any sound which might either warn him of danger, or indicate the direction in which he ought to strike out in order to make the shore.

Presently Boris heard the sound of oars, and remained where he was until the boat should pass. It was a party of fishers putting out to sea, and Boris judged that by going in the opposite direction he would reach land; so he struck boldly out for the point whence the boat had come. Soon his intently listening ears caught the sound of the twittering of sand-pipers, and Boris guessed that he neared the shore. This was the case, and in some twenty minutes from the time of his plunge the hunter had the satisfaction of feeling the bottom, and of wading, drenched and somewhat cold, but exceedingly rejoiced, ashore. There was no one about. The city lay to the left; he could hear the crowing of cocks, and caught the occasional glimmer of a light. Boris took the opposite direction, and walked along what seemed to be the edge of an arm of the sea or of a large river. All night he toiled along, sometimes swimming or wading, in order to put possible pursuers off the track.

When morning came, Boris found himself on the skirt of a large forest, and here he concealed himself, and dried his clothes and his food in the sun. Then, deep in the shade of a birch thicket, he lay down and enjoyed a good rest until the evening, when he rose up and recommenced his flight, always keeping to the shore of the river, which, as he afterwards discovered, was the Don. Thus Boris travelled for three days, pushing on at night and resting during the day, until his food was well-nigh exhausted. Then, to his joy, he reached a rough-looking village where he found the Russian language was understood. Here he was received kindly and entertained hospitably by the rough but good-hearted inhabitants, a tribe of Don Cossacks; and here he rested for several days, and collected his exhausted energies amid his kind Cossack friends, in preparation for the long journey for Moscow and home!

CHAPTER XVI.

HOME AGAIN.

One day, early in November 1695, when the palace of the Tsar in the Kremlin was thronged with officers and dignitaries awaiting audience in the ante-chambers, and crowding one another in the halls and passages, discussing the news and transacting various matters of state business, a tall but ragged-looking figure strode in at the principal entrance of the palace, pushing aside the doorkeepers, and elbowed his way through the crowded entrance-hall. Up the wide stairs he went, taking no notice of the protests and smothered curses of those whose toes he trod upon, or into whose sides he had insinuated his sharp elbows. Many of those who had turned round to see who this audaciously rough individual might be, stopped open-mouthed when they beheld him, the protest half-uttered, and gazed after him with wide eyes, muttering prayers, as men who believe they see a ghost. But the ragged courtier looked neither to the right hand nor to the left, but pursued his reckless march over the toes of the highest dignitaries in the realm, without noticing the fact or the persons, and making straight for the private cabinet of the Tsar as though, until he should reach that haven, there could be no thought for anything else.

Arrived at the ante-chamber, wherein were assembled Lefort and Menshikoff and a few others of the inner circle of favour, the new arrival paid no more heed to these august personages than he had done to the rest, but elbowed them out of his way and went straight to the door which led into the sanctum of the great Peter, altogether disregarding the exclamations of surprise and awe which were all that these found time to utter as he passed rapidly through the room and in at the Tsar's own door.

Peter was sitting alone at the writing-table, busily penning letters to foreign potentates—applications, in fact, for the loan of talented engineer and artillery officers for the new campaign against the Turk on the Black Sea; a project upon which his mind was so fixed that his whole time was spent in planning and organizing it in advance. The Tsar raised his eyes as the ragged figure entered the room and stood before his table. But though Peters eyes fixed themselves upon the strange, wild object before them, the speculation in them had nothing to do with the object of their regard. Peter lowered his head again and wrote; he finished his letter, and signed it. Then, once more he raised his eyes, and this time those orbs were looking outwards, not inwards. Peter started, and spat on the ground; then he crossed himself, and shaded his eyes, and stared at the figure that stood before him. For a moment the strong face looked scared and bewildered; then the Tsar rose with his big laugh, and walking round to the other side of the table caught the man by both shoulders and shook him till his teeth rattled.

"It is true flesh and blood," he cried, "and no ghost! Boris, my most miraculous of bear-hunters, whence come you, and why is this ragged body of yours not eaten by Turkish rats? This is the best and most wonderful thing that mortal man ever heard of." Peter drew the grimy traveller to his own broad breast and embraced him in the most approved Russian manner, kissing both cheeks and his forehead.—"Here! Lefort, Menshikoff, all you fellows in there!" continued the Tsar, shouting aloud, "here's Boris come back, our faithful, Streltsi-sticking, Turk-spitting Bear-eater!—Come, sit down, my Boris, quickly, and tell us all about it. Why are you alive—have you a plan of Azof—how did you get out of the place—has that Yakooshka had his sneaking German tongue cut out of him yet? Tell me that first of all, quick!"

Boris replied that as far as he knew the head of Jansen was still upon his shoulders with his tongue in it.

"Then," said Peter, "we shall have at least the satisfaction of removing it ourselves instead of relinquishing the privilege to the Turk, as I had feared." Peter took two or three turns about the room, looking his blackest; then he recovered his equanimity. "Come," he said, "let's talk of pleasanter subjects; tell us all about your adventures."

Boris told his plain tale amid frequent interjections from the four or five men present. Peter roared with laughter over the account of how Boris with his sword had kept at bay for ten minutes any number of Turks who chose to come on, and how he was ultimately scragged by a pasha while in the very act of fainting from sheer exhaustion. "Bravo, Bear-eater," he cried, "and bravo again! Ho, if I had but five thousand bear-hunters like you, my son, I should attack Sweden to-morrow! But there is some good in the Turk after all; for think how easily any one of a thousand of them might have blown your brains out with musket or pistol. Yet they preferred to see a good fight out to the end; but, ha! ha! that pasha. You shall scrag that same pasha with your own hands, my son, next summer, as sure as I am standing here. Go on!"

"Out sprang Boris, and alighted with terrific force upon Menshikoff's back."

Peter's pleasant mood underwent a great change when Boris went on to tell of his interview with Jansen in prison. His face worked in terrible contortions, and he rose and paced the room once more without a word. "So you would have throttled him, would you?"

he said at last. "I am thankful that you did not interfere with what is my privilege. Enough about Yakooshka. Go on."

But the Tsar fairly roared with laughter as Boris described how he had leaped upon the back of the sentinel, a distance of fifteen feet, and stuck the poor fellow with his little broken bit of sword-end. He must have that little weapon, he said, as a keepsake from his good bear-eater. But nothing would satisfy the Tsar with regard to the mighty spring upon the back of the sentry but a rehearsal of the feat then and there, in that very room.

Menshikoff said the thing was impossible; no man, he said, could leap five yards from a cramped position upon a window ledge. Boris must have miscalculated the distance. But Menshikoff regretted this remark a moment after he had made it; for Peter declared he believed the bear-eater could perform the feat if no one else could, and that he should try it at once, in order to put this sceptic to confusion. Menshikoff should act the part of sentry, and walk along while Boris jumped on him. Afterwards they would all try it. Then two tables were piled together, and Boris was instructed to bend himself into the original position as far as possible, and thence spring upon the unhappy Menshikoff, who paced the floor at a distance of fifteen feet. Menshikoff eyed the heavy figure of Boris, soon to be launched at him, with gloomy foreboding; but there was no help for it, Peter was in earnest. As Menshikoff reached the necessary point, out sprang Boris, and without difficulty covering the distance, alighted with terrific force upon Menshikoff's back. Over rolled the favourite, and over went Boris with him, amid the boisterous laughter of the Tsar and the rest, the crash making such a commotion that frightened courtiers from the room beneath presently rushed in to see what had happened to his Majesty.

Peter insisted upon attempting the feat himself, and insisted also that Lefort and Menshikoff should leap as well. The Tsar easily accomplished the leap; but so tremendous was the shock of his descent, that poor Lefort, who was detailed to receive the ponderous imperial body after its flight through space, was well-nigh wiped out of the land of the living. Both Menshikoff and Lefort failed to accomplish the feat, and Boris was obliged to repeat it, in order that the Tsar might try the sensations of the sentinel, as a "bolt from the blue," in the shape of some thirteen stone of humanity, came crashing down upon his shoulders. Peter was better built to stand the shock than the unfortunate Turkish soldier, and Boris's big body hardly caused him to stagger; though when the two changed places, and the huge Tsar sprang through the air and alighted upon the back of Boris, that hardy young hunter, for all his sturdiness, rolled over like a rabbit.

Then at length the Tsar, now in the highest good-humour, permitted Boris to finish his tale—how he had plunged into the dark waters of the Azof Sea, and found his way to land; how he had been befriended in a village of the Cossacks of the Don—Peter making a note of the name of the village; and of his long adventurous journey through moor and forest, where he supplied himself with food from day to day by means of his knowledge of woodcraft, until he reached Moscow that very morning. Then the Tsar informed Boris of his own designs for a renewed siege of Azof by land and sea, and of all that had happened in the regiment and out of it since his disappearance. The officers had all mourned him as certainly lost, the Tsar said, and had even included his name in their service for the repose of the souls of those slain beneath the walls of the city; they would be overjoyed to see his face again. Then Peter told of how little Nancy Drury had come to scold him for losing "her Boris," and of how he had promised faithfully to go and fetch her friend home again in the summer. When Peter mentioned Nancy, the face of Boris flushed, but his eyes glowed with great tenderness; and presently he asked leave to retire, in order to visit his fellow-officers, "and others." The Tsar permitted him to go, on condition that he went first to see "those others;" for, said Peter, those others might be even more rejoiced to see him home again than the officers of the regiment, who, at least, had not blushed whenever his name had been mentioned. Then Boris blushed again, and thanked the Tsar, and went out to do his kind bidding.

When Boris reached the house of the Drurys, and was ushered into the sitting-room by the frightened servant, who took him for a ghost, and did not announce him because his tongue refused to speak for very fear, Mrs. Drury was busy over her needlework, while Nancy sat at her lessons at the same table. Mother and daughter looked up together, but their first impressions were entirely different. Mrs. Drury had never felt the slightest doubt that her little daughter's faithful friend was long since dead and buried in the far-away Tartar city, and had mourned his death in secret, while concealing her convictions from Nancy, in the hope that when the truth must be known time would have softened the blow. When, therefore, the door opened noiselessly, and the scared servant, speechless and pale, admitted the ragged figure which so strongly resembled the dead friend of the family, Mrs. Drury was taken by surprise, and screamed and hid her face in her hands. But Nancy's instincts did not err. No sooner did she raise her eyes than she knew that this was no ghost, but her own beloved and familiar friend; and with a cry of great joy and surprise she sprang to her feet, and was in his arms in a moment, her head buried in his tanned neck, sobbing and laughing, and conscious of nothing excepting that here was her Boris alive and well and come home again.

When Mrs. Drury recovered her equanimity, which she did in a minute, her English ideas of propriety were a little shocked at Nancy's undisguised demonstration towards her friend, and, after warmly greeting Boris, she reminded her little daughter that her fifteenth birthday was at hand, and that she would shock Boris Ivanitch by her demonstrativeness. But Boris begged her to let Nancy be as affectionate as she pleased, for, he said, he had sadly needed the comfort of a little love for many a long and dreary month. So Mrs. Drury let matters be as they were, and Nancy clung to her friend's neck, and cried and laughed in turns, though saying but little, until Boris gently detached her arms from about his neck and placed her upon his knee to hear the stirring tale of his adventures and escape and return home.

Boris left the Drurys' house presently with a new conviction looming large and prominent in his inner consciousness, and that was that there was nothing in all the world quite so good as the love of an innocent girl; neither the delights of bear-hunting, nor the glory of successful fight, nor the favour of a great king, nor the applause of his fellows, nor rank in the army, nor wealth, nor the pride of great strength, nor anything else. All these things were good, especially the praise of a beloved master and Tsar; but the clinging arms of this child had revealed a new yet a very old thing to him, and Boris walked towards the barracks of the Preobrajensk Guards on feet that felt not the wooden pavement beneath them, and with his manly heart so full of tenderness towards that other confiding and loving little heart that he almost wished all the world would rise up and menace that one little child, that he might rise also and defend her.

Then Boris went and proved for a third time that he was no ghost, but a solid and able-bodied bear-hunter, and retold once again the story of his adventures for the benefit of an admiring mess. Here Boris learned also from the officers of his regiment that he had narrowly escaped a shot in the back as he stood alone upon the wall of Azof; for a former companion of the Streltsi, one Zaitzoff, had deliberately taken a shot at him, in order, as he had declared, to pay off old scores. Another member of the corps, one Platonof, being wounded to death, and horrified at the dastardliness of the proceeding, had communicated Zaitzoff's words to the surgeon who attended him. The surgeon in his turn reported to the officers of the Preobrajensk, and these took summary vengeance. They had gone in a body to the Streltsi quarters that very evening on hearing the surgeon's tale, had pulled Zaitzoff out of his tent, held an improvised court-martial on the spot, and shot the miscreant then and there, and in the presence of all his comrades, who did nothing to protect him, being themselves horrified with his action.

One more danger escaped, added to the many, was as nothing to this man returned, as it were, from the very gates of death; yet Boris did not fail to offer thanks for the erring flight of Zaitzoff's bullet when he counted up the mercies of God on this first evening of his return, and knelt long and fervently within the cathedral of the Kremlin. Neither did Nancy forget to be grateful when she knelt at her bedside and said her daily prayers, which were the old English ones, in spite of the fact that Colonel Drury and all his house were now within the fold of the Russo-Greek Church and naturalized Russians.

CHAPTER XVII.

OFF TO ENGLAND.

Bombardier Peter Alexeyevitch entered with all his impetuosity and marvellous energy into the preparations for the second attack upon Azof. During the whole of the winter and spring he was busy superintending the work of ship-building in the south of Russia. Every little river harbour on either side of the Don had its own improvised ship-building yards, and its hundreds of workmen from all parts of the country, engaged in the setting up as quickly as might be of galleys and rafts and every kind of floating vehicle. "We live, as old Adam did, in the sweat of our brow," wrote the Tsar to one of his intimates in Moscow, "and have hardly time to eat our bread for the pressure of work." Dockyards burned down, and destroying in their own destruction the work of many months; gangs of labourers deserting and disappearing when most required to complete their work—nothing could discourage the great Tsar, or turn him by the fraction of an inch from the path he had laid out for himself. Galleys and boats quickly took shape, and gradually approached completion. Peter was everywhere, swearing, scolding, encouraging, organizing, never weary, and never losing heart because of the misfortunes of the moment. The Don waters rose and carried away many half-completed vessels and much valuable timber; but the forests of Voronej were not so far away nor so poor but that inexhaustible supplies of birch and oak and pine and beech might be had to replace what was lost; and these same waters of the Don which had swept the timber away should be utilized to carry down on their broad bosom as much again and more than they had stolen and cast into the sea. Then Peter himself fell ill; but even sickness could not quell his ardour for the work he had set himself, and the building was not delayed for a moment. At last, when the long nights of midsummer were near at hand, the flotilla was ready and slipped down the broad river straight for the doomed city. There were twenty-two galleys, and one hundred large rafts for carrying ordnance, and some seventeen hundred smaller vessels, boats and lighters.

By this time the regiments from Moscow and the Streltsi, who had never left the neighbourhood, were once more assembled beneath the walls of Azof. The Preobrajensk were there, and among them our friend Boris, who had spent a delightful winter and spring in Moscow, and was now ready and anxious for adventure again. All the troops which had taken part in the former unsuccessful attack upon the fortress were now present again to retrieve their laurels, which had faded before the breath of Turk and Tartar.

But many new faces were to be seen among the old ones—veterans, chiefly, of tanned and foreign appearance; experienced engineers and gunners from France, and Hanover, and Brandenburg. Under the orders of these men a high wall of earth was built beneath the very ramparts of the city, so that the soil, when the wall was finished, trickled over the ramparts of Azof, which it overtopped, and fell into the streets of the city. At the same time the ships and rafts blockaded the town from the water side, so that there was no escape this time by way of the Black

Sea. Then, when all was ready for the attack, preparations were made for a combined assault both by land and sea.

But the hearts of the Tartars failed them, and the city capitulated before the storming was commenced, greatly to the disappointment of many young heroes who had intended to perform deeds of valour, and especially of the valiant Boris, whose arms ached for another brush with the Turkish swordsmen, especially with those who had been so unfortunate as to be instructed in the art by himself, with whom he had promised himself much entertainment.

The Tsar spared no pains to discover Boris's friend the pasha, whom, when found, he placed at the service of Boris. The hunter, remembering the palanquin, but recollecting also that he owed to the pasha, in a fashion, his deliverance from death by the sword, was merciful, and did but take his fun out of him for a day or so, after which he released him altogether and let him go free. But for one day that poor pasha afforded much amusement to the officers of the Preobrajensk and to the Tsar also; for Boris harnessed the poor fat manikin to a light hand-cart, and, himself sitting as a coachman in front, drove him up and down the camp, whipping him up with a horse-lash when he tired, till the wretched Turk was ready to fall between the shafts and expire from pure exhaustion.

Jansen, who was captured also in the streets of the city, though disguised in the garb of a common Tartar tradesman, did not escape so easily. He was carried in chains to Moscow when the troops returned to the capital, and there his head was struck off his shoulders and exhibited on a pole as a warning to traitors.

The army entered Moscow in triumph, under festal arches made to represent Hercules trampling Turkish pashas under foot, while Mars, on the summit of a second triumphal archway, pitched Tartars over in large numbers. The principal generals were drawn into the city upon gilded sledges placed on wheels; while

Bombardier Peter Alexeyevitch, now raised, however, to the rank of captain, walked in the procession as befitted his humbler grade in the service. Boris was there, too, in all the glory of a major's epaulets; and if he had glanced up at a certain balcony in the Troitski Street as he passed beneath, there is no doubt that he might have seen two bright eyes for which he was the centre of the procession, if not the only figure in it, and which did not fail to notice with pride the new insignia of rank and promotion which he bore on either broad shoulder. There, too, in the midst of the happy marching host, was the wretched prisoner Yakooshka, hooted and spat upon by the crowd as he dragged his heavily-ironed feet over the stones of Moscow.

Thus the first triumph of Peter's new army and navy was achieved with scarcely a single blow struck; for, with the exception of a brilliant assault upon redoubts by the Don Cossacks and an easily-repulsed sortie by the inhabitants, during which but few lives were lost on the Russian side, there had been no fighting done. But the prestige of the foreign troops was won, Peter's policy was justified, the enemies of Christ and of the true faith had been overthrown, a seaport had been gained for Russia, and the beginning of her expansion had become an accomplished fact.

Peter was thoroughly and entirely happy, for he had made the first move in the great game he had come into this world to play, and it was a good move. The Mussulmans had been hustled out of Azof, and a garrison of Streltsi left in the city to take care that they did not return; and now three thousand Russian families were sent to the town, there to abide for ever, they and their descendants. Ship-building was commenced wherever docks could be conveniently erected, and all classes were heavily taxed in order to pay for the ships to be built in them.

Meanwhile, young Russians of talent were despatched to Venice, to the Netherlands, to London, and to Paris, in order to learn the newest things, whether in ship-building, or in gunnery, or in drill and uniform. Their orders were to keep their eyes open and to see and learn everything worth learning.

And now Peter felt that he might conscientiously undertake that trip to foreign lands which he had long promised himself, and to which he had so ardently looked forward. He was to travel incognito, in order to avoid the worry of publicity and the tedious attentions of courts. The journey was to be undertaken under the ægis of a great embassy, Peter following in the train of his ambassadors in the character of a humble *attaché* or secretary. Boris was to go, as the Tsar had long since promised him; for he would be extremely useful, in England at least, if they ever got so far, by reason of his knowledge of the language. Besides, Peter liked to have his faithful bear-eater, as he still loved to call him, constantly at his side, and would not have thought of leaving him behind under any circumstances.

There was one little heart that was sore indeed when Boris came to take his leave before the departure of the embassy. It was always good-bye, Nancy said wistfully, as the hunter tore himself regretfully from her side: would there never come a time when she would not continually be looking forward with dread to his departure somewhere?

Boris gazed long and earnestly into the sorrowful blue eyes raised to his own. "Perhaps there will, my Nancy, perhaps there will," he said at last, "when you are a little older—God knows; but I must always be a soldier and serve the Tsar wherever he will have me go."

"And I shall always love you and be miserable when you go away," said Nancy, in perfect sincerity.

Nancy had intrusted to Boris many letters and presents to her friends and relations in England, letters in which she had not failed to enlarge upon the greatness and heroism of the bearer; for she had extracted a promise that Boris would deliver with his own hands certain of the packages. There would be frequent couriers backwards and forwards, so that she could write to her friend, and he would write too; so after all Nancy felt there would still be some comfort in life in spite of the envious fate which so constantly took her idol away from her.

Then began that historical journey of Peter and his suite through the Baltic provinces, and Königsberg, and Hanover, and the Netherlands, where Peter left his embassy to follow him at leisure while he hastened on and lived for some weeks at Zaandam as a common Dutch labourer, in order to learn thoroughly the rudiments of ship-building, and to set a good example of industry and self-denial to a lazy and self-indulgent people at home. The details of Peter's life at Zaandam are known to the "youngest schoolboy." I need not therefore dwell upon this hackneyed subject.

Boris had passed with wonder and admiration through the various foreign lands and courts visited by the great Muscovite embassy; but there was far too much eating and drinking and wearing of fine clothes to please him, and he soon began to weary of it and think of home and the simplicity of his life in Moscow, and of hunting expeditions, with Nancy for companion. Especially after the Tsar left the suite and went his own way, Boris found life desperately dull and monotonous. Right glad was he when the embassy reached Amsterdam and the spell of the Tsar's presence was once more upon him. Peter had just been informed that, good as the Dutch ship-builders were, they were very inferior to those of England. This had been quite sufficient for the energetic Tsar, and Boris found that arrangements had already been made for a visit to the latter country.

"So get ready, my bold Bear-eater, for to-morrow we cross the water. You will be sea-sick, of course; but then you will see Nancy's native land—ha, think of that!"

Boris did think of that, and it rejoiced his heart to reflect that his eyes should look upon the country which could produce so wonderful a thing as Nancy Drury.

So, on the following morning, Peter, with Boris and fifteen other Russians, took ship in the private yacht of his Majesty William III., which that monarch had sent for his accommodation, together with three ships of war, the whole under the orders of Admiral Mitchell of the British navy, and crossed the seas for this hospitable land of Britain. The weather being rough, Boris was sea-sick, as foretold by the Tsar; but Peter himself was as happy as a schoolboy out for a holiday, for that sail in his Majesty's beautiful yacht, escorted by such ships of war as he had never yet beheld, was the most delightful thing he had ever experienced. Such being the case, Peter arrived in this country in the highest good-humour, having familiarized himself on the way with the name and use of every single object on board the yacht, as well as with the names, ages, duties, and salaries of every man and boy that went to make up her crew.

Once on shore, the Tsar would hear no talk of palaces and luxury and the idle life of courts, but went with two or three chosen followers and pitched his tent in a country house close to the shipping at Deptford, where he was soon busy among the skippers and sailors, inquiring into and laying to heart everything that he saw which was likely to prove of service to him in his own country. And ever at his right hand, ready for work or for play, though preferring the latter, was Boris the Bear-Hunter, whose prowess in all athletic matters Peter was never weary of showing off to his English friends.

CHAPTER XVIII.

HOW BORIS THREW A BIG DUTCHMAN OVERBOARD.

But busy as the Tsar was during the daytime, visiting and inspecting the ships and trade, and examining the skippers and sailors of all nationalities as to maritime affairs and other matters connected with the various countries from which they hailed, he nevertheless found time at night for much conviviality and jollification. Menshikoff was always at hand to bear his master company, but Boris, being now practically a teetotaller, was allowed to go to bed instead of taking his share of drinking and revelling. There were generally guests at these entertainments—skippers from English and Dutch ships, or English friends of low or high degree who had been fortunate enough to scrape acquaintance with the big Russian Tsar.

One night there was a guest present, the mate of a Dutch vessel then lying in the Thames, to whom the Tsar was much attracted by reason of his great size, of which the man was exceedingly proud. He was almost, if not quite, as tall as Peter himself, who, according to Russian chroniclers, measured six feet seven inches in height. This person, by name Otto Koog, had taken his full share of the good cheer provided by his royal host, and his tongue was freed so that it spoke many vain things, both of his own prowess and of the feebleness of other people. There was no man on this earth, the fellow boasted, whom he could not put down in fifteen seconds. The Tsar expressed a great desire to witness an exhibition of Koog's strength, whereupon Koog said that, with his Majesty's permission, he would carry Peter and Menshikoff together three times round the room, like two babies, one upon each arm. This feat he performed with ease, though he declared the Tsar to be one of the finest babies he had ever lifted. Then Peter said that this was all very well, but could he carry in his arms a strongish man who was unwilling to be so carried? To this Koog replied that there breathed not a man whom he could not lift and carry, whether willing or unwilling, as easily as a four days' puppy.

"That being so, mynheer," said Peter, "there is one asleep in the room above us in this very house whom I should like to see brought downstairs in your arms. You shall wake him first and pull him out of bed. Tell him I sent you to bring him down in your hands as you would carry a baby."

Nothing loath, the big Dutchman left the room, and soon the Tsar and his guests could hear him blundering up the wooden stairs. Then came the sound of his heavy feet upon the floor above, after which a ponderous bump, as of a great body falling upon the ground, this being followed by the noise of talking.

Next began rushings to and fro, bumpings and thumpings on the floor, crashing of glass, and smashing of crockery and furniture; then more jumping and tumbling, with occasional loud shouts. Then came the banging open of a door, and the stumbling and sliding footfall as of one descending the stairs with difficulty. Next there was much struggling at the door of the room, with kickings at the panels of the door; and presently the hinges flew asunder and a big Russian boot appeared through the panels, and into the chamber walked Boris, carrying in his arms Mynheer Otto Koog, whose kickings and strugglings scattered many bottles as the young Russian deposited his burden upon the supper-table before the Tsar in the centre of a large dish of stew.

Then the Tsar and his guests began to laugh and applaud, and laugh again when Boris wiped his brow with his hand, and with mock gravity said, "Supper is served, your Majesty."

Koog declared that he must have drunk more than was good for him, or no man on earth could have done what Boris had done this night. But the Tsar laughed, and maintained that drunk or sober Koog would find his bold bear-eater a pretty tough customer.

Then Koog, in the smart of defeat, challenged Boris to a wrestling match on board his own ship, the match to take place on the following morning, and the victory to belong to him who should first succeed in pitching the other overboard into the water. The Tsar did not wait for Boris to express any opinion on this matter, but immediately accepted the challenge in his name for ten o'clock on board the *Zuyder Zee*.

When the morning came rain was falling heavily, which made the deck of the Dutch ship, upon which this wrestling match was to take place, very wet and slippery. Koog had put on his string slippers, which would give him a far better hold of the wet deck than would be afforded by the thick Russian boots which Boris wore. Nevertheless, the hunter made no objection, and took his stand opposite to his antagonist, both being stripped to the waist.

The Dutchman was by far the taller and heavier man, but what Boris lacked in weight he made up in the spring and agility of his movements. At the word to commence, given by the Tsar himself, the big Dutchman sprang at Boris, and clasping him by the waist raised him some inches from the ground, and actually made as though he would end the battle in its earliest stage by carrying the Russian to the side of the ship, and fairly hoisting him over the bulwark. But the hunter had no intention of allowing the fight to close before it had fairly begun. He struggled in Koog's arms until his feet were once more upon the ground, when he, in his turn, clasped his antagonist by neck and waist, and the wrestle began in earnest. For full half-a-minute neither Dutchman nor Russian obtained any advantage; if Otto succeeded in pushing Boris a few inches nearer to the ship's side, Boris quickly recovered his lost ground. Then, of a sudden, the hunter's foot slipped on the wet deck, and in an instant he was prone at the feet of the other. Koog was all ready to take advantage of this misfortune, and before the Russian champion could recover himself he seized him in his arms, as though he carried a baby, and sprang with him to the side of the vessel.

"Boris lifted his kicking legs and slid them over the bulwark."

For a moment Peter and the crowd of spectators thought that it was all up with the chances of poor Boris, and looked over the side to see him go splashing into the water beneath.

But Boris was far from being beaten yet. He laid hold of a rope which formed part of the rigging of the ship, and to this he clung so tightly that all the efforts of the mighty Dutchman could not compel him to relax his hold. Suddenly, however, he did relax his hold, and this just as Koog gave so violent a pull that when the resistance unexpectedly failed, he staggered backwards. At the same moment, Boris twisted in his arms, and feeling the ground once more with his feet, pushed so vigorously at his antagonist that Otto fell violently backwards with Boris on the top of him. They both rolled about for many minutes, first one being uppermost and then the other, until by mutual consent they both rose to their feet in order to start fair once more; and thus ended the first round.

Then began the final stage of the contest. Three times Boris forced Koog to the bulwark, but could get him no further; and twice the bear-hunter was himself well-nigh hoisted over the side. Then, at his fourth attempt, Boris drove Koog backwards till his back touched the bulwark; there, closing with him, with a desperate effort he lifted the ponderous Dutchman till Koog sat upon the rail. Then Otto, in desperation, hitched one foot around an iron stay which stood up against the bulwark, and pressed forward with all his weight and strength upon the champion of Russia, who, in his turn, did all that lay in his power to force the Dutchman backwards; and so the pair remained for upwards of a minute, straining, and hissing, and panting, and sweating, while the fate of Koog hung in the balance.

Then suddenly Boris relaxed, for an instant, his pressure upon Otto's shoulders, though without losing his grip. The strain removed, Koog's body fell forwards, while his leg flew up, having released itself from the stay. Instantly Boris stooped, and with one hand laid hold of the Dutchman's baggy trouser leg, while with the other he continued his pressure upon the shoulder. Backwards went the Netherlander, slowly but surely; his balance was lost, and so, for him, was the fight. Deftly Boris lifted his kicking legs and slid them over the bulwark, bending them back over the body, which was now in full retreat towards the water, and in an instant the big man splashed into the waves and the muddy Thames closed over his head. So fatigued was the Dutchman with his exertions that he could barely keep afloat, and was quite unable to swim a stroke; he floated away gasping and sputtering, and the crew of a neighbouring vessel fished him out with a boat-hook and ropes.

Great was the joy of the Tsar over this victory of his champion. Peter hoisted Boris upon his own shoulders, and carried him round and round the ship, amid the cheers and laughter of many spectators, not only on board the *Zuyder Zee*, but also upon many other vessels anchored near her.

After this triumph, the Tsar was still more anxious to pit his Russian champion against those of other nationalities, and involved poor Boris in many defeats by reason of this passion. As an instance, a coal miner from Cumberland, and a champion wrestler of that county, was hunted up by the Tsar and pitted against Boris for a match. In the skilled hands of this man, poor, untutored Boris was as a child in arms. The Cumbrian threw him again and again, adopting at each attempt a new device of the many known to him, and every one of them sufficient to topple over the Russian like a nine-pin. Boris, and Peter also, were to learn that mere strength and activity were insufficient to cope with equal, or even inferior strength, scientifically exercised. But in spite of this, Boris, after having fallen heavily six times, ended the fight in a manner unexpected by his adversary, and little to his taste. The match took place on the deck of a collier, and at the seventh round Boris, suddenly bending before his antagonist could lay hold of him, caught the Cumbrian champion by the knees, and lifting him by a tremendous effort, sent him flying over his shoulder, and over the side of the ship also, into mid-river, where the poor man would have been drowned had not Boris himself gone to his assistance.

Peter gave the Cumbrian champion a present in money, and offered him handsome wages to come over to his country and teach the Russians to wrestle. But the man of Cumberland looked knowingly at the Tsar, and refused the offer; he would rather stay, he said, in a country "where men did not eat their own kind," even though at a lower rate of wages. In vain the Tsar assured him that in Russia men are not cannibals; the sturdy north countryman only looked the more knowing, and the negotiations ended where they began.

Then, again, Boris was required to run races with sundry champions, who easily defeated him, as was natural; though he held his own in jumping. At swimming, however, even the best of his English competitors were obliged to take a second place, for Boris excelled any who were pitted against him, especially in the longer races.

In the noble science of self-defence Boris, though untutored, surprised every one by his aptitude. It was not that he was skilled either in defence or in attack; but his eye was good and his natural guard excellent, while his enemies, or rather antagonists, declared that it was one of the most disagreeable things in the world to receive a blow straight from the Russian's shoulder.

Thus, though often worsted in the competitions wherein, by the desire of the Tsar, he tried his strength and agility against the best foreign exponents, Boris on the whole held his own against all comers, and the Tsar declared himself well satisfied with his faithful bear-hunter, who had upheld, to the best of his ability, the claim of far-away Muscovy to compete with the rest of the world in trials of strength and pluck and endurance. It was, indeed, a matter of no little pleasure and encouragement to Peter to find that he was able to produce a picked man who had proved himself as good as, and sometimes better than, the picked men of other nationalities. The circumstance led him to hope that his Russians, when instructed by qualified tutors, would show themselves worthy to take their proper place in Europe, and to hold their own whether on the battle-field or on board ship, as he would assuredly call upon them to do ere many years were past.

Besides all this, Peter saw and did much, during his stay in London, with which our bear-hunter was not so immediately connected; but for a short account of his doings and seeings among our forefathers in this merry land of England, I must refer my readers to the following chapter.

CHAPTER XIX.

BAD NEWS FROM MOSCOW.

To Admiral Carmarthen, of the British Navy, Peter of Russia was indebted for one of the supremest pleasures of his life. This was a review, or naval sham-fight, which the admiral organized for the Tsar's benefit at Spithead. We can imagine how Peter, whose heart was so set at this time upon ships and all matters connected with the sea and maritime affairs, must have gazed in rapture and delight at the beautiful battle-ships that manœuvred before his eyes; how he must have knit his strong face, and bent his eagle glance which nothing ever escaped, upon each turn and evolution of the vessels, and watched each manœuvre, drinking in for his future guidance the reason for every movement made and the probable result, had this been actual warfare, of every gun fired. There is no doubt that the young autocrat learned much from this memorable scene, and laid to heart many hints to be utilized afterwards when he himself, in command of a Russian fleet, engaged and overcame a stronger fleet of the King of Sweden.

Peter's delight with the day's entertainment may be gauged by his conversation, when it was ended, with Admiral Carmarthen. "Admiral," he said, "you are a lucky man! I would rather be the admiral of a British fleet such as this than the Tsar of all the

Russias!"

Probably Peter's excited state of mind was responsible for this somewhat exaggerated manner of expressing his satisfaction; but there is no doubt that his enthusiasm and delight were perfectly sincere at the time. Boris was present also, and his delight was no less than that of his master. He, too, felt that it must indeed be a delightful position to be in command of so magnificent a sea-army as this.

"Boris, Boris!" said Peter, as the two tall men stood side by side watching the beautiful spectacle, "shall I ever own a fleet like this, and a good seaport to keep it in?"

"That depends upon your Majesty," said Boris. "Every one knows that Peter Alexeyevitch will perform anything to which he puts his hand and sets his heart!"

"Ah, Boris," said the Tsar, "I thought so too before we left Russia; but I am humbler now! Oh, for the sea, my Bear-eater—the sea! that is what we must fight for and live for. Our poor Russia is cramped and stifled for want of windows; we must break through her walls, Boris, and that as quickly as possible. I can build a fleet, there is no fear of that. If we had but a hundredth part of the seaboard that these happy Britons possess, I should be blessed indeed!"

"Never fear, your Majesty; we shall have seaports yet!" said Boris, to whom the matter presented no difficulty whatever, for did not Peter desire it?

As the Tsar and his henchman walked through the streets of London, they attracted considerable attention by reason both of their size and of the conduct of Peter, whose actions were at times very eccentric. He would stop people in the street, in order to ask questions as to the make of their clothes and hats and watch-chains. Once he seized the wig of a passing pedestrian, to that individual's surprise and alarm, who thought he had to deal with a gigantic lunatic. Peter carefully examined the wig, which was of a new-fashioned shape and did not please him, gave a short laugh and a grunt of disgust, and clapped it back upon the man's head so violently that the unfortunate fellow nearly fell forward upon his nose. He would enter jewellers' and other shops, and question the artificers very minutely as to their trade and craft, frequently ending the conversation by inviting the shopman to remove his business to Moscow, where he should be assured of a fine trade among Peter's subjects. Sometimes these offers were accepted, and numbers of goldsmiths, blacksmiths, gunsmiths, joiners, and other skilled workmen were prevailed upon to travel to the far north, where they were subsequently well treated and made fortunes for themselves, while they were useful in teaching their crafts to the Russian people.

Couriers frequently passed between London and Moscow, and through their good offices Boris was able to keep up a constant communication with his friend Nancy. The hunter was no great hand at letter writing, though he had long since learned the arts of reading and writing, of which of course he had been ignorant while still the bear-hunter of Dubinka. In one of his epistles Boris wrote to this effect, the letter being partly in English and partly in Russian:—

"His Majesty is exceedingly pleased with this city [London], wherein are more people than would fill a score of Moscows. The people are kind and hospitable, but somewhat boastful, and think but little of the Russians. His Majesty deigns to take his pleasure in causing me to wrestle and otherwise contend with great wrestlers and swimmers and fighters of the English. In these matters there are some experter than I, excepting in swimming. I have seen your friends and delivered your letters and packages, wherewith all were greatly pleased. Your friends made much of me, far more than I deserve. For their kindness I am indebted to you, and also for many good words spoken of me in your letters, portions of which they read to me.

"The Tsar and I had an adventure last night which might have ended in bloodshed, but ended actually only in laughter; for we were fallen upon by robbers, of whom there were five, in an outlying, lonely part named Hampstead. The robbers surprised us in the midst of this place, and would, no doubt, have cut our throats, but that his Majesty and I, being armed with thick oaken sticks, kept them at bay, and in process of time banged two of them on the head. The rest his Majesty, with some assistance from me, pitched into a small pond covered with green ooze, whence they issued half-drowned, and ran to their homes."

Nancy, on her part, told all the Moscow news and the progress of the ship-building throughout the country, of which she heard much talk, for every one spoke of it. Nancy also mentioned that many reports were being disseminated in Moscow by the priest party to the effect that the Tsar had been drowned on his way to England. Others said that he had been captured by the Queen of Sweden, placed in a barrel, and rolled into the sea. The motive of these reports was obvious. If Peter were dead, his widow, or his brother, or his son would be proclaimed head of the realm, and in any case his policy would be reversed; foreigners would be sent out of the country, and Russia given back to the Russians. It may be mentioned in this connection that so deeply was the belief in Peter's death at this time rooted in the minds of hundreds among the lower classes, both in Moscow and throughout the country, that to their dying day many of these believed that the man who returned eventually from abroad, and assumed the government of the realm, though he certainly resembled Peter, was an impostor and a pretender, and that the real Tsar lay drowned at the bottom of the North Sea.

During his stay in London, Peter had many opportunities of conversation with all classes of the subjects of William III. He visited country houses, where he startled the sober rural folks by the eccentricity of his manners—loving to amuse himself in rough and barbarous ways, such as causing Boris to wheel him, afterwards himself wheeling Boris, in a barrow through a massive holly hedge at Saye's Court. The Tsar could not endure the ways of refinement and luxury, and preferred to sleep on the floor rather than in a grand bed, and loved to drink quantities of English beer, which he condescended to admire.

Boris thought little of England from the point of view of the hunter. There were no woods, he said, fit to hide a bear or a wolf; as for hunting the fox, it was poor sport. The country was well enough, but not in his line; he preferred the broad forests of his native land, and the excitement and danger of hunting big game. In a word, Boris was well tired of England when, at the end of a few months, Peter declared that he had seen enough, and would now depart homewards, taking Vienna on the way, and travelling slowly in order to see as much as possible of every country visited.

The English king made Peter the most acceptable of presents at parting, in the shape of a small frigate of twenty-four guns. The delight of the Tsar in his new possession was immense, and his return voyage to Holland was made aboard of this vessel. But Peter, too, desired to offer a memento of his visit to the hospitable British sovereign, and did so in a characteristic manner; for, while bidding William farewell, he pressed into his hand a small object wrapped in a piece of dirty brown paper, which he took out of his waistcoat pocket. This proved to be a magnificent ruby, and was valued afterwards at ten thousand pounds.

So the Tsar and Boris and the rest took ship and set sail for Holland in the frigate which the English king had presented to his Russian brother. And that voyage came well-nigh to being the last that any of the party were to undertake; for a terrific storm arose in the North Sea, and for a day or two they were uncertain whether they should live or die. The Tsar's suite were greatly concerned at their master's danger, knowing well that the destiny of Russia was kept by this man in the hollow of his hand. But Peter himself professed to have perfect confidence in the happy outcome of the voyage; he inquired of his long-visaged companions whether they had ever heard of a Tsar of Russia being drowned in the North Sea? All admitted that they certainly never had read of such a disaster! "Very well then," said Peter; "I don't intend to be the first to set the example!" Whereupon the suite took heart of grace, and trusted to the good luck of the Tsar to pull them through, which it did; for the good ship sailed safely into port, and was then sent round to Archangel, while the Tsar and his embassy continued their journey by land, and in due course arrived at Vienna.

Here Peter had intended to stay some little while, in order to learn whatever the Austrians might have to teach him; but disquieting news came from Moscow, which compelled him to give up the contemplated visit, and to make all the haste he could towards his own capital. So bad was the news, indeed, that the Tsar was at his blackest and most savage during the whole of the hurried journey home, and those pleased him best who talked least, and left him most alone to his gloomy thoughts. Like a storm-cloud that rushes over the face of the sky, the angry Tsar flew over the hundreds of miles that lay between him and the objects of his wrath; and like the piled-up masses of black vapour that burst and vomit forth water and lightning, so burst the anger of Peter upon those who had vexed him, when, a very few days after receiving the news, he dashed into Moscow with a few attendants only, the rest following as quickly as they could.

The purport of the letter received by Peter in Vienna was certainly disquieting enough, for the epistle contained an account of a military revolt, and of a march upon the capital by the Streltsi. It appeared that these regiments, ever on the watch for opportunities of interfering in existing affairs, had sent a deputation to Moscow to inquire into the truth of the rumours as to the absence or death of the Tsar, and to demand of the authorities orders for the immediate return of all the Streltsi regiments to Moscow. Their wives and families were still in the capital, and they had been absent long enough at Azof and elsewhere. Besides, political affairs demanded their presence in the capital.

The deputation were unable to obtain the ear of the authorities, and were dismissed with scant ceremony from Moscow—very loath to leave the city, and extremely angry with those who would not listen to their grievances.

Meanwhile the main body of the Streltsi had become impatient, and sent word that, if not summoned to Moscow in compliance with their request, they intended to come without waiting for an invitation.

It was at this stage of affairs that letters were despatched to the Tsar at Vienna, summoning him to his capital, which was menaced by a descent upon it by the dissatisfied Streltsi regiments.

Meanwhile, however, the two generals, Schéin and Gordon, whom Peter had left at the head of military affairs in his absence, proceeded wisely to take the bull by the horns. They prepared a moderate force, selected from the new regiments, and marched towards the seat of disturbance.

Before they had gone very far they met emissaries from the Streltsi, who informed them that the massed regiments of that body were in full march upon Moscow, with intent to chase the foreigner from the soil of holy Russia; to place the Grand-Duchess Sophia, late regent, upon the throne in lieu of the Tsar Peter, who, they had heard, was dead; and to restore the old *régime* and the good old days of a Streltsi-dominated Moscow, without a foreigner in the place to set everything upside down and worry the souls of the priests.

Gordon sent these men back with a message to their comrades to get home as quickly as might be to their quarters, and there to pray Heaven to so rule the heart of the Tsar Peter (who was quite alive enough to cut the throat of every Streletz in Russia), that he might be led to look with indulgence upon their foolish imaginings, and forgive them in consideration of their instant and complete submission, tendered from their barracks.

But the Streltsi would not believe the words of Gordon, and declared that they must and would come to Moscow in order to see with their own eyes that all was well with the Tsar and the country.

Thereupon Gordon and Schéin met these misguided men half way as they marched upon Moscow. The Streltsi would not surrender at demand, and therefore a volley was fired over their heads. This set the brave fellows running, which proved that their courage was scarcely equal to the noise they made in the world. Three thousand of them were taken prisoners and brought to Moscow; the rest were permitted to escape and return to their own quarters.

Such was the state of affairs when the enraged young Tsar dashed into Moscow in his angriest and blackest mood, and with his mind set upon making a terrible example of this body of men, who had been a thorn in the flesh to him since his first experience of their eccentricities, at the age of ten.

How he carried out his intentions, and the bearing which this affair had upon the career of our bear-hunter, shall be treated of in the following chapter.

CHAPTER XX.

BORIS IN DISGRACE.

The page of the history of Peter of Russia which I must now briefly refer to is stained and blurred with the records of ferocity and brutality, and I am sure my readers will thank me if I give as cursory an account of the Tsar's terrible mood of cruelty as is barely necessary for the thread of my own tale. This is the blackest period of Peter's life, if we except perhaps his persecution in later years of the unfortunate Grand-Duke Alexis, his utterly unworthy son; and for those who are sincere admirers of the genius and self-denial of the great Tsar, and of his many remarkable and wonderful gifts and graces of mind and disposition, the record of his treatment of the Streltsi at this time affords extremely unpleasant reading.

Peter's first step was to form a court of inquiry, or inquisition, on a gigantic scale. For many weeks this court continued its labours of investigation, examining the captured soldiers and officers at great length and with extreme persistency, in the hope of extracting from them minute details of the conspiracy which had culminated in the revolt and march upon Moscow. The object of the Tsar was to obtain the names of all those connected with the plot who were outside the ranks of the Streltsi, and more especially to discover proof of the participation of his sister Sophia, the late regent, in the affair.

To this end horrible tortures by scourge and fire were daily inflicted upon the unfortunate Streltsi, who very soon confessed all they knew, which was the very simple fact that the priests had persuaded them that Peter was dead, and that they had therefore determined to come to Moscow in order to request Sophia, the Grand-Duchess, to take in hand measures for the legal succession to the throne. Also, they were anxious to see their wives and families, from whom they had been, as they imagined, unfairly separated. Not a man among them, either by torture or of free will, could be made to say that the Grand-Duchess had stirred up or in any way encouraged the rising. They had, indeed, brought a letter for Sophia, begging her to act as regent and to reinstate themselves in Moscow, dismissing the foreigners and disbanding the new regiments; but Sophia herself had known nothing of the letter or of their intentions.

The Grand-Duchess and those around her were exhaustively

examined, though not by torture, as to the truth of these statements; and the investigators could find no reason to believe that it was otherwise than as declared by the Streltsi.

Foiled in his attempt to dig down to the roots of this matter, but unconvinced that his sister and others were innocent, Peter then proceeded to wreak his vengeance upon the Streltsi themselves. The Tsar was determined that this festering sore in the side of Russia should be healed once for all. The Streltsi, if allowed to remain in their old strength and numbers, and with their traditions of privilege and license of interference undisturbed, must for ever be a fruitful source of disturbance, and an element of danger to the state. They must be exterminated, root and branch, as an institution. But first these ringleaders must be dealt with; and here Peter determined to make a terrible example. Nearly two thousand of the unfortunate prisoners, together with a number of priests who were proved to have been implicated in the rising, were put to death in the streets of the city. One man was left hanging close to the window of the Grand-Duchess Sophia, holding in his dead hand the letter which the Streltsi had intended to present to her, in order to show Peter's half-sister how little he believed in her protestations of innocence.

It is not my intention to enter into any details of the horrors of this time, but one circumstance must be mentioned in connection with all this brutality and bloodshed, because it bears upon the career of our friend Boris, who was at this time forced into taking a step which was pregnant with changes in his life and prospects.

The Tsar, lost in these dark days of vengeance and brutality to all sense of propriety and moderation, decreed that his nobles and favourites should all take a hand in the barbarities being enacted —should, in a word, assist in the death of the mutineers. Some of Peter's intimates, either brutal enough to enjoy the work or else anxious to please the Tsar, cheerfully consented to do as he had requested them. Others protested, and with tears besought his Majesty to exempt them from so unworthy a duty. But the maddened young autocrat was firm, and insisted upon the carrying out of his commands.

What misguided motive Peter can have had for this outrageous piece of brutality it is impossible to determine; but since he never acted without motive of some kind, it is charitable to suppose that he believed he fulfilled some subtle purpose in commanding these men to do his savage will. Perhaps he desired to impress upon his favourites the awful consequences of treason to his person, by means of an object lesson which would linger in their minds as long as they lived, and thus effectually deter them from ever entertaining the idea of disobedience. It was a terrible lesson, whether required or not, and we may safely suppose that no man who was concerned in those scenes of violence and cruelty ever forgot the experience. The Streltsi behaved with exemplary bravery, and laughed, and sang soldier-songs, and prayed aloud upon the scaffold, until death stilled their tongues.

But there was one man who neither at the request nor at the command of the Tsar would take a hand in the horrors of the day, and that man was Boris. Among the captured and condemned Streltsi were several members of the hunter's old regiment (which had revolted with the rest), one or two of whom had in former days crossed swords with Boris on a memorable occasion; indeed, two of them were of the party who had lurked in the dusk of the Moscow street-corner in order to assassinate him.

One morning, when Boris paid his usual visit to the cabinet of the Tsar to hear his Majesty's commands for the day, he found the latter pacing rapidly up and down the apartment, black and gloomy, as he ever was at this time. None had ever known the Tsar's savage mood to last for so long as it had continued on this occasion. Since the day when, in Vienna, the letter of Gordon had been brought to him, the "black dog" had sat upon his Majesty's shoulder, and there had been no gleam of even transient sunshine to dispel the clouds that overcast his soul. Peter was not himself. He had been worked up by his passion into a condition of mind in which his own intimate friends failed to recognize their rough but ever kind and indulgent master.

At this present moment Boris could plainly see that rage had full possession of his Majesty's spirit. He took no notice of him beyond glaring fiercely at him as he entered, and said no word of greeting. Boris had been bitterly affected lately, not because of Peter's neglect of himself—for that, he knew, would mend with brighter days—but because the dreadful savagery which the Tsar had shown at this time revealed his beloved master in a character which the hunter had not seen before; a revelation which filled him with a shocked sense of pain and disappointment very hard to bear.

Peter continued to stride up and down the room, muttering to himself, and spoiling the rugged beauty of his features by twisting them into contortions and grimaces as the passion worked within his soul. At last he stopped. Then he raised his eyes and saw the hunter, who lingered near the door.

"Ah! it's you, is it?" he said. "It is as well you have come, for I have special work for you to-day. There are some old friends of yours, I find, among these accursed ones, the Streltsi prisoners."

The heart of Boris sank, for he guessed what was coming; many of the Tsar's intimates having already been told off to do his savage will, and he knew that his turn was come.

"I have reflected that it would be only fair," continued the Tsar, "to allow you the privilege of paying off old scores. Since these men are sentenced to death, there is none who could so fitly carry out the sentence as yourself."

"Your Majesty must excuse me," said Boris, who was more of the athlete and soldier than the orator; "I am an officer, not an executioner."

The Tsar's face worked. He glared savagely at Boris for the space of half a minute; then he laughed, but not in his old hearty way.

"You are a bold man, whatever else you may be," he said. "Now listen. It is my desire that you take this axe"—here his Majesty produced a workman's hatchet from a grim pile beside his table —"and with it proceed to that corner of the Uspensky where these men or others of the same regiment once attempted your life. There you will find a block already erected, and upon that block you shall execute these three men—Michael Orlof, Vladimir Donskoi, Feodor Latinski." The Tsar read these names from a slip of paper which he took from his table.

But Boris still preserved a bold front. He raised himself to his full height, looking very proud and very handsome, and almost as big as the Tsar himself, who appeared somewhat bent and borne down by the evil days and more evil passions which had fallen upon him.

"I have told your Majesty I am no executioner," repeated the hunter, regardless of the passion of the Tsar. "Command me to fight these men, all three at once if you will, with the sword, and I will obey your bidding this very hour, and your Majesty knows enough of me to accept my promise that not one of them shall remain alive; but as for beheading them in cold blood with yonder axe, I cannot and I will not do the deed."

Boris felt that in taking this bold course he was probably, in the Tsar's present humour, signing his own death-warrant; yet he knew also that he would sooner die than do this detestable thing that Peter would have of him.

The Tsar bit his lip till the blood showed red on the white. "Boris Ivanitch, I entreat you," he muttered, "do not anger me more. By the mercy of Heaven, I know not myself at this time. I repeat to you that I am to be obeyed. Take this axe and do my bidding—go!"

But Boris stood straight and firm, and looked the Tsar boldly in the eyes. His blood was up and his stubborn spirit was in arms. He seized the axe which Peter held out to him and flung it crashing to the farthest end of the room.

"No," he said, quietly but with firm lips and erect form, "I am not a slave. I love your Majesty, but your way this day is not God's way. Not even the Tsar shall force me into doing this ungodly and detestable deed!"

The Tsar recoiled, his face livid and bloodless, and his features convulsed with the passion that beset him—drawing his sword as he stepped backwards.

Boris thought that his end was come; yet even at this supreme moment he felt as cool as though he were going to step out of the chamber next moment and go about his usual business.

For a full minute the Tsar and Boris faced each other without a spoken word from either—Peter, with drawn sword half raised to strike, his breast heaving, his breath drawn in with hissings, his face working with evil passion, his eyes ablaze, and the infinite generosity and manhood of his nature struggling beneath the passion that had so long suffocated and cramped it; Boris, calm and cool, thinking, like a good Russian, of his soul, but thinking also of Nancy, who was so soon to be deprived of a friend as tender and true as the best.

At length the Tsar's arm fell to his side and he tossed his sword upon the table.

"Be it so," he said; and then, "There is not another in all Russia for whose sake that sword should have been held back. Boris Ivanitch, I remind myself of your good service—we have been friends and brothers—you have even saved my life at the risk of your own. For these reasons I forbear to strike, as you deserve. But you have disobeyed me—" here the Tsar's face worked once more, and he was silent for a moment. Then he continued, "You have disobeyed me; you can serve me no longer, you are no servant of mine from this hour. Thus I tear you from my heart for ever. Give me your sword." Peter tore the epaulets from his shoulders, and took Boris's sword, laying it beside his own upon the table. "Now go from my sight; I will never see you more. I can never forget your disobedience; it is for me the unpardonable thing. Away—out of my sight!"

Boris had been prepared for death, but he had not expected this—disgrace and banishment from the face of his beloved master; for at the Tsar's words Boris had felt all his old love come swelling into his heart.

The poor hunter burst into tears and seized the Tsar's hand to kiss it ere he left his presence for ever.

But the Tsar repelled him. "Go," he said sternly—"out of my sight; you sicken me with your woman's ways; I am not to be softened by hand-kissing and crying—go!"

Thus befell the first and only quarrel between the bear-hunter and his much-loved master, and the pair were destined, in consequence of it, to be parted for many a long year.

Boris realized at once that he must leave Moscow. There was little object and much danger in remaining in the capital. Once in disgrace with the Tsar, there was no certainty but that the madness of Peter might cause him to treat Boris with scant ceremony should he meet the hunter in the streets or elsewhere. Whither, then, should he go?

Boris went to his apartment, and, with aching head and dazed intelligence, sat down to think out the problem. Why not return to Dubinka? That was his first idea; but he put it from him at once. Dubinka was too far away from Moscow; for Boris could not allow himself to banish entirely the hope that the Tsar might yet forgive him when these evil days had passed and all was forgotten. Besides, there was Nancy. He could never bear to live so far away from her home; how should he ever do without her love, now that he had come to realize that it was, if not all in all to him, at least a large proportion of his all?

Boris ended his cogitations, which resulted in nothing, by setting out to walk to the Drurys' house, to inform them of the melancholy turn which his affairs had taken, and to ask their advice. No one was at home excepting Nancy, and to her Boris then and there confided his tale.

Nancy's face flushed as her friend told of how he had refused to obey the Tsar's bidding, of his disgrace, and of the loss of military rank and the Tsar's service. To the surprise of Boris the girl burst into tears and kissed the torn places upon his tunic where the Tsar had violently removed the epaulets. "I thank God you did what you did," she cried, "for, O Boris! I could never have loved you quite so well again if you had executed those poor men!"

Then Boris felt a great flood of comfort and encouragement come welling into his heart, and he went on to tell Nancy, with recovered spirits, of his determination to leave Moscow, and his reasons for taking the step.

Nancy grew very pale as he spoke of this, and when he was silent she, too, said no word for some little space. Then she placed her little hand in his big one and said,—

"If you leave Moscow, I shall go with you."

"Where to, Nancy? I am not going for one day," said obtuse Boris, playing with the little hand in his, and speaking sadly enough.

"Anywhere—I care not whither; but wherever you go, my Boris, I shall go too." Nancy smiled through her tears. "Won't you take me—won't you have me, Boris?" she said.

Then the hunter understood what the child wished to convey to his dense mind, and all his soul came rushing to his lips as he gathered her to his breast and said a thousand incoherent and tender and ridiculous things. For it had not dawned upon Boris that she was no longer a child, but a very beautiful and tender maiden of seventeen; and that it was now possible, if nothing untoward prevented it, to carry her away with him, even as she had, in her innocent candour, suggested, to be his lifelong companion and helpmate.

So Boris and Nancy passed a happy hour together, and all things miserable and unfortunate were forgotten in the new light which was thus shed upon the prospect. How different now seemed the idea of leaving Moscow! How could Boris have been so blind? Fate could not have been kinder. The Tsar would have forgiven him long before he should grow tired of indolent married life and wish to return to service and the imperial favour.

When Colonel and Mrs. Drury returned home and heard the story of Boris, and Nancy's declaration that she would not suffer him to go alone into exile (which in no wise surprised them), they had a new plan to propose. They possessed a country house, set in its own corner of the forest, some twenty miles from Moscow. Why should not the whole party retire to Karapselka for a while? The priest of the village could perform the marriage ceremony as well as the high ecclesiastics of Moscow; and probably Boris would prefer to have a quiet wedding, in order to escape observation. After the ceremony Nancy and her husband could take up their abode permanently at Karapselka, and there await the dawn of happier days, while the old people returned to Moscow, where they would at all times be within easy reach of their daughter. Boris would find plenty of congenial occupation among the bears and wolves in the forest.

This plan was hailed with joy by all concerned; and it need only be added that Nancy and Boris were duly married, and took up their abode at Karapselka, as the parents of the bride had suggested and as destiny decreed.

CHAPTER XXI.

NANCY AND THE BIG BEAR.

There was, as Colonel Drury had promised, plenty for Boris to do at Karapselka; so much so, indeed, that the hunter scarcely was aware of the flight of time, so happily did the days and the weeks and the months come and go. Nancy was the sweetest of young wives, and in her company Boris soon forgot his disgrace, and the sorrow and regret which the quarrel with the Tsar still caused him whenever he recalled it. Away from drills and service and the countless engagements and amusements of city life, the bear-hunter soon recovered all his old passion for the life of the forest. From morn till night he was afoot, tracking, hunting upon his trusty snow-shoes, stalking capercailzie or blackcock among the rime-embroidered pine trees, and revelling in the free and wholesome air of his oldest friend, the forest. Nancy often accompanied him on his excursions, when the distance was not too great; and the evenings passed as happily as mutually agreeable society could make them.

During these months and even years of peaceful life at Karapselka, Boris had many adventures with those animals which had furnished him his original title, as well as with wolves. In these adventures he found that his old skill in the chase was in no wise diminished, nor his nerve shaken, nor his strength and activity abated; he was still the bear-hunter all over. Sometimes it appeared to him that all his military career and his many adventures by land and sea were nothing more than a dream, and that he was back in Dubinka chasing the wild animals as a paid employé of his liege lord, the owner of the land and village in which he lived. But a word from Nancy, or a look into her sweet face, soon put matters into shape, and he knew himself for what he was—a once-favoured servant and soldier of the Tsar, now living under a cloud; a state of affairs which should have made him very miserable, whereas there was no denying the fact that he was nothing of the sort, but, on the contrary, exceedingly well content with his present lot.

One day, when they had been married for the better part of a year, Boris and Nancy met with an adventure which might have had fatal consequences for both of them.

Boris had allowed his wife to accompany him, as he often did, into the woods, driving in their comfortable kibitka, or covered sledge, to a point at a distance of a few miles from the house, and thence proceeding on snow-shoes for a mile or two further in pursuit of hares or foxes, or perhaps with an eye to a partridge or two to replenish the larder.

The day was magnificent—one of those glorious February days when the sun is bright but not warm, and the air rare and invigorating; when every pine is a marvel of subtile filigree-work in silver rime, and the snow beneath one's feet is dazzling with innumerable ice-gems, and has so hard a crust upon it that it will bear the weight of a man.

Nancy and her husband had enjoyed their drive, and were now drinking in the intoxicating fresh forest air as they slid easily along upon their snow-shoes, Nancy having by this time become quite an expert in this graceful fashion of getting over the ground.

The larder at Karapselka happened to be empty at this time, for there was no system of obliging bakers and butchers to call for orders in that out-of-the-way spot, nor indeed in Moscow either in those days; and Boris was intent upon whistling up tree-partridges, to provide food for the establishment at home. Three of these beautiful birds had come swooping up in response to his call, but had swerved and settled a hundred paces to the left. Boris immediately and cautiously followed them, in hope of getting a shot at the birds before they should take fright. On crept Boris, Nancy cautiously following him at a distance.

Suddenly, to the surprise and alarm of Nancy, and certainly no less of himself, Boris disappeared in a cloud of snow—disappeared as completely as though the earth had opened and swallowed him whole.

For a moment Nancy stopped short in consternation and uncertainty, so sudden had been the disappearance of her lord, when, to her still greater amazement and horror, there came from the spot where her husband had disappeared first terrific roars and growlings, together with much upheaving of snow and pine boughs, and next the ponderous figure of a large bear. Boris had fallen into a *berloga*, which is Russian for the den which a bear makes for himself during his hibernating period, and in which he remains more or less fast asleep from November until the thawing of the snow in March or April.

This was the first occasion upon which Nancy had seen a live bear at close quarters; and though she was as courageous a little person as you will meet in a day's march, yet the unexpected sight filled her with terror, which was largely increased when the great brute caught sight of her, and with renewed roarings made straight for the very spot where she stood helpless and motionless.

What had happened is easily explained and in a few words. Boris had stepped upon the top of a berloga, the roof of which immediately gave way beneath his weight, precipitating him upon the top of the sleeping tenant. The bear was not so far gone in somnolence but that the sudden descent upon his person of so heavy an individual as Boris not only awoke but irritated him exceedingly. Boris, finding himself upon the bear's back at the bottom of Bruin's own premises, felt quite at home; indeed, he was never more so than when in the company of a bear. He felt about for his knife, but found to his annoyance that he had left it at home. His axe was at his side, but there was no room to use it except by getting off the brute's back and allowing it to scramble out of the den, when he might get a stroke at it as it went, wounding it sufficiently to prevent its escape, and finishing the business as soon as he could climb out also.

Meanwhile, the bear was doing its utmost to rid itself of the incubus on its back. It heaved itself up and wriggled, and at last tried to bolt through the aperture which the new arrival had made in the roof of the den. By this move it rid itself of Boris, who slid off backwards, but could not recover himself in time to aim the blow at Bruin's hind-quarter which he had intended to deal it.

By the time Boris was upon his feet the bear had disappeared, and it only then struck Boris that Nancy was outside, and might be in danger of receiving injury from the frightened and angry creature. Full of this fear Boris darted upwards in order to follow the bear and see to Nancy's safety. But the roof gave way as he attempted to climb out, and he fell backwards a second time to the bottom of the berloga. At the second attempt Boris was more successful, and reached the surface in safety.

But when he did so he saw a sight which filled him with fear and horror, for the huge brute was in full pursuit of his young wife, who fled before it upon her snow-shoes, uttering cries of alarm and calling on Boris to help her.

"Bear round this way to me—to me, Nancy!" shouted the poor hunter in agony, starting to run after the pair in desperate dread.

His snow-shoes had been broken in his tumble into the bear's den, so that he was now on foot and trusting to the hard crust of the snow to support him. The animal turned at the sound of his voice, and for a moment seemed to pause, as though doubtful upon which of the two enemies to wreak its passion; then it turned again and resumed its pursuit of poor Nancy. Boris saw with anguish that whenever Nancy endeavoured to edge round in order to come towards him, her pursuer seemed to comprehend her design, and prevented it by cutting the corner to meet her.

Then Boris thought in his agony of mind of another plan. Nancy was gliding beautifully on her light shoes, and could easily keep her lead of the bear so long as her breath held out; while he, run as fast as he might, could scarcely keep up with the chase, without shoes to help him along. It was plain that at this rate he would never overtake bear or wife, and could thus do nothing to assist poor Nancy.

"Make for the sledge, Nancy," he shouted; "go straight along our old tracks—'tis but a short half-mile away!"

Nancy heard and understood, and went straight on, looking neither to the right hand nor to the left, but only straining every nerve to gain upon the brute behind her, so as to reach the sledge sufficiently well ahead of him to allow time to unfasten the horse, which was tied to a tree.

On rushed Nancy, and on came the bear behind her, she gaining slowly but steadily; and after them came panting Boris, with difficulty holding his own, for all that he was a good runner and in fair condition, for at every third or fourth step the treacherous snow surface gave way and plunged his foot and leg deep in the powdery ice-covered stuff.

And now the sledge came into view, and a glad sight it was for more than one of the party. Nancy took heart at seeing it, and made a renewed effort to gain a yard or two, reaching the horse's head—the horse struggling and tugging for terror of the bear the while—with a lead of thirty good yards. Deftly she untied the noose and freed the snorting, terrified animal, and as deftly she threw her body across the side of the sledge, and the horse, feeling himself free, dashed with it homewards. Then she slipped into the seat, just at the very moment that Bruin arrived upon the spot to find his bird flown.

"Bravo, bravo, my Nancy!" shouted Boris, as he watched with unspeakable relief and joy how the swift little sledge bore her instantly out of danger.—"Now, Mishka," he added, "come back and settle accounts with me; you won't catch that bird, she's flown."

"The huge brute was in full pursuit of his young wife."

The bear, who was still standing and watching the sledge as it glided away from him, seemed to hear and comprehend the invitation of Boris. It turned sharp round upon hearing his voice, and with a loud roar accepted the challenge thrown out to it. It looked very large, and certainly a terrific object, as it bore down upon Boris, half mad with fury that Nancy should have escaped its wrath, and roaring aloud as it came.

But the hunter cared nothing for its roarings, nor yet for the ferocity of its appearance, though such fury as it had shown was somewhat rare in a bear which is suddenly awaked from its winter sleep. He stood very calmly, axe in hand, and awaited the onslaught.

When the bear came close up it raised itself upon its hind-legs, whereupon Boris aimed a terrific blow with his axe at the head of the brute. The axe was sharp and the aim was true, and the iron crashed through Bruin's head with so mighty a shock that in an instant this monster, who had been so terrible but a moment since, was more harmless than the smallest creature that flies and stings.

Then Boris looked, and perceived that his wife had returned from the sledge and was at his elbow with the gun, which she had found and brought in case he should require help in his dealings with the bear. She was pale with her fright and panting with her run, and Boris took her very tenderly in his arms and bore her back to the sledge, praising and encouraging her. And it so fell out that on this very night was born their little daughter Katie, of whom I shall have something presently to tell.

CHAPTER XXII.

A WOLF-MAIDEN.

Happy as she had been before, Nancy was now in the seventh heaven of content. There was no more dulness and waiting for her now, when Boris had set forth for a full day's hunting in the forest and left her to look after household matters at home. That little baby was companion and occupation and amusement to her, all in one tiny person, and the days passed right joyously at Karapselka.

When spring came, and the frost and snow had disappeared from the woods, Nancy loved to take her little companion in the tiny hand-cart and pass a pleasant hour or two wandering beneath the waving pine trees, enjoying the fine air, and listening to the thousand and one sounds of awakening forest life. The little birds populating the tree-tops were noisy at this time of year, and there were the crooning of the amorous blackcock to listen for, and the tok-tok of the gluhar, or capercailzie, while in the distance might always be heard the screaming of cranes in some damp corner of the woods, as they kept up their constant sentry-cry. There was plenty both to see and hear in these glorious woods—there always is for those who have eyes and ears, and know how to employ them to advantage—and Nancy was never weary of strolling with her baby asleep in her cart into the delightful glades which lay within easy reach of her home.

Since her adventure with the bear, Boris had insisted that she should go armed, and had presented her with a neat hunting-knife, without which she was never, he said, to stir from home, were it but for a hundred paces into the forest and back again. So Nancy went armed, though she declared she would be far too frightened to use her dagger if she were to encounter a second bear anything like the first. But Boris explained carefully how the knife should be used in emergency, and how not to use it, of which there appeared to be a great many ways.

One day, while out strolling as usual in the forest, Nancy suddenly caught sight of two small animals whose aspect was quite unfamiliar to her, which was odd, for she was as well acquainted with the life of the forest by this time as any Russian peasant-woman who had lived in it from childhood. The little creatures were somewhat like puppies, with a suggestion of fox, and when Nancy ran after them they scuttled away with comical little barks.

Nancy mentioned this matter to Boris on his return from hunting.

"What colour were they?" Boris asked.

Nancy said they were of a yellowish gray.

"They were young wolves, then," said Boris; "and if you see them again, catch one for me if you can—I long to possess a tame wolf-cub; but have your knife handy in case of the mother interfering."

It so fell out that a few days after this conversation Nancy did see these same little creatures again, four of them together; whereupon, mindful of her husband's great wish to possess one, she left the baby asleep in its hand-cart and gave chase. The wolflings scampered bravely, and led her up and down and about in every direction, until Nancy bethought herself that she was getting winded, and besides that she might easily get confused, if she went further, as to the position in which she had left her precious little Katie. So she gave up the hunt, and returned towards the place whence she started.

Then she realized how just had been her fears, for it was with difficulty that she succeeded at last in retracing her steps to the place where the hand-cart had been left. To her surprise and alarm she saw that the cart lay over upon its side; and hastening towards it she perceived, to her unspeakable consternation and horror, that it was empty.

Poor Nancy was not the person to sit down and do nothing in an emergency; but the horror of the discovery she had just made bereft her for some few moments of the power of action as well as of thought. Her mind instantly flew back to the words of Boris telling her to beware of the mother-wolf, and for several minutes these words danced in her brain. The mother-wolf, it was the mother-wolf! it had taken her darling child in order to feed those detestable little gray scuttling things which she had chased through the trees! While she had been senselessly hunting the cubs, the mother-wolf—some lean-looking, gray, skulking brute —had crept secretly up and carried away her Katie, her darling baby.

In another moment Nancy had drawn her sharp little dagger, and with shriek upon shriek had rushed wildly into the forest and disappeared among the pines, whither she knew not, but full of a wild determination to find that gray thief and force her to deliver up to her the priceless thing she had stolen.

When Boris returned home late in the afternoon he was somewhat surprised to find that Nancy was not at home. She and the baby had gone for a stroll in the woods, the old servant explained, and had not been home to dinner.

"God grant the *lieshui* [wood-spirits] have not got hold of them, or done them some injury!" the old fellow concluded, sighing deeply. "The forest is a terrible place, and for my part I have always warned the barina."

Boris did not stay to exchange words with his faithful old serf, but taking a horse from the stable galloped off as fast as he could into the forest, shouting Nancy's name in every direction. Up and down, and through and through every glade and pathway, wherever there was room for the horse to pass, Boris rode; and ever as he rode he shouted Nancy's name, until his voice grew hoarse, and the cob waxed weary, and the light began to wane, and still he neither found trace nor heard sound of his lost wife and child.

Still he rode on and on, and would have ridden all night rather than return home to misery and uncertainty; but when he was upwards of twelve miles from the house, and his heart was despairing and his spirit mad within him, he heard at length a faint reply to his calling. Lashing up his tired horse he dashed on, and presently, to his infinite joy and relief, he came upon Nancy sitting worn and utterly fagged out beneath a tree, crying bitterly, and nursing in her arms a portion of her baby's frock which she had picked up in the forest.

For many minutes poor Nancy could do no more than cling to her husband's broad breast, and sob and weep as though her very heart were melted within her for sorrow. At last she held up the tiny torn dress, and murmured, "The mother-wolf," and then betook herself once more to her bitter crying.

Boris realized at once what had happened—realized also that he had arrived far too late to do any good; for the wolf, even if it had not at once eaten the poor baby but carried it away to feast upon at leisure, must now be far away beyond the reach of pursuit. In his great joy and thankfulness to have found Nancy safe, Boris did not feel in all its poignancy, in these first moments, that grief for the child which he was destined to suffer acutely afterwards. His chief thought was for Nancy; she must be got home and at once, that was the most important duty of the moment. As for the baby, it was gone beyond recall, and would assuredly never be seen again by mortal eye.

"Come, Nancy," he said, when he had comforted and petted his poor stricken wife, "let me get you home, and then I will scour the forest on a fresh horse. You need food and rest. If our Katie is alive, I shall not cease searching till she is found; if not, I shall not rest until I have killed every wolf within fifty miles of the house!"

But Nancy would not hear of it. "Oh no, no," she cried, "I shall never go home till we have found our darling. She is alive, I am sure of it. See, there is no blood on the frock; the wolf has not hurt her. It stole her away because I was wicked to chase her little ones. It is wrong to catch the wild animals of God's forest and enslave them. We ought to have known it, Boris."

The frock had no stain of blood, that was true enough; and the circumstance gave Boris some slight hope that it might be as the stricken mother had suggested, though the chances were much against it. Boris had heard often enough stories of how wolves had taken and befriended babies, allowing them to grow up with the cubs. His own experience of the ferocity and greed of these animals, however, had always led him to laugh at such tales as old women's yarns, unworthy of a moment's serious consideration. Nancy had heard of them too, that was evident, and was now leaning upon the hope that in poor little Katie's disappearance was living evidence of their truth.

No persuasions would induce the sorrowing mother, therefore, to give up the search. All night long Boris walked beside the horse, supporting his weary little wife, who could scarcely sit in the saddle for weakness and fatigue; and not until the horse was unable to go further would she consent to pause in the work of quartering the ground in every direction, and riding through every clump of cover, in case the beloved object of her search should have been concealed in it.

When morning came, and the sun rose warm and bright over the aspen bushes, Boris found a place where the horse could obtain a meal of coarse grass, and where Nancy, upon a soft couch of heather, could lie down and take the rest she so greatly required. He was lucky enough to find and kill a hare, and with the help of a fire of sticks, which no man in Russia was better able to kindle than he, an excellent improvised breakfast was soon prepared. Afterwards, Nancy slept for several hours while Boris watched, listening intently the while in the hope of hearing the sound of a wolf-howl, which might possibly indicate the whereabouts of the thief. But the hours passed, and there was nothing to guide him to take one direction more than another, and poor Boris knew well enough that he had set himself a hopeless task; nevertheless, for Nancy's sake, he agreed to continue the search for the rest of that day, and the forest was hunted as it had never been hunted before, until his feet ached with walking, and Nancy was but half-conscious for sheer weariness. Then Boris took the law into his own hands and directed the horse for home, and the weary trio reached Karapselka as the shadows of night fell upon the forest behind them.

The next morning a peasant came early and inquired for the barin. Boris, who was about to set out once more upon his hopeless search, received the man unwillingly, as one who is in a hurry and cannot stop to discuss trifles.

"Well?" he said; "quick, what is it?"

The man scratched his head for inspiration, then he cleared his throat and began the business upon which he had come. He had been in the forest yesterday, he said, collecting firewood. The winters were cold, he proceeded, and the poor peasants must spend a good deal of their time during summer in laying up a store of fuel for the winter. But it was God's will that the peasants should be always poor.

"Get to the point," said Boris impatiently, "or I must go without hearing it."

That would be a pity, the man continued, for he believed that when the barin heard what he had to tell, the barin would give him a *nachaiok* (tea-money) for the news. He had been in the forest collecting wood, he repeated, when suddenly he saw a sight which filled him with fear—nothing less than a great she-wolf with a whole litter of young ones following at her heels. The man had at once thought to himself, "Here now is a chance of a nachaiok from Boris Ivanitch, who is a great hunter, and will love to hear of a family of wolves close at hand." But the moment after, said the peasant, he saw something which quite altered the aspect of the affair. When the wolf saw him, she had stopped and picked up from the ground where it lay close to her a small creature something like a human child, and which cried like one, but which was of course one of the lieshui, or wood-spirits, which often enough take the form of babe or old man. The she-wolf took up the creature in its mouth and trotted away with it into the forest. "Oho," the man had thought, "still more shall I earn a nachaiok from Boris Ivanitch; for now I must warn him that if he meets with this particular she-wolf and her brats he must give them a wide berth and be sure not to shoot or injure them, for this wolf is the handmaid of the lieshui, and woe to him who interferes with the favoured creatures of those touchy and tricksy spirits, for they would assuredly lure him to his destruction when next he ventured deep into the heart of the forest."

Boris hastily bade the man follow him and point out the exact spot where he had seen this wonderful sight. The peasant showed a place within a short distance of the house, and added that the wolf family had passed at sunset on the previous evening.

Here then was joyous news for Nancy; her babe had been alive and well some thirty-six hours after its disappearance, and had actually been seen within call of its own home, while its distracted parents had scoured the woods for a score of miles in every direction, little dreaming that the child was left far behind.

Nancy received the news calmly, but with the intensest joy and gratitude. "I was sure our darling was alive," she said; "but oh, Boris, if only it were winter and we could track the thief down! What are we to do, and how are we to find the child before the she-wolf carries her far away, or changes her mind and devours her?" And Nancy wailed aloud in her helplessness and misery.

There was nothing to be done but to search the forest daily, taking care to do nothing and permit nothing to be done in the village to frighten the wolves, and scare them away far into the depths of the forest, where there would be no hope of ever finding them again. Accordingly no day went by but was spent by Boris and his ever-hopeful but distracted wife in quartering the woods far and near, the pair going softly and speaking seldom, and that in whispers, for fear of scaring the wolves away.

But the days passed, and the weeks also, and a month came, and slowly there crept over their souls the certainty that their labour would be in vain, and that they had seen the last of their beloved child. Still, they would never entirely lose hope, and day by day they continued their wearisome tramping, sometimes going afoot, sometimes riding when their feet grew sore with the constant walking. Another fortnight went by, and it was now high summer, and still they were childless.

CHAPTER XXIII.

A NOTABLE DAY AMONG THE WOLVES.

Then, at length, when their bodies were wearied with the fatigue of constant tramping, and their souls worn out with disappointment, and their hearts sick with hope deferred, there came a day of great joy for Boris and Nancy.

It befell on this wise. They were out, as usual, quartering the forest, and hunting every clump of birch cover and grove of young fir trees, Boris being in front, and Nancy behind on the left, when a cry from his wife caused the hunter to start and look round, fingering his axe, for he knew not what might befall in these dark depths of the forest. Nancy repeated her cry and rushed forwards; and Boris knew at once that it was no cry of terror, but of ecstasy and joy. He too sprang forward to rejoin Nancy, and a wonderful sight met his eye.

There, close before them in an open space between the trees, a huge she-wolf was trotting across the glade, followed by her six cubs, and chasing after the tail of the procession was a tiny human child, hurrying along as fast as it could make way on hands and knees, losing ground, however, rapidly, and crying because it could not keep up with the rest.

With swift inarticulate cries of great joy Nancy rushed open-armed in pursuit, and Boris was not far behind.

The old wolf stopped once, and turned and snarled savagely at Nancy; but its heart failed, and it quickly disappeared among the trees, followed by its four-legged cubs, leaving the little foster-child. Her the true mother, frantic with love and happiness, caught quickly up and hid close in her bosom, bending over it and calling it every sweet name in the English language, and in the Russian also, and cooing and talking nonsense to it.

But the child snapped, and scratched, and growled, and struggled, and fought, as though it were no human child but a very wolf born and bred. So fiercely did it fight and kick out for its freedom that Nancy was obliged presently to set it down, when it instantly made off on hands and knees in the direction taken by its companions.

Boris fairly roared with laughter in the exuberance of his delight to see the child alive and well; and Nancy in her joy could do nothing wiser than laugh also, as they both walked quickly after the little crawling thing, easily keeping up with it, though it went far quicker than they would have believed possible. This time the father picked up the wild tiny creature, and well he got himself scratched for his pains, of which he took no heed whatever. Presently the poor babe, finding that her captor had no intention of hurting her, lay quiescent in his arms, and after a while fell asleep, tired of crying and fighting, and doubtless feeling very comfortable.

Nancy meanwhile walked beside her husband, feeling no ground beneath her feet. All her weariness and her heart-soreness had vanished entirely, and the lines of care which had set themselves upon her face, and caused her to look old and worn in the May-time of her life, had vanished also. She danced and sang as she went, and in all that forestful of gay singers there was none that was so happy as she. And at home, what though the little savage bit and snarled and refused to be fed or washed, and for many hours thought of nothing but how to escape back into the woods —why, a mother's love and care would soon recover it to herself, she said, and she could well afford to wait for a few days longer for her full happiness, she who had waited so long and wearily in tears and sorrow!

As a matter of fact, the faithful Nancy had not to wait very long before matters began to mend. The little wolf-girl soon found that she was well off, and that no one wished to do her hurt. After this it was merely a matter of patience, for the little one became more human, and showed less of the wolf every hour, until, at the end of a week, she permitted herself to be washed and dressed and fed and petted with no more opposition than is generally shown by people of the age of four or five months! What opposition she did make to anything she disapproved of was perhaps more savage than that of most babies; but there the difference ended.

One peculiarity remained for many a day—an intense love of the woods and of the open air generally, as well as a marked taste for scuttling about on hands and knees, which she managed to do at a very great speed considering her size. Nancy was wont to declare that for neither of these characteristics was she indebted to her sojourn among the wolves, but that she simply inherited both her love of the forest as well as her nimbleness from her father. I who write these lines am inclined to believe that her wolfish infancy is a sufficiently good reason for both.

Thus ended happily the most terrible experience that a devoted father and mother could pass through; and if the child was loved before, she was ten times as dear to both parents after her almost miraculous recovery from the very jaws of death. Boris declared that he could never kill another she-wolf unless it were to save his own or another life; and this resolution, I may add, he kept until his dying day.

Thus the months and the years went by at Karapselka in peace and happiness, with but an occasional adventure to break the monotony of such an existence. Boris was perfectly happy; but for all that he was conscious from time to time of a feeling of regret for his old days of activity in the Tsar's service, and of honour fairly won and unfairly lost, and he felt that this fleeting sensation might at any moment strengthen into an irresistible desire and longing to be up and about once more among his fellow-men. This sort of life was all very well for a time, but, after all, it was an inglorious sort of existence, and Boris knew that even his devotion to Nancy and her babies—for she had two now—would not suffice to keep him at Karapselka very much longer, especially if anything should happen to reawaken his old spirit of enterprise, or to bring him again within the magic of the Tsar's presence and favour. Of this last Boris had but little hope, for Peter's displeasure had been too deep for forgiveness; but there were rumours of war with Sweden, which Colonel Drury, who brought the news, said would be a long and terrible struggle if the threatenings came to anything; and Boris in his wanderings through the forest continually found himself turning over in his mind the idea that if war broke out with Sweden he must have a share in the business, ay, even if he enlisted as a soldier of the lowest rank to do it. Had not the Tsar himself started at the very foot of the ladder? then why not he? He was barely twenty-eight; there was plenty of time to carve himself out new honour and a new career with the sword. And if, *if* he were so fortunate as to gain the notice of the Tsar, by some feat of arms, for instance, or some act of bravery on the battle-field—and the Tsar's eye saw everything, so that it would not escape his notice—who knows? As a new man his beloved master might take him into new favour.

Occupied with these thoughts, Boris walked one winter day through the forest, looking for the tracks of any beast that should have had the misfortune to pass where he too wandered. Suddenly the hunter was pulled up in his reflections, as also in his stride, by a largish footprint in the snow. He knew it at once for what it was —a wolf's; but the experienced eye of Boris knew also at a glance what a less expert woodcraftsman would not have known—namely, that here had passed not one wolf but several, for wolves prefer to tread in one another's tracks, in order to save themselves the trouble of plunging into the snow and out again.

Boris examined the track, and judged that there must have been five or six wolves, at least, travelling in a procession, and also that they must have passed this spot but a very short while ago, for the loose snow-powder still sifted into the holes left by the animals' feet.

The sporting instincts of Boris never required much to arouse them when dormant, and in a moment Boris had forgotten all about the possible Swedish war, and enlistment, and everything else, excepting the fact that here was a family of wolves, and here was he, the hunter, and that the sooner he followed up and engaged those wolves the greater would be his happiness. So away went Boris upon the trail, flying like the wind upon his light Archangel snow-shoes, which are the best in the world, and the use of which Boris understood perhaps better than any man in all Russia.

Before he had gone very far the hunter noticed that the track of a man, without snow-shoes, came into that of the wolves, cross-wise—that is, the wolves had come upon the track of this man, and had turned aside to follow it. "Hungry wolves," said Boris to himself; "going to run in the man's tracks—perhaps to attack him if they get a good chance!" Accordingly Boris hastened on, for he scented fun in this, and his life of late had been terribly lacking in incident.

The tracks meandered about in the most curious way, now heading in one direction, now in another, and at last travelling round in a complete circle and recrossing a point where they had passed before; and wherever the man went the wolves had gone also. "Lost his way," thought Boris. "How frightened the poor fellow must have been when he crossed his own track and saw there were wolves after him!" Then the hunter could see that after crossing the old tracks the wanderer had greatly accelerated his pace. "Frightened," thought Boris; "and small wonder."

Soon there was audible at no great distance a noise of yelpings, such as wolves make when they grow excited in the pursuit of their prey; and Boris rightly concluded that these wolves were very hungry, and not likely to hold back from attacking a single man, unless he should be provided with fire-arms. He had better make all speed, or the matter might end unpleasantly for one of the members of the hunt.

And presently Boris ran suddenly into a stirring sight. There, before him, with his back to a tree, stood a big, kaftaned man, armed with a dagger, keeping at bay as best he could a band of seven wolves, who, to judge by their demeanour, had every intention of pulling him down. If there was one thing in all the world that Boris would have chosen, it was such an enterprise as this. His very soul was athirst for a good slashing fight with man or beast—it was four or five years since he had engaged in a real scrimmage against odds, such as this promised to be; so Boris flourished his axe and rushed into the thick of it with a shout of real exultation. Right and left he slashed, and right and left again, and two wolf-lives had gone out in a moment, while two other gray bleeding creatures crawled yelping and snarling away to die in hiding. Another rush in, and the foe would wait no longer, but turned, and in an instant were skulking away into the forest.

Then for the first time Boris looked up at the man whom he had saved from the unpleasant position of a minute or two ago, and as he raised his eyes the axe fell from his hand, and his heart gave a great bound of surprise and joy, and then stood still.

Of all the men in the world least likely to be met with in this place, of all men in the world that Boris loved the dearest and honoured the most, and most ardently longed to see and to speak to, it was he—the Tsar—Peter!

For a full minute neither spoke. The heart of Boris was too full for words, and his tongue refused to utter sound of any sort. When at length the silence was broken, it was the Tsar who spoke, and his voice seemed to Boris unlike the old boisterous voice of three years ago; it was quieter and a little tremulous.

"Boris," said the Tsar, "this cannot be accident; we are but puppets in the hands of a mightier Power which overrides our puny will and laughs at our dispositions. This is the fourth time, I account it, that you have directly or indirectly stood between me and death; how can I possibly continue to hold aloof from you, my brother?"

At these words all the old love and devotion that Boris had felt for his master completely overcame him, and he fairly flung himself at Peter's knees and hugged them, weeping.

"No, no; get you up, my Bear-eater," said the Tsar, raising him. "It appears to me that we were both somewhat wrong upon a memorable occasion; I have since thought so more than once. And having said this much, I will neither say nor hear another word in respect of those events, which are done with and lie buried in the past. As concerning the present, my Boris, what brought you so miraculously here at the precise moment when you of all men were the most needed? I had you in my mind as you appeared, and had but that instant bethought me that I would you were with me as of old; and at that same instant you came."

Then Boris, his heart bursting with great joy, began to tell the Tsar how that his house was but a few miles away, and that in this same house he and Nancy had dwelt for the last three years. Peter knew nothing of all this, for the name of Boris was never breathed at court since the day of his disgrace, seeing that the Tsar himself never spoke it. Then Peter in his turn explained how he had wandered from his suite in pursuit of a roebuck, but had lost his way; and how he had not thought of danger until he found himself pursued by wolves and armed with but a knife. And both thanked God that Boris and his axe had chanced to wander in the same direction.

Then the pair got to talking of old days and their many adventures together as they walked towards the house; and the Tsar graciously said that now he had found him again, he could only wonder how he had contrived to do without his faithful bear-eater so long, and would Boris, forgetting all that had been unpleasant in the past, return to his service once more, and things should be as they had been at the return from England? And Boris could only weep for joy, and this foolishness was the wisest thing he could find to do.

CHAPTER XXIV.

WITH THE TSAR AGAIN.

Supper at Karapselka that night was a happy meal for Boris and his wife, though Nancy, as a matter of fact, preserved her secret private opinion as to the rights and wrongs of the quarrel over the Streltsi, and did not altogether forgive Peter for his conduct at that time. But Boris was happy in his restoration to the Tsar's favour —that was enough for Nancy to think of to-night; and the Tsar was certainly all kindness and cordiality and friendship towards her husband. And so the evening was a right joyous one to herself as well as to Boris.

Peter declared that now he was here he should stay and have one more hunt with his bear-eater before returning to Moscow. As for his suite and their feelings, they deserved a lesson for their awkwardness in losing their master in the forest. They might roam the woods in search of him all night and to-morrow morning as well. If one or two of the lazy hounds were eaten by wolves, so much the better; there would be vacancies for better men!

Accordingly, arrangements were made for the Tsar to sleep at Karapselka, and Nancy went upstairs to prepare the best bed and the most luxurious coverings and decorations that the house afforded. And an extremely good piece of work she made of it; for Nancy was a young person of some taste in these matters. But when the Tsar was shown, with pride, to his chamber, the very first thing he did was to gather all these Turkish coverings and Persian silk draperies and fineries together and pitch an armful of them outside the door; after which he dragged the hardest of the mattresses from the bedstead, laid it upon the floor, and slept upon it.

In the morning, Tsar and hunter had a great spin on snow-shoes. They found a lynx track, which was great good luck, Boris said, for lynxes are rare; and following it for miles, they eventually came so close upon the animal's heels that it was forced to run up a tree to avoid being caught and killed from behind. No shaking of the tree from below could bring the lynx to the ground, and it appeared that the animal must either be shot in the tree or fetched down by hand—which is an exceedingly unpleasant process, and not to be recommended to the amateur.

"Now, Boris," said the Tsar, "shall it be you or I? We are both fairly good at climbing the rigging!" But the hunter could not think of a Tsar of Russia climbing a pine tree after a lynx, and was half-way up before the words were well out of Peter's mouth.

The lynx looked down the tree and up the tree, and ran up a little higher, till the top of the pine bent with its weight like a fishing-rod. Then it looked at the next tree, which was the better part of ten yards away; and glared down at Boris, and hissed like a great cat at bay to a dog. Suddenly the creature jumped straight for the nearest tree, and alighted fairly upon an outstanding branch; but, alas, the branch was a dead one, and broke with the weight, and down came the lynx with a thud to the earth close to the feet of the Tsar. Down came Boris also, almost as rapidly, and he and the Tsar threw themselves upon the animal almost at the same instant.

Though stunned with its fall, the infuriated lynx, which vies with the tiger for ferocity when at bay, instantly seized the Tsar by the leg—the imperial limb being clad, luckily for the imperial feelings, in thick Russian thigh-boots—whereupon Peter caught the animal's neck with one great hand, and deftly passed his knife across its yellow throat with the other. The sharp teeth loosened their hold of the leather hunting-boots, the terrible claws relaxed, the wicked, yellow-green eye grew slowly dim, and the lynx lay dead at Peter's feet.

The Tsar was as pleased as a schoolboy with his success, and together he and Boris skinned the creature as a memento of the exploit.

Afterwards, as the pair strolled together through the woods, the talk fell upon politics and the projects of Peter. War was certain and imminent, the Tsar said; Poland had joined with him in an engagement to drive the Swede out of the Baltic.

"Only think of it, my Bear-eater," said Peter, "the Baltic!—ports, Boris, seaports! How we shall fight for our windows. If it takes us a score of years, we shall have them!"

The Tsar spoke more prophetically than he knew of; for those ports were won indeed, but the final winning of them actually did cost Russia twenty years of fighting by sea and land, so stubborn was the struggle.

Then came the question as to what part Boris should play in these weighty projects which were so soon to be embarked upon; and at this point the hunter's exultation received a check, for Peter spoke as though it must be taken for granted that Boris would recommence his career at the foot of the ladder—he must enlist. That, the Tsar explained, was indispensable; for he could not stultify himself by taking Boris back straight into all the ranks and dignities of his former position. What would the rest of the officers of the Preobrajensk think? Yes, Boris must enlist.

Boris looked foolish, but said nothing. For the life of him, he could not tell whether the Tsar was pleased to joke with him or was serious.

"I am only a major myself, you know," continued Peter, "and I cannot have officers admitted into the regiment at a grade senior to my own; that would delay my promotion."

"Very well then, your Majesty," said Boris, simply because he could think of nothing else to say, "then I enlist."

"Come, come, then," said Peter, "we've made a start. I congratulate you, Mr. Private-soldier Boris Ivanitch, and may your promotion be speedy!"

Boris began to think that the Tsar was scarcely treating an old friend very generously. He grinned, however, weakly, because there was nothing else to do, and said he was "much obliged."

"Let me see," Peter continued, after a pause; "was it you or was it another who saved me from an old she-bear at Archangel some years since?"

Boris began to fear for the Tsar's reason, but he replied,—

"It was I, your Majesty; but then you had befriended me a few days before, so that we were quits for that."

"What! the bear you ran away from? Dear me! yes; so I did. Well, well, never mind that. As I was about to observe, in consideration of the service you did me on that day, I think you might be allowed a step in rank—say a corporal. You are promoted, Mr. Corporal!"

"I am extremely obliged," said poor Boris, bewildered.

"Who was it behaved rather well that afternoon when the pack of wolves attacked us?" asked Peter, with perfectly-assumed seriousness, a minute or two later. "Was it you or old Ivan the driver?"

"Oh, Ivan, your Majesty," said Boris, nettled at the Tsar's levity.

"Ah, modest as usual!" said the Tsar. "But it won't do, Boris; you must be promoted, whether you like it or not! Sergeant of the Preobrajensk, I congratulate you!"

"Thank you, your Majesty; but surely I have already received all the recognition those services deserved, for you rewarded me well at the time with many favours."

"Well, now, there's a good deal in what you say," said Peter, still quite serious, "and perhaps you are right. Your promotion, Mr. Sergeant Boris Ivanitch, should, properly speaking, follow some signal achievement of the present time, and not be awarded for services long past. Now, see what I have in my mind. You were a good jumper in the old days; I daresay you are stiffer now, for want of practice. Here I lay my cap on the ground: for every foot you can jump beyond the distance of five yards, you shall have a step in rank. There, now, that's fair enough; only don't jump yourself into a major-general, for I have too many of them on my hands already."

"Come, come!" thought Boris, "if the Tsar is in this playful mood, I'm his man!" So the hunter stripped off his kaftan and laid aside his heavy long-boots, and chose a spot where the snow was hard enough to bear him running over it, and stood ready to jump for his rank and position in life.

"Three jumps," said the Tsar, "and I'll measure the best. My foot is just an English foot, without the boot."

Boris girt up his loins, took a good run, and launched himself into space. But he was stiff, and barely cleared the five-yard mark planted by the Tsar.

"Only just got your commission," Peter remarked. "That won't do; you must leap better than that."

At the second attempt Boris cleared a foot and a half over the mark.

"Better!" said the Tsar; "but leap well up for your last!"

This time the hunter, who was getting into the way of it now, sprang so lightly and powerfully that the Tsar ran up excitedly to measure the distance. As he placed his feet down one behind the other, measuring, he ticked off the promotions thus:—

"Sub-lieutenant, lieutenant, captain, major, and a bit—say brevet lieutenant-colonel. Bravo, bravo, Colonel Bear-eater, 'tis a good jump—nineteen and a half feet—and it has landed you one grade above me! A good jump indeed!" And so pleased was the Tsar with his pleasantry, that he caused Boris's commission to be made out endorsed with all these promotions, "for special service."

Boris found great changes in Moscow. As he and the Tsar reached the western gate of the city, the hunter was immensely surprised to observe hanging upon a large post what at first sight appeared to be a human being, but which proved, on closer inspection, to be a suit of clothes such as he had seen worn in London by the people of the country. Written underneath the clothes, in large letters that all might read, was a notice to the effect that it was the

Tsar's will that all his subjects above the rank of peasant should wear clothes of a cut similar to the suit here represented. Any who left or arrived in the city by any gate thereof, at any time after the 1st January 1700, without having previously complied with this ookaz, should be condemned to pay a heavy fine, or submit to have their kaftans cut short to the knee by the gatekeeper.

Peter informed his companion that most people had quietly submitted to the change, but that there were still many who would neither wear the new clothes nor pay the fine which would be payable at each passing through the gates of the city, whether leaving or returning; and that these men went with kaftans cut short to the knee, to the huge delight of the people.

Boris saw the gatekeeper in the act of cutting down a kaftan; and certainly the appearance of the obstinate gentleman who wore it was funny enough to justify the amusement which it caused to the yelling and hooting crowd who watched him leave the place. Boris laughed till the tears ran down his cheeks, as he stood with the Tsar and looked on at the comedy; nor did he stop laughing until the Tsar jogged him by the elbow and said, "Come, Bear-eater, your turn; will you pay up or be cut short?" Then Boris laughed no more, but paid up with the best grace he could.

And this was the Tsar's method of teaching his people the way to dress *à l'Anglais*. Boris noticed, further, that beards were no longer worn in Moscow, and found that this also was the result of an ookaz from Peter, which ookaz cost Boris himself a very fine specimen of a patriarchal Russian beard; indeed, when he rode down next day to Karapselka, poor Nancy did not recognize him in his new style of apparel and without the flowing ornament to his chin, though she was bound to admit, when she became used to them, that both the changes were great improvements to his personal appearance.

The officers of the Preobrajensk greeted Boris as one returned from the grave. He had always been a favourite with his fellows, and their delight to have him back among them was cordial and sincere. From them Boris learned that the Tsar's evil humour had lasted for long months after the hunter's banishment from Moscow; and that his bitterness against Boris must have been deep indeed, for that he had never once mentioned the name of the bear-hunter in all the three years of his absence. Accordingly, they congratulated him the more sincerely upon his return to favour; and when Boris described to the mess, or rather to the assembled officers at the favourite eating-house, where his return was celebrated, how he had literally jumped from non-commissioned rank to that of brevet lieutenant-colonel, they fairly roared with laughter in their delight, for, they said, the Tsar must be quite coming round again to his old *status quo ante Streltsi*, and they had not heard of so "Peterish" an action on his part for many a long day.

So, at last, after three years of quiet life in exile at Karapselka, Boris was restored to favour, and entered once more upon an active military career. For the next three or four years he enjoyed many opportunities of distinguishing himself in arms, and of engaging in the kind of stirring adventure which his soul loved; for, a few months after his arrival, with Nancy and her babies, in his new Moscow home, war was declared with Sweden, and the entire army lately raised by Peter and carefully drilled by himself and his trusted veteran officers at Preobrajensk, together with the four old regiments raised by Lefort and Peter for the siege of Azof, marched away for the Swedish fortress of Narva, and with them went Boris the Hunter.

CHAPTER XXV.

BORIS HAS A NARROW ESCAPE.

The formation of the twenty-nine new regiments which were to take part in the war had been an arduous undertaking. While Boris was in exile at Karapselka the Tsar had lost two capable assistants, as well as dear friends, in Lefort and Gordon, both of whom had died during that interval of time. Had these men lived to assist him at this emergency, there is no doubt that the raw peasantry now sent up for training at Preobrajensk would have emerged from their months of drill in a higher state of efficiency than that in which they actually marched out of Moscow in August. Nevertheless much had been done, and the Tsar had worked as few but he could labour to make soldiers of them. In this matter Boris was of inestimable service to him; and many a time did Peter declare that he would not for half his empire that those wolves had not run him down in the Karapselka forest and in doing so brought him back his bear-eater, for what could he have done without Boris at this time?

Nancy was sensible enough to see that, happy as she had been with her husband for three long years of country life at Karapselka, she must accept the inevitable, and allow him to do now as his duty and his manhood dictated. So Boris bade farewell to his young wife, and the little wolf-maiden and her tiny brother, and marched away from Moscow with a feeling that life was recommencing for him—stern, workaday, adventurous life—and that the idle paradise of Karapselka had been nothing but a dream.

The possession of Livonia and Esthonia, of Ingria and Karelia was the darling object of Peter's ambition. He longed for the mastery of the Gulf of Finland and a grip of the Baltic coast as a hungry man longs for the food he sees in a shop window. Without some outlet to the sea in this direction, he well knew that Russia could never develop her trade and take her proper position in Europe as a European power.

But Sweden at this time was strong and courageous, and there sat upon her throne a young prince who had been devoted from his earliest infancy to the study of war and its practice in the playground—Charles XII.; who at this very moment was proving to the allies of Russia—Poland and Denmark—that in picking a quarrel with him they had attacked a hornet's nest. Charles had not as yet attained to his full reputation as a soldier; but he was formidable already, and his name was feared and respected by all who had had dealings with him in the field. For this reason, Peter knew well that he must proceed with caution.

No sooner was war declared than he marched away towards Narva, the nearest Esthonian fortress occupied by the Swedes; for, could he but possess himself of this stronghold, he foresaw that the Neva and the opposite coasts of the Gulf of Finland would be practically at his mercy, for both Livonia and Esthonia would be cut off from direct communication with those parts.

Thus Narva became the first objective for the armies of Peter. But the journey from Moscow to that fortress, undertaken at this late season of the year, proved long and tedious. The transport service was crude and inefficient, and the want of stores delayed the march; the roads were frightfully bad, as any one who knows Russian roads, even at this day, may well believe; hence it was not until the first days of November that the first detachment of troops with a portion of the artillery arrived before the walls of Narva.

The Tsar himself superintended the placing of the guns in position, and fired the first shot. It was soon found that the gun-carriages had been so knocked about that they would not stand more than two or three discharges, and then broke in pieces. By the 14th November all the powder and shot had been used, and the troops were obliged to sit and wait for new supplies with the best grace they could muster.

During this tiresome period of waiting the garrison of Narva made several gallant sorties. During one of these, Peter's own regiment, the Preobrajensk, was engaged, Boris and the Tsar both fighting at their posts. One of the foreign officers, a certain Major Hummert, at one period of the engagement, finding himself pressed by the Swedes, became alarmed, and gave the word to retire; thereupon the whole regiment turned and fled in sudden panic, in spite of all the efforts of the officers to keep them in their places. The Tsar was furious, and sent for Hummert in the evening, when the day's fighting was over, in order to treat him to one of those ebullitions of passion in which he indulged on provocation. But poor Hummert could not face the ordeal, and escaping from the lines under cover of the darkness, deserted to the enemy. Peter hung him in effigy; but the Swedes themselves improved upon this by hanging the deserter in the flesh. Shortly after this episode, the Tsar left the Russian troops at Narva and departed to attend to other duties, and while he was absent a great and unexpected misfortune befell the Russians.

No sooner did Charles of Sweden hear of the action of Peter in laying siege to Narva than he took ship with nine thousand troops for Revel and Pernau. Landing at these ports, he marched with all his characteristic energy and marvellous expedition straight across country to Narva, falling upon the Russians from the rear like a sudden terrible tornado. The Russians, with the exception of the Preobrajensk and Semenofski—two of the veteran regiments —ran like sheep, hardly striking a blow in self-defence. They rushed hither and thither headlong, shrieking that the "Germans had betrayed them," and making matters very unpleasant for their foreign officers, many of whom they killed, or chased over the field. The Preobrajensk, with Boris among them, held out bravely, and Boris had the honour of crossing swords with Charles XII. as the latter rode by slashing right and left with his weapon, and doing execution at each passage of his terrible blade. Boris barred his way, guarded a tremendous downward cut at his helm, and lunged fiercely back, striking the Swedish king full in the breast-plate, and causing him to grab with his left hand at the horse's mane in order to prevent himself falling over backwards. Charles was furious, and smote at Boris with such energy that, though Boris guarded the blow, the sword cut his tall Preobrajensk helmet clean in two, but fortunately left his head untouched. Then the hunter's blood was thoroughly up, and he slashed back at the king with such good will that his Majesty was knocked clean off his horse by the force of the blows, though his body remained unwounded. At the same moment the horse itself received a flesh wound and dashed away in terror and pain. But Charles was quickly placed upon a second horse by his people, who thronged around when they perceived his dangerous position, and the king, though he endeavoured to get back to Boris, was unable, because the crowd separated them. Charles turned in his saddle and smiled and waved to Boris. "Well done, Russian," he shouted. "I am glad there are not many of them like you! We'll finish this another day!"

But Boris, together with the rest of his regiment, was being forced back at this moment, fighting for every yard of ground, and he had no time to respond to his Majesty's kind attentions. Bravely the Preobrajensk fought, but the weight of numbers drove them back surely and steadily; and now they were upon the bridge which the Russians themselves had built in order to connect the two portions of their camp, which occupied both sides of the river. Suddenly, the bridge being crammed at the moment with crowds of Russian soldiers and gun-carriages, all retiring face to foe, there was a terrible sound of crashing and rending timbers, which rose above the din of musketry fire, the shouting of officers, and the cries of the wounded, and in an instant Boris found himself struggling in the half-frozen waters of the river, one of several hundred Russians in the same predicament.

As we have had occasion to see during the course of his adventurous career, water had no terrors for Boris; but to the danger of drowning was added on this occasion a far greater peril.

The banks were lined with Swedish soldiers, and these men immediately opened fire upon the unfortunate Russians in the water. As Charles wrote to a friend after the battle, "The greatest fun was when the bridge broke and tumbled the Russians into the water. The whole surface of the river was crammed with heads and legs of men and horses sticking up, and my men shot at them as though they were ducks."

It may have been very amusing for Charles XII. to watch, but it was very poor fun for Boris and his unfortunate companions, who were drowned around him in scores, while hundreds of others were killed by the rain of bullets poured upon them from the banks.

Boris felt that this was indeed a critical moment in his career, for if he allowed his head to remain a moment above the surface his life was not worth a moment's purchase. Accordingly, the hunter allowed himself to sink to the bottom, and then swam under water down the current, as fast and as far as his breath would hold out. The water was freezing cold, and he was much hampered in his swimming by the numbers of drowning men whom he was obliged to circumvent as far as possible for fear of being seized and drowned before he could escape from the grip of despair.

Boris came to the surface some twenty yards from the bridge, but the bullets were falling upon the water like hailstones in a sharp shower, and after taking a gulp or two of air he sank once more. He was instantly gripped by a drowning man, who clung to his throat with both hands. Boris felt that his last hour was come, and said the prayer of the dying; nevertheless he gripped the man by the neck also, and it became a strangling match. For ten seconds or so, which seemed an eternity, both men throttled each other in this strange and unnatural duel, and then Boris saw the man's mouth open wide and the water pour in, and the poor fellow's grasp relaxed and let go, and he floated away.

Boris rose to the surface a second time, but little further from the bridge than before. Finding a dead body floating beside him as he rose, he used this as a screen from the fire while he took four or five deep lungfuls of air. He was used to the water now and did not feel it so cold. He dived again, and this time he swam under water for a long distance, coming to the surface far enough from the bridge to be out of the great crush of struggling humanity.

From this point his progress was much easier; and though he was shot at several times, none of the bullets struck him. One Swedish soldier ran down the bank after him, and fired twice as he rose. Boris was obliged to pretend that he was hit in order to rid himself of this tiresome individual. He raised his arms and gave a cry as of one sorely struck, and sank; but came to the surface ten yards further up stream and close under the bank, whence he watched the soldier look out for him to appear at a point lower down, his musket ready to shoot again. Presently the man, satisfied that Boris was "done for," came slowly along towards the bridge, and the hunter bobbed beneath the current, though he stood in shallow water close to the low bank. As he came up again the Swedish soldier was just passing him, but he did not see him, for he was gazing towards the bridge, looking out for more Russian ducks to wing. Boris could not resist the temptation, but stretched out his arm and seized the man by the leg, pulling him violently as he did so. The Swede slipped and fell with a cry of surprise and alarm; but Boris dragged him remorselessly down into the cold stream before he could recover himself, and pushing him out into deep water drowned him then and there as a punishment for his cruelty in shooting poor, struggling Russians as they battled for life with the river.

Almost worn out, Boris, by swimming and diving, succeeded in making his way to a turn of the stream where he was out of sight of the bridge and its tragedies, and he came to the shore for a good rest.

He was numb and cold and stiff, and finding a dead Swedish soldier he took the liberty of divesting him of his uniform and of putting himself into it, leaving his own wet garments on the ground. He took the man's sword and pistol also; and thus provided, Boris felt that, all things considered, he had come fairly well out of this adventure.

After resting a while, the hunter took careful observations from a neighbouring tree to discover in which direction the Russian army had fled, and how best to avoid the Swedish troops which, he imagined, would be sure to have followed in close pursuit. But Boris soon found that he had little to fear from the Swedish forces. They had by this time all returned to the Russian camp, and were now making free with the Russian provisions, which they much needed, since they had marched for nearly three days without resting and with scarcely any food to eat, thanks to the energy and military ardour of their young king, who was determined to reach the Russian position before rumours of his landing should have spoiled his game.

That night every Swedish soldier in his army was drunk with Russian vodka; and had the Russians known it, they might have returned and made short work of their late victors. But the troops of the Tsar were now far away, heading for home as rapidly as they could get over the ground, in terror for their lives, and imagining that the Swedes with that terrible young king at their head would overtake them and cut them to pieces at any moment.

Thus Peter's first attempt to wrest a fortress from Sweden proved a terrible failure; but the experience was by no means an unmixed disaster for Russia, because of its different effect upon the minds of the two sovereigns concerned. Charles was puffed up with pride and vainglory, and from the day of his victory at Narva imagined himself to be invincible, and the Russians to be mere sheep who would scatter at any time at the barking of a dog. The Tsar, on the other hand, took his defeat coolly and sensibly. It was an object lesson, and he recognized it as such. His men were, he knew, mere recruits; the troops of Charles were veterans. He studied the details of the fight as reported to him by his generals, and learned, by careful comparison, where the Swedish generalship had been superior to the Russian, and made a note of it. "We shall learn to fight by-and-by!" he said; "and when we have learned what Charles has to teach us, we shall practise our knowledge upon our teacher!" Events proved that Narva was a blessing in disguise to the vanquished Russian troops, and that this was so is due to the greatness of Peter.

CHAPTER XXVI.

HOW BORIS OUTWITTED THE SWEDISH ADMIRAL.

His reverse at Narva aroused the Tsar to tremendous exertions. He met the remains of his beaten troops at Novgorod, where he ordered every portion of the scattered army to assemble and report itself. The town of Novgorod first, and afterwards those of Pskof and Petcherski—the site of the famous monastery—were strongly fortified and garrisoned, as the frontier to be defended against a possible advance of the enemy. For the work of fortification every man, woman, and child in the several districts was employed; the services in the churches were suspended in order that the priests might be free to assist in the business of national defence; houses and even churches were pulled down if they in any degree impeded the work; the bells of cathedrals and monasteries all over the country were melted down to supply metal for the forging of cannon; and through it all Peter himself worked like a common labourer in the trenches, except that he did as much work as any three other men. His disposition towards those generals who had been beaten at Narva was kind, and he did not this time allow his passion to get the mastery of his judgment; so that all men worked in harmony for the defence of the fatherland.

Gradually the troops dribbled into Novgorod, arriving sometimes in bodies of several hundreds, and occasionally in small companies of ten or a dozen men.

One fine afternoon a small company reached the town, bringing with them a Swedish prisoner, whom they led straight to the Tsar as he stood working in the trenches, exceedingly proud of their achievement in having secured and retained the fellow, for he was a big man, much bigger than any of themselves, and a good deal too big for his clothes. The men marched up to the trench where the Tsar was busy with his spade, and stood at attention. Peter looked up after a while. "Well," he said, "what is it?"

"A Swedish prisoner, your Majesty," said the men.

Peter was all attention immediately, for this was the first prisoner brought in, and he might prove an exceedingly valuable source of information as to Charles's intended movements. The Tsar fumbled in his pocket for loose cash, intending to bestow a gratuity on those who had effected the capture. But as he did so his eye fell upon the face of the prisoner. Peter stared at the fellow. Suddenly his countenance changed, and he burst into one of his loudest laughs.

"Bear-eater," he said, "I shall never believe you dead again, until I bury you with my own hands.—Get out there, you idiots, and report yourselves to your colonel; your prisoner is about as much a Swede as I am.—Here, Boris, my wonderful Bear-eater, come into this ditch, if you aren't a ghost, and tell me all about it. Don't think I am not mighty glad to see you; but there's no time for chatting idly. Get a spade and come in; we can talk as we dig."

So Boris was obliged to do half a day's work in the trenches while he told the Tsar his story, part of which we know.

"At last," Boris continued, having described his adventures in the water, and how he had travelled half the night in pursuit of the retiring Russian troops—"at last I overtook those heroes there, who, seeing that I was in a Swedish uniform, were at first for catching up all they were possessed of and continuing their headlong flight; but finding that I was but one belated man, and without a musket besides, they gallantly surrounded me and discussed my throat as a suitable whetstone for their swords. I informed them in my purest Russian that I was of their own way of thinking—not as to my throat, but politically; but they were not to be taken in, and declared that I was a Swedish spy, and as such ought to be shot. I pointed out that, even if this were so, it would be far better to make me a prisoner and take me straight to the Tsar, who would give them a handsome gratuity for their service. What would they gain by shooting me down? There would be no nachaiok [tea-money], and no glory either; for none would believe them, and they could not well take along my body for evidence, with the Swedish troops in full pursuit behind them; it would hamper their movements and prevent their escape! This last consideration decided them, and they took me prisoner, and bound me hand and foot. One of them had secured a horse, and as I found it awkward to walk all tied up like a bit of boiled beef, they put me on the horse and gave me a pleasant lift to Novgorod; and here I am."

"Well done, my Bear-eater," said the Tsar, delighted with the tale. "I thought we could trust you to take good care of yourself, and, believing this, I did not send word to Nancy of your death—which is just as well. And now I have plenty of work for you!"

There was indeed work, not only for Boris but for all those who had the safety of the country at heart. Besides the fortifying of the frontier towns, there was much recruiting to be done. The Tsar would have nine new regiments of dragoons formed at once; this being one of the results of his object lesson at Narva, where the cavalry of Charles had swept Peter's timid footmen before them like autumn leaves before the storm-wind. Then the infantry regiments must be patched up with new men to fill the gaps. And the drilling of all these soldiers, new and old, must be taken in hand by men like Boris qualified to undertake it. All this necessary work was set agoing without a moment's delay by the never-weary Tsar; and so well did it proceed that, within a few months after the rout at Narva, Peter found himself in possession of a far better army than that which he had left beneath the walls of the Swedish fortress to be cut to pieces by the enemy as soon as he had turned his back.

Boris was as busy as man could be over his various occupations, but found time to write continually to Moscow, where his letters comforted and entertained his wife amazingly, whose faith in the star of Boris was so great, that even his narrative of the adventures at and after Narva alarmed her less than they amused her. She felt, as the Tsar had declared that he also felt, that under any conceivable circumstances her husband was well able to take care of himself.

But with the spring came a change for the hunter. News arrived that the Swedish fleet meditated a descent upon Archangel as soon as the disappearance of the ice should have rendered navigation possible. Boris, to his delight, was sent up north to superintend the fortification of the old town which had been the home of his boyhood and early youth. The hunter received his new commission with joy, and started at once, passing through those forests and villages which were memorable by reason of his adventures with the Tsar nearly ten years ago. Though there was no time to waste, Boris managed to enjoy a day or two in the woods, after his old friends the bears and wolves, and reached Archangel early in April, when he commenced the work of fortifying the place without further delay.

And now the hunter was to experience one of the most exciting of all the adventures of his chequered career. Scarcely was the ice away, and the mouth of the Dwina open to navigation, than one fine day in May there appeared a fleet of, seemingly, English and Dutch merchant vessels, which sailed in from sea and anchored off the island of Modiug. Suspecting nothing, a boat containing fifteen soldiers, acting as custom-house officials, made the usual visit to the foreign ships to collect the harbour dues, receive the reports of cargo, and go through the ordinary commercial formalities in connection with the port. These men did not return at once; and when night fell and they were still absent, the authorities were obliged to conclude that the Dutch or British skippers had proved too hospitable, and that the officials were still occupied in drinking the health of the first arrivals of the year. But in the middle of the night Boris, in his capacity of commissioner of the Tsar, was awakened from his sleep by a half-drowned, dripping person, who stated that he was one of those who had been sent on board the supposed English and Dutch merchantmen. He had swum ashore at Modiug, he said, having escaped from the cabin in which the company had been confined. But the rest were still on board, and likely to remain so; for the ships were not merchantmen but vessels of war, and their crews were not good Englishmen and Dutchmen but blackguardly Swedes, sailing under false colours in order to steal a march upon the forts and capture the city unawares as soon as the first glimmering of light should render such an enterprise possible. The man had climbed out, by the help of his companions, through the skylight, choosing his time when the sentry had his back turned, had crept to the side, let himself down by means of a rope, and swum to the island. There he found a boat, and got himself rowed quickly to the town; and here he was! The man added that he had overheard it said that three of the vessels would signal for a pilot in the morning, and sail into port; the remainder of the fleet were to wait where they were, in case of accidents, and would come on if required.

Boris made glad the heart of this dripping hero by rewarding him handsomely in money, and promising to mention his conduct to the Tsar at the first opportunity. Then the hunter sat down to think matters out, and the result of his cogitations was, first, a visit to the commandant of the fort, to whom he gave his instructions. After this Boris got himself ready for the further development of his plans, and took up his position in the pilot-house, whence a good view of the foreigners would be obtained as soon as it became light enough to see. Boris had concocted a delightful plot, and hugged himself with joy to think how the Tsar would roar with laughter when he told him of it, after its successful outcome. It did not occur to Boris that he ran about as good a chance of having his own throat cut as ever man deliberately set himself to run; but then Boris was a great believer in his own star, and would have laughed at the very idea of danger in his scheme.

When morning came, Boris soon observed the usual signal flying from the deceitful flag-ship's mainmast indicating that a pilot was required. Then he arrayed himself in an over-garment, which caused him to look as much like a pilot as any other man, stepped into the pilot-boat, and had himself conveyed on board the Swedish admiral's ship, to the great astonishment of the real pilot, who could not imagine why the Tsar's commissioner usurped his duties when he had plenty of his own to look after.

When Boris stepped aboard the frigate, the Swedish admiral did not pretend to be other than he really was, but roughly bade the "pilot" take the vessel into Archangel harbour. The pilot, simulating great fear and distress of mind, did as he was told—the frigate, followed by its two companions, sailing gallantly forward on a light wind direct for port.

But that deceitful pilot did not intend that those Swedish ships should ever reach the harbour save under the Russian flag, and before a mile of water had been covered they were all three suddenly brought up by running straight upon a sandbank which jutted out from the island of Modiug. When the admiral and the rest of the Swedish gentlemen who happened to be on deck at the moment of the catastrophe had picked themselves up from the undignified attitudes into which they had been thrown by the shock, they learned two extremely unpleasant things. One was that their pilot had left them the legacy of his topcoat, and had taken a neat header into the water, whence he was now addressing certain remarks to them in the English language, remarks of a valedictory nature, coupled with flattering expressions of the hope that he would soon have the pleasure of meeting them again on shore; and the other that the forts were in the act of opening fire upon them as they lay helpless and immovable upon the sandbank.

Within half a minute of the first discovery a dozen furious Swedes had snatched their muskets, and a dozen Swedish bullets whistled through the air and sent up little fountains of spray as they struck the water somewhere near the spot where the head of that pilot had last appeared. But the head was no longer there. When it appeared again it did so in a direction where it was not expected; and though the bullets sought it once more, they did not find it. The furious Swedes even went so far as to train a gun upon the vanishing black spot, and banged away merrily at it with musket and cannon as long as it was in sight, but never went within several yards of the mark; for Boris dived so deftly and dodged so cunningly that he invariably had plenty of time to fill his lungs before he was seen and shot at.

Meanwhile the fort blazed away at the stranded ships, with such success that these soon hauled down their colours; after which a party of Russians from the fort put off in boats to take possession, picking up the swimming pilot on their way. Once on board, the Russians turned the ships' guns upon the four remaining Swedish vessels and quickly drove them from their moorings.

Boris was not mistaken as to the Tsar's delight upon hearing of his exploit. Peter wrote him an affectionate and appreciative letter, in which he congratulated him on his out-foxing the old Swedish reynard, presented him with a gratuity of two thousand roubles, and gave him a commission in the navy. Peter himself was at this time a boatswain in the same service, having risen, some say, from the humble position of cabin-boy, in which capacity he had insisted upon entering the navy in order that he might experience the duties of every grade of both branches of the service.

CHAPTER XXVII.

SMALL BEGINNINGS OF A GREAT CITY.

Boris lived on at Archangel during the whole of the summer of 1701; but his Majesty of Sweden did not venture to send a second force to Russia's only seaport, the first lesson having proved a salutary one. Boris had therefore plenty of time for the indulgence of his passion for hunting, and during those pleasant months he was fully occupied in clearing the country around, including his own native village, of the bears which infested it. The peasants declared that they had suffered from a plague of bears since his departure, for there had been no one to rid the place of them. Accordingly, the hunter had a grand summer of it among the members of the Bruin family, who must have regretted his reappearance as fervently as the peasants rejoiced over it. Nancy with the little ones had joined Boris at Archangel, and the pair enjoyed many days together in the woods, days which reminded them of old Moscow times and recalled the three quiet years at Karapselka.

With the approach of winter, however, came letters from the Tsar appointing Boris to the command of one of the new regiments of infantry, and requiring his immediate attendance at the head of his men to act under the orders of General Sheremetieff, who had already had a brush with the Swedes at Rappin in Livonia, and was now waiting to follow up his success there with a more important affair. In January the opportunity arrived, and a serious engagement was fought at Erestfer, Boris being present with his regiment. On this occasion the Russian troops gained a victory which went far to efface the memory of Narva. Three thousand of the troops of Charles XII. were left dead upon the field, after both sides had fought for several hours with the greatest courage and determination. Every officer engaged in this fight was promoted or decorated, Sheremetieff being made field-marshal, and Boris receiving the decoration of St. Ann. The troops marched into Moscow in triumph, and a solemn Te Deum was chanted in the national cathedral in the Kremlin.

The Russians followed up this success with a second brilliant victory at Hummelshof, which decided the fate of Livonia; and this unfortunate province was given over to devastation, from the effects of which it took many years to recover. Swedish prisoners became so common that a boy or a girl of fifteen years of age could be bought for the sum of fourpence.

Boris was not present at this second battle, for he had at this time accompanied the Tsar to Archangel, whither Peter had travelled on ship-building intent. Here the pair had a small adventure with a bear. Boris had introduced the Tsar on this occasion to a new method of hunting the bear—that of sitting in ambush over the carcass of a horse or a cow, in the hope that the bear will scent the delicacy and arrive to make a meal of it. On the occasion in question the Tsar and Boris had sat up in the branches of two pine trees opposite each other for two nights without result, and were in the midst of a third, which Peter vowed should be the last—for the carcass was by this time so very unsavoury that nothing would induce him to sit there another night—when of a sudden the watchers became aware by sundry gruntings and shufflings in the distance that the guest for whom the feast had been set was approaching.

It was a moonlight night, and Peter, being anxious to secure the brute while he could see to shoot, sighted him as best he could, and pulled the trigger. The bullet passed through one of the bear's ears, and only served to enrage it. Seeing the smoke hanging about the tree in which the Tsar sat, the angry brute rightly guessed that its assailant lurked amid the branches, and with a roar of rage and defiance it dashed to the foot of the tree, intent upon climbing it and fetching down the rash person who had dared to burn its ear with a hot iron.

The Tsar had nothing but his knife to protect himself with; and remembering this, Boris was somewhat concerned to observe the course which events had taken. He was not long in making up his mind, however, that he must shoot and that quickly, for the bear was already half-way up the trunk of the pine. Boris hastily put his gun to his shoulder and fired, but his bullet did nothing better than hit the furious brute in the foot, redoubling its fury.

The Tsar was now in a somewhat serious position, for it is never pleasant to be obliged to face a bear with no weapon excepting a knife, and from the insecure position of a pine branch it is even less agreeable than on *terra firma.* Peter nevertheless drew his knife and settled himself in his place, resolved to make things as unpleasant as possible for the visitor, as soon as he should come within striking distance.

Up came Bruin, hand over hand, climbing very fast, and already the Tsar was slashing at him, though as yet without reaching him, when suddenly, with a loud roar of rage, the bear let go his hold of the tree trunk and slipped down to the ground, clutching at the stem of the tree as he went. Boris, seeing the Tsar's danger, had slipped down from his perch, and with a bound just succeeded in catching hold of the bear's hind feet, from which he dangled and swung with all his weight. This sudden mysterious tugging from below had so startled Bruin that he let go and fell together with poor Boris to the ground, the hunter being undermost. The bear caught him by the leg as he attempted to crawl away from beneath, and inflicted a nasty wound. But just at this moment the Tsar dropped from his perch to the ground, and stepping behind the bear as it tore at the poor hunter's leg, he deftly inserted his sharp blade in the brute's windpipe and ended the fray.

Soon after this last episode, Boris having recovered from his wounds, the Tsar left Archangel with the hunter, full of plans for a great *coup* to be directed at that portion of the Swedish king's territory which he coveted far more than any other. Peter went south through the Onega lake, thence by the river Svir to Lake Ladoga, where he met by appointment Sheremetieff with his army of thirteen thousand men, still flushed with their great victory at Hummelshof. After a few days' rest, Peter fell upon the small fortress of Noteburg, which stood upon a tiny island just where the Neva flows out of Ladoga. This fortress was attacked with great spirit, and was defended with equal gallantry by its Swedish garrison. On the second day, Peter received a letter from the "ladies of Noteburg," begging that they might be allowed to leave the place, the Russian fire being rather warmer than they liked. The Tsar, however, returned a characteristic reply to the effect that he could not think of permitting the ladies to travel alone in these troublous times; they were quite at liberty to depart, however, if they took their husbands with them. So on the third day of the siege, the ladies actually persuaded their lords to escort them to the nearest Swedish stronghold, and the place was evacuated.

The capture of Noteburg was most important, since it furnished the Tsar with the mastery of the Neva, so far as its upper waters were concerned, and there now remained but one small fortress between him and the open sea. This was a day of joy for Peter. The fort at Noteburg was rechristened Schlüsselburg, and the Tsar caused the key of the castle to be fastened to a bastion as an indication that here was the *open sesame* to the Neva, which was the gate of the sea.

Having proceeded thus far towards the attainment of his ends, the conqueror, leaving a strong force in possession of his newly-acquired fortress of Schlüsselburg, and with it our friend the hunter, hurried away to Voronej in order to see to the ship-building on the Don, and to keep an eye upon the movements of Turkey, whom he suspected of designs upon his city of Azof, the Tartar stronghold whence Boris had escaped on a memorable occasion.

Boris found life at Schlüsselburg very pleasant. It was winter time, and the forest in this part of the country was full of game, so that he had ample opportunity both to enjoy himself and also to instruct his fellow officers in the delights of the chase. Wolf hunting became the fashionable occupation among the garrison of Schlüsselburg, and many were the exciting hunts and adventures which occurred during those months, not always to the final triumph of the hunters; for more than one inexperienced sportsman met with his end at the teeth of a desperate wolf, or in the close embrace of a bear who would not be denied the pleasure of hugging one of his Majesty's subjects. But my readers will pardon me if I do not enter into details of these events in this place, for there is matter of more moment to be described.

The Tsar, having satisfied himself that all was right in the south, returned to Schlüsselburg in the early part of the year 1703, and without loss of time proceeded to do that which set the seal upon Russia's greatness by providing her for ever with that window into Europe, to attain which was the main object of his life. Peter marched down the flat banks of the Neva with an army of twenty thousand men until he came to a spot where a small stream called the Ochta mingles its waters with those of the larger river. Here was situated the Swedish stronghold of Nyenkanz, which was quickly bombarded by the Russian troops, and captured the following day. Peter rechristened this fort Slotburg, and from this small beginning there arose in a very few years the city of St. Petersburg, which was built around the nucleus afforded by this little fort.

Soon after the capture of this all-important *pied-à-terre*, the garrison were startled to hear one day the sound of two cannon shots coming from the direction of the Gulf of Finland, which opens out almost from the very city of St. Petersburg. Peter, guessing rightly that this was a signal from a Swedish fleet which approached in ignorance that the place was in the hands of the Russians, immediately replied with a similar discharge of two pieces. Within an hour a row-boat appeared, and was allowed to approach close up to the walls of the fort, when its crew were made prisoners, to their unbounded astonishment. From these men Peter learned that the fleet consisted of nine ships of war. Soon after two large vessels were observed to leave the fleet and sail up the Neva as far as the island now forming the northern half of the city, and known as Vasili Ostrof (William, or Basil Island). Here they anchored by reason of the darkness. They had come to see why their boat had not returned, and what was the meaning of the suspicious absence of the usual courtesies between garrisons and maritime visitors.

That night Peter prepared thirty large flat-bottomed boats, and when morning came loaded these full with two regiments of the Guards, and made the best of his way, by a circuitous route, towards the Swedish frigates. The Neva, just before throwing itself into the gulf at St. Petersburg, spreads out into several branches, like the fingers of a hand, the spaces between these fingers being occupied by islands. Hidden among these islands, the barges of the Tsar had no difficulty in keeping themselves out of sight, and after a thorough inspection of the Swedish strength it was resolved to make a dash and, if possible, board the vessels. Accordingly the long oars were got out, and the barges glided silently around the eastern end of Basil Island, massed just at that corner where the Bourse now stands, and at a given signal dashed round the corner and were upon the astonished Swedes in a moment. Before the enemy could do anything to prevent it, boarding-ladders were placed at the ships' sides, and crowds of the Russian Guards swarmed up and over the bulwarks, sword in hand, Peter and Boris among the foremost.

From the first the Swedes were at a hopeless disadvantage, and in half-an-hour or less the sailor Tsar found himself in possession of two very fine specimens of the warship of that day, and, what was still better, the undisputed proprietor of a fine natural harbour, with outlet to the sea, to keep them in.

There was no happier man inhabiting this planet that evening than Peter Alexeyevitch; and if he demonstrated his delight by dancing upon the supper-table after that meal was over, we must regard with indulgence this characteristic manner of working off the exuberance of his feelings in consideration of the momentous importance of his achievements of the past few days. For Russia had won her first naval engagement, and from this day would commence to rank as a maritime power, and to draw into her bosom the wealth and the commerce of other nations. Truly there was something to dance for, even though it were among empty bottles and upon the top of the supper-table.

CHAPTER XXVIII.

HOW THE SWEDES ERECTED A GIBBET FOR BORIS.

Now that Russia was, or would be, a maritime power, the Tsar was determined that those around him, of every grade, should learn something of naval affairs. While, therefore, the beginnings of the city of St. Petersburg were in progress, the sovereign devised means whereby as many as possible of his favourite companions and officers, as well as humbler classes of his subjects, should at least have the opportunity of learning the use of sails and oars. Peter organized entertainments for his people, inviting large numbers to sup with him each evening in a tent upon an island, which could only be approached by means of boats or sailing yachts, for of course there were as yet no bridges. Peter provided the craft as well as the supper, but the guests were obliged to navigate for themselves. Many, the majority indeed, of these had never set foot in a boat of any sort in their lives, and, notwithstanding the honour which an invitation to his Majesty's board undoubtedly carried with it, they would gladly have gone without both the honour and the sailing, too. The Tsar's guests were invited to step into the first boat that came, and whether this happened to be a rowing or sailing boat they were expected to find their way unassisted by experts to the imperial sea-girt pavilion. If this plan was productive of confusion and exciting incident while the unfortunate guests set out supperwards, it is easy to imagine that the scenes when these same gentlemen returned after their meal and its accompanying potations must have been doubly entertaining. Wrecks and drenchings were the rule; prosperous journeys and the haven safely won the exception. The Tsar stood upon his island and watched the approach of his expected guests as one who goes to the play; their frantic efforts to manage oar and sail gave him the most exquisite delight, his happiness reaching its culmination whenever one of them, more awkward than the rest, was upset. No one was permitted to drown, for either the Tsar himself or Boris or other competent persons were ever at hand to rescue the shipwrecked; and many a poor dripping wretch was brought ashore by the hunter, to eat his supper in the miserable anticipation of more boating to be done afterwards.

Meanwhile a new fortress began to take shape, close to the old one, and the city of St. Petersburg was commenced.

Boris returned to Moscow in the autumn, and spent the winter with his family, to the great content of his devoted Nancy. But his peaceful home-life did not last very long; for with the return of spring the troops were called out once more to finish that which had been so well begun in the previous year, and the hunter bade farewell to his belongings, little thinking that he should come very nigh, during this summer's campaign, to forming a meal for the Swedish crows—nearer, indeed, than ever before.

There were two fortresses which the Tsar felt must be his before he could feel quite secure in the possession of the Neva—namely, Dorpat, and his old friend Narva, where the Russian arms had received their first salutary check, and where Boris had so nearly had his brains blown out as he swam for life in the blood-stained river whose surface hissed in the hail of the Swedish bullets.

With the siege of Dorpat we are not concerned, for Boris was not present. Suffice it to say that it fell before the Russian assault during the summer months, and that its fall greatly encouraged the other half of the Russian army which sat before the walls of Narva, among which latter was Boris. Weeks passed, but Narva, mindful of former achievements, still held out, and besiegers and besieged alike grew very tired of the weary business of bombarding one another, and longed for something more exciting. Then the ingenious spirit of Menshikoff devised a plan which promised at least the chance of a few lively moments. Early in August the Russian troops before the city divided themselves under cover of night into two portions. One half retired out of sight of the city, where they arrayed themselves in Swedish uniforms, and returning when it became light, with drums beating and flags flying, fell upon the Russian lines, to the intense delight of the beleaguered ones within the city, who imagined that history was here repeating itself, and that Charles himself had arrived once more in the nick of time to relieve his faithful city, and to cut the Russians to pieces. Their delight was still greater when the supposed Swedish hosts hotly pressed the Russians, who slowly but surely gave way before them towards the walls of the city. So well did the Russians perform this wholesale piece of play-acting, that not for one moment did the troops within the city doubt the reality of the victory which their friends outside appeared to be gaining over the besiegers. With the intensest excitement they watched the progress of the fight; and when there was no longer any doubt as to which side was winning, they threw open the gates of Narva and sallied out to assist in the rout of the enemy. Then the fleeing hosts turned savagely upon them, and what was a thousand times worse, the late assailants of the latter, Swedes though they appeared to be, now took sides with their defeated foes and fell upon them also. The brave Narva garrison fought well, though they were surprised and demoralized by the deception of which they were the victims. They fell back in good order towards the town; and though they lost several hundreds of their men, they succeeded in getting home again and shutting their gates in the face of the Russians, of whom they carried away one or two prisoners.

Boris had acted as one of the pseudo-Swedes, and had fought with his usual dash, both while the cartridges had been blank ones and the swords ash staves, and also afterwards when the curtain fell upon the opening farce and the real play began. He had pressed, at the head of his men, to the very gates of Narva, and was fighting desperately to effect an entrance, when something crashed upon him from the walls above, the gates of the city turned black in his eyes, and as he fell senseless at the almost-entered haven, the last retiring squad of Swedish soldiers picked him up and carried him into the city, his men vainly struggling to effect a rescue, and many of them falling as he had beneath the showers of large stones and sand-bags hurled upon their heads from above.

When Boris recovered his senses he found himself in a small cell in the citadel, aching all over, and sick and weary. He was still in the Swedish uniform which he had donned for the purpose of carrying out the ruse of Menshikoff. A tall Swedish guardsman stood at the door. Boris was visited during the day by many of the leaders of the garrison troops in Narva, and was questioned by them at great length as to matters upon which he had not the remotest intention to enlighten them. One of the officials who thus catechised the poor hunter recognized him as having been the sham pilot in the Archangel affair of a year or two ago—the Swede having been at that time on board the frigate captured by means of the hunter's successful deception. Boris was unwise enough to laugh heartily as the official recalled this circumstance, a proceeding which much incensed his interviewer. It appeared that the commandant of Narva and his officers were not in the best of humours, by reason of the trick played upon them by the Russians, and were inclined to make an example of Boris, especially now that he was recognized as having already outwitted them on a previous occasion.

Every day Boris was examined by the authorities, but all to no purpose. Gradually it dawned upon the governor that there was nothing to be done with this long-limbed Russian, whose legs stuck out of his Swedish garments, and whose tongue could not be induced to wag. He might just as well be hung on the ramparts at once, as a warning to other Russian deceivers who presumed to play-act in Swedish uniforms. So Boris was given to understand that he might prepare for his end, which would be brought about on the gallows, and in the uniform which he had dared to desecrate.

Even to Boris, who believed so implicitly in his own star, this communication came with somewhat of a shock. To be hung on the gallows like a common spy, and in full view of his own people too—for the execution was to take place upon the ramparts—this was rather more than even Boris could contemplate with serenity! One thing was certain—he must escape, if he was shot a thousand times in the attempt; anything would be preferable to hanging on a gibbet.

But there was no question of escape at present. The window, so called, was too small to admit of the passage of a full-sized human being; and Boris was certainly full-size. The door of the cell was but the entrance to a stone corridor which, in its turn, was jealously locked and guarded, and led into a courtyard full of soldiers. Besides this, the poor hunter was heavily chained. There could be no talk of escape here. However, they could not rear a gallows in this little room and hang him here; they must take him outside to die—and then! Well, then, Boris promised himself, he would have a merry five seconds or five minutes with somebody's sword, or, failing that, with his own fists, which he had learned to use with some skill while in England.

Meanwhile the Russians outside the walls were growing deadly tired of this long siege. A new general, a foreigner named Ogilvie, had been brought down by the Tsar to watch the siege. Ogilvie declared that if the Russians peppered away at Narva until doomsday, in the present disposition of their guns, they would never take the city. The guns must be placed differently. If this were done, and a sharp fire kept up for two days, he would guarantee that the place could be stormed with success on the third day. Ogilvie's advice was taken. The guns were brought round to the eastern side of the walls, and a terrific bombardment was commenced and kept up for two days.

On the morning of the third day, at sunrise, the Tsar, with his new general and a group of officers, was up and about preparing for the attack upon the besieged city which was to take place that day. The fire of the last two days had been marvellously successful, and the Tsar was in the best of spirits as he visited the guns which had been so well served on the preceding day. Peter distributed rewards among the gunners, and bade them recommence their practice immediately. He swept the walls with his telescope, considering which spot should be selected as the breach to be stormed by his brave soldiers; for there were several weak places, and it would be well to concentrate his fire upon one or two.

"Ogilvie," said Peter, after a prolonged stare through the glass, "what do you make of the erection upon the eastern ramparts?

What are they doing? It looks to me more like a crane than anything else—probably to raise stones for patching their walls. They really might save themselves the trouble."

Ogilvie took the glass. "It's no crane," he said; "it's a gallows. Some poor fellow going to be hung, I suppose."

"Then why on the walls?" said the Tsar. "That must be for our edification. They haven't another Hummert, have they, or any deserter from us; or—" Peter's countenance suddenly changed —"it can't surely be for Boris Ivanitch! They would never dare!— Here, men! a hundred roubles to the gunner who brings down yonder gallows on the walls—fire, quick, every one of you!"

Crash went the big guns one after the other, sending the stonework flying around the spot indicated, and scattering the crowds of people who could be distinguished surrounding the gibbet; and, finally, a shot struck the gallows itself, either full or at a ricochet, and the erection disappeared. Peter gave orders that the fortunate gunner should receive his reward, and hurried away to see after the immediate despatch of the storming party.

Meanwhile Boris, on the evening preceding the events just narrated, had been informed by a friendly sentry that he was to be publicly executed on the following morning. He did not sleep the worse for this information. He had lived up till now with his life in his hand, and had stood many a time face to face with death, and yet survived it. If by the mercy of God he should escape this time also, why, so much the better; if it was decreed that he should die, well, that was no reason why he should fret all night and destroy his nerve, in case it were wanted in the morning.

At sunrise Boris was led out upon the ramparts; and certainly his heart sank when he caught sight of the gallows upon which these Swedish fellows meant to suspend his long body. He was still bound at the wrists as he marched up to the place of execution; but they would not surely hang him in thongs? Boris vehemently protested as the final arrangements were being made, imploring the officer of the guard to loose his wrists; but in vain. When all was ready he was seized by soldiers, and in another instant would have been carried to the gibbet and set swinging there, when, at this critical moment, big shot from the Russian lines began to fly high and low and in every direction, and soldiers and crowd were scattered in an instant to all points of the compass.

"Bringing up his clenched fists together against the fellow's chin."

Boris thought this a good opportunity to make his first move for freedom. He raised his foot and tripped up one of the men who held him by the arm, the guards with Boris between them being in full run at the moment. The man fell. Thus freed of one hindrance to his movements, Boris quickly turned upon his second custodian, and bringing up his clenched fists together with tremendous force against the fellow's chin sent him flying backwards.

The crowd were fortunately too busy rushing hither and thither for shelter from the Russian cannon-balls to take much notice of the prisoner and his doings, and Boris was able to dodge round the corner of a house and into a yard with a gate to it before his bewildered guards had recovered their feet. Kicking the gate shut behind him, Boris rushed down the yard and into the back door of a house. Here he found himself within a kitchen, in which a woman was busy preparing food, presumably for some one's breakfast Boris appealed to her to cut his thongs, which she (he being still in his Swedish uniform) immediately did, without asking questions. Having heartily thanked the amiable cook, he went back to the yard and prospected through the key-hole of the gate.

The Russian gunners had made good practice, he observed, during the last few minutes. The crowd was dispersed; the gallows had disappeared—shot away, doubtless; many dead soldiers lay about the walls and in the street below—there was one just outside the yard gate.

This was the very opportunity the hunter required. He opened the gate and dragged the man inside, where he despoiled him of his sword. He recognized the fellow as one of the guards from whose hands he had escaped a few minutes since: clearly he had been in the act of following Boris into the yard when he was shot down.

Now Boris was ready for anything. If they came to fetch him here, at this gateway—well, it was narrow, and, barring accidents, he thought he could defend it against swords all day!

As a matter of fact he was not again molested, for the garrison had enough to do in defending the breaches in their walls from the storming party to have any time to search for the escaped prisoner. When his fellow-officers and the men of his regiment came scouring into the town an hour afterwards, flushed with victory, and on plunder and prisoners intent, some of them rushed into the house which had been the hunter's shelter since the early morning, and there they found our friend Boris seated in the kitchen over an excellent breakfast, of which some of them were invited to partake, and waited upon by his benefactress, the Swedish cook.

CHAPTER XXIX.

MAZEPPA.

And now the Tsar of Russia, well satisfied with the success of his arms, was for making peace with the King of Sweden. He had made himself master of Ingria and Livonia, but was ready, if necessary, to restore the latter province if he might be allowed to retain the Neva with its two forts of Schlüsselburg and Slotburg.

But Charles XII. would not hear of peace. He would have the Neva forts, he declared, if it should cost him his last soldier to regain them. Then Peter sent ambassadors to the court of St. James in London, to petition for the mediation of Queen Anne. But the ambassadors found the British statesmen, as they declared, too diplomatic and tricky for them, and could get no decided answer. Then the Duke of Marlborough was approached, and handsome bids were made for his good offices, if only he would consent to be peacemaker. The Tsar offered to the duke the title of Prince of Siberia, or of Kief or Vladimir, a large sum of money in gold, and "the finest ruby in Europe." Marlborough did not at once refuse to act as mediator, but, though he seriously considered the proposition, nothing came of Peter's offer, and the matter dropped.

Then the Tsar regretfully realized that there was to be no peace, but that he must make himself ready for war.

The year 1705 began with a victory for Sweden at Gemanerthof, near Mitau; but Peter, hastening up to the front with fresh troops, stormed Mitau and made the honours equal. Neither was there much advantage to either side in 1706, though the Russians were lucky in retiring from the fortress of Grodno, hard pressed by the Swedes, without serious misfortune. Charles himself had awaited the moment when the Russian troops must retire in order to follow them and cut them to pieces, which he probably would have succeeded in doing, but he was delayed for a week by the breaking up of the ice on the River Niemen, and this delay saved the Russians from destruction.

The following year was without military movement on either side, but was spent chiefly in diplomacy—Peter striving for peace, Charles insisting upon war; and when the year went out, it left the latter young monarch occupied in making preparations for the invasion of Russia, and the Tsar equally busy in putting his forces into order for the defence of the fatherland.

Meanwhile Boris, after his terrible experiences in Narva, had been but little engaged in the few military movements of the following year or two, and had spent most of his time at home in Moscow, or rather at Karapselka, with Nancy and the children. His little wolf-maiden was now seven years old, and there was very little of the wolf about her seemingly; for she was as pretty a child as could be found in all Russia. Nevertheless she was strangely and passionately devoted to the woods, and was never so happy as when allowed to accompany her father and mother upon their drives into the forest. In the summer time she would spend the entire day there, wandering about among the pines, or lying couched in a heathery bed at their roots. She was never in the least afraid of wild animals, and loved nothing better than to hear repeated the oft-told tale of her own sojourn among the wolves as a helpless baby. If the truth had been known, she longed in her heart to see a big wolf, and she would undoubtedly have offered to play with it then and there had one appeared, without an atom of fear.

Her little brother Boris, aged six, was a fitting companion to this forest-loving maiden. The boy was the bear-hunter in miniature, strong and hearty, and a stranger to all cravenness.

Nancy and her husband were proud of their children, and were right glad, moreover, to have spent this quiet year with them at Karapselka; for the little ones had not seen much of their father during those troublous war-years. Next year there would be more fighting—any one with his eye on the signs of the times could see that; indeed, half Europe was convinced that 1708 would close with the Swedish king dictating terms of peace from the Kremlin. Why this should have been the opinion of Europe it is difficult to say, for the balance of success up to this point had undoubtedly rested with the Russian arms; but Charles was making great preparations, and was very much in earnest, and his reputation as a successful soldier was very great, and, since he would conduct the new campaign in person, those who knew best made no secret of their conviction that he would carry all before him. As for Charles XII., he himself was perfectly sure that there could be but one end to the struggle. He gave out far and wide that Russia was to be subdued, and that he intended to do it. She was to be forced to disband her new regular armies, and Peter was to be made to restore to the country the Streltsi whom he had abolished, and the old order of things generally. The Neva was to remain, of course, a Swedish river; and as for Dorpat and Narva, and the rest of the places which his fools of generals had allowed Peter to become temporarily possessed of—why, Charles would soon make him disgorge them.

Meanwhile Boris was summoned to the Tsar, who was busy at St. Petersburg building that city under difficulties. Peter wished to send him, he said, on a mission to the hetman of the Cossacks of the Ukraine, to inquire what force the latter could put into the field for the approaching campaign of defence. The hetman bore a name familiar to my readers. He was no other than that Mazeppa whom Voltaire and Byron have made so familiar to readers of poetry as the hero of one of the most romantic episodes ever sung by bard or told as sober truth by historian.

I regret to say that the real Mazeppa was very far from being the romantic hero he is generally supposed to have been. His ride, strapped to the back of a wild horse and pursued by numbers of wolves, is little better than a myth, though founded upon a slight substratum of truth, as will presently be shown.

Born of Cossack parentage, young Mazeppa appears to have served as page to King John Casimir of Poland about the year 1660, twelve years before the birth of Boris; but by reason of his quarrelsome disposition he soon got himself into trouble at court, and retired to his father's estate in Volhynia. Here again Mazeppa fell into disgrace, this time with a neighbouring Polish gentleman. This is where Mazeppa's ride comes in. The Polish neighbour, infuriated at the young Cossack, caused his attendants to strip Mazeppa of his clothes, and to fasten him with thongs to the back of his own horse. In this undignified and uncomfortable position Mazeppa was conveyed to his home, which lay but a mile away, the horse galloping straight to its own stable with its naked master tightly secured to it. After so disgraceful an exposure, Mazeppa disappeared, and he is next heard of as a man of light and leading among the Cossacks of the Ukraine.

The Ukraine was a sort of no-man's-land, lying between Pole, Russian, Turk, and Tartar. To this happy retreat fled, in former years, every kind of freebooter, robber, and bad character who had made his own home, whether in Russia or Poland or elsewhere, too hot to hold him. These were the first Cossacks of the Ukraine. As time went on and the Cossacks became numerous, large portions of the fertile soil of the country were reclaimed, and a great proportion of the inhabitants gradually settled down as peaceful agriculturists, tilling their own land. Those Cossacks nearest to Poland became independent vassals of the kings of Poland, and were called "registered Cossacks," because their names were entered in a book as "subjects" of the Polish monarch, though they insisted throughout on their absolute independence, and their hetman or chief considered himself the equal of the king, and brooked no condescension or patronage from him. Towards the middle of the seventeenth century, however, the Cossacks threw off the Polish connection and espoused the cause of Russia; the tribe having decided by their votes whether they should enrol themselves under the protectorate of Russia, Poland, or Turkey. Thus the Ukraine became Russian territory, and the Cossacks, though "preserving their privileges," acknowledged the Tsar as their head.

This was the position of affairs when Mazeppa appeared among the Cossacks of the Ukraine.

At this particular juncture there were two hetmans, one being at the head of that larger half of the population which had embraced the protectorate of Russia; the other, chief of a portion of the Cossacks who still coquetted with Pole and Turk and Russian, faithful to none of the three, but always on the look-out for betterment. Mazeppa became secretary to this latter chief. In this capacity he was, a year or two later, despatched to Constantinople with letters to the Sultan containing proposals for the transfer of the allegiance of his wavering master from Russian to Turk.

But Mazeppa never reached Constantinople. He was arrested, papers and all, by agents of the Tsar, and carried off to Moscow. Here, by his diplomatic gifts, Mazeppa not only succeeded in exculpating himself, but contrived so deeply to impress the reigning Tsar, Alexey, Peter's father, with a belief in his merits, that both Alexey and afterwards Peter himself remained his truest friends and benefactors, in spite of every attempt of his enemies —and there were many—to dethrone the idol.

Mazeppa now realized that the Russian was the real "strong man," and that he had espoused the wrong cause. His late employer was arrested and exiled; but a place was found for Mazeppa with the rival hetman, Russia's faithful vassal, Samoilovitch, in whose service he so greatly strengthened his position that in 1687, when Galitsin returned from an unsuccessful campaign in the Crimea, and in order to shield himself threw the blame upon Samoilovitch and his Cossacks, who had been employed to assist him, Mazeppa found means to overthrow his late chief and to get himself elected in his place as hetman of the Cossacks of the Ukraine.

One of Mazeppa's first acts was to hasten to Moscow in order to assure the young Tsar Peter of his loyalty, and, if possible, to make a personal friend of the monarch. In this he proved so successful that, once having accepted and pinned his faith to the Cossack chief, Peter never could be persuaded to doubt his honesty, in spite of every effort to convince him of Mazeppa's perfidy. For many years there was a constant stream of correspondence reaching the Tsar from various sources, warning him of the treacherous disposition of his trusted hetman. All these letters Peter invariably forwarded to Mazeppa, with assurances to the effect that his faith in the latter was quite unshaken. Frequently the Tsar added that the Cossack might consider himself free to deal with his traducers as he pleased. Mazeppa was never backward in taking the hint, and many of his enemies were thus removed out of his way, some with great barbarity.

As for the rights and wrongs of these matters, it is impossible to judge whether Mazeppa was or was not so bad as he was painted. His name is execrated to this day in the national songs and ballads of the Ukraine, where his memory appears to be cordially hated, while the names of his enemies are crowned with all the tribute of honour and love that song can offer. An intimate personal acquaintance of Mazeppa has placed on record his conviction that the famous hetman was always at heart a Pole and detested Russia, and that all his life he was on the look-out for a good opportunity of casting off his allegiance, and transferring it to

Pole or Turk or Swede, as soon as any one of these should have proved himself the stronger man. At the same time, in justice to Mazeppa, it must be mentioned that he undoubtedly received more than one invitation from the King of Poland to break with the Tsar, and that he invariably forwarded such proposals to Moscow for Peter's perusal. Probably Mazeppa was a time-server, and was faithful to Russia only so long as Russia appeared to be the rock upon which his house was built. As will presently appear, he eventually, in his old age, made the one great mistake of his life, when his political sagacity, which had befriended him and guided him aright for many a long year, at last failed him and brought about the ruin which his treachery undoubtedly deserved.

Mazeppa received Boris with every mark of honour and respect as the Tsar's emissary. His court at Batourin was that of a king, far more luxurious and refined than that of Peter himself; and Boris was surprised to see the gorgeousness and magnificence of this man, whom he had been accustomed to think of more as a wild Cossack chief than as a monarch surrounded by every luxury and refinement of western civilization.

Mazeppa spoke with tears in his eyes of his love and devotion for Peter, and quite charmed the simple-minded Boris by his eloquent declaration that he would rather be the bear-hunter himself (of whom he said he had heard), and be ever about the person of that most marvellous man, his master, than hetman of the Cossacks of the Ukraine, honourable and dignified though the position might be.

To Boris's questions as to the forces at his disposal and their loyalty to the cause of Russia, Mazeppa replied,—

"My dear man, I have fifty thousand lances; and I would rather each one was buried in my own flesh than turned against the throne of my brother Peter. Why has he sent you? Does he not know that we are brothers, and more than brothers, and that all that I have is his?"

Boris was perfectly satisfied. He could not doubt this man, whose voice shook with feeling as he spoke, and whose eyes were filled with tears when he told of his devotion to the great Tsar, their beloved master.

Then Mazeppa entertained Boris with much talking, of which he was a master, and with a review of those fifty thousand lances of which he had made mention, or as many of them as he could collect at Batourin. Boris was delighted with their wonderful feats of horsemanship. Whole squadrons would dash forward at the charge, the wiry little ponies holding up their heads till their ears touched the Cossacks' bending figures; then, suddenly, every man would dip down sideways till his hand swept the ground, and again with one accord the entire body would recover their original position. Then a company would gallop past, every man kneeling in his saddle; followed by a second, of which each Cossack stood upright. Then a body of men would dash by, spring from their saddles while at the gallop, and spring back again. Then the entire corps would burst into wild, stirring song, and charge, singing, at an imaginary foe. It was a fine sight, and gave Boris much sincere pleasure; and he returned to give his report to the Tsar, convinced that in Mazeppa and his lances Peter possessed a friendly contingent which would prove of immense service during the coming Swedish attack. How Mazeppa acted, and what is the exact value to be attached to moist-eyed protestations of love and faith from a Cossack of the Ukraine, will be seen in the following pages.

FOOTNOTE:

Russian, "At the borderland."

CHAPTER XXX.

RUSSIA'S GREAT DAY.

In the autumn of 1707, Charles XII. made the first move in the great game which was to decide for ever the supremacy of Sweden or of her great rival of the north of Europe. Charles left his camp near Altstadt with forty-five thousand men, marching through Poland; twenty thousand were sent under Lewenhaupt to Riga, and fifteen thousand to Finland; in all, the Swedish king put in the field eighty thousand of the finest troops in the world.

Passing the winter at Grodno, Charles appeared early in the following summer at Borisof. Here he found a Russian army ready to contest his passage over the river Beresina; but he drove the Tsar's troops before him, and defeated them again at Moghilef, and a third time at Smolensk, which point he reached about September 1708.

He was now but ten days' march from Moscow, and there is no doubt that, had he pushed straight on at this time, he might have, as he had promised, dictated terms of peace from the Kremlin. There is no doubt, also, that the Tsar himself began at this period to entertain grave fears for the final outcome of the struggle, and made proposals of peace which would practically have annulled his successes of the past few years. Had Charles either accepted these terms or marched direct to Moscow, the history of Russia from that day to this would have been written very differently; but, fortunately for the Tsar and for Russia, he did neither the one nor the other, and the reason for this was the conviction of a certain individual of whom we have lately heard that the run of luck which had attended the arms of Russia had received a check.

Mazeppa, watching events from his castle at Batourin, observed with disquietude the rapid and victorious advance of the dashing young soldier whom all Europe at that time hailed as a second Alexander of Macedon. He saw his lord the Tsar, in the person of his advanced guards, driven from pillar to post, and flying before the soldiers of Charles like sheep before the sheep-dog; and the politic soul of Mazeppa quaked within him. Still he waited on, unwilling to take decisive action until there remained no doubt whatever as to the final issue of the struggle. When, however, the Swedish hosts arrived at Smolensk, Mazeppa deemed that the moment had come when it behoved him to declare for the stronger, and he despatched letters secretly to Charles at his camp in that city, offering to place at the disposal of the Swedish monarch his entire strength of fifty thousand lances.

On receiving this communication, Charles immediately altered his plans. He quitted the highroad to Moscow, and turned aside into the Ukraine in order to effect a junction with the Cossacks of Mazeppa.

This movement proved a fatal mistake. The Tsar had not been idle during the last few months, and though his troops had met with no success in their efforts to stop the onward march of Charles's hosts, Peter, with his best officers and an army of about one hundred thousand men, had still to be reckoned with before his Majesty of Sweden could carry out his threat of dictating peace from the palace in Moscow.

No sooner had Charles turned aside into the Ukraine, thereby exposing his flank to the Russian attack, than the Tsar saw his advantage, and hastened towards the Borysthenes, or Dnieper, with all the speed he could, at the head of a strong force of fifty thousand picked troops. His object was to cut off the main Swedish body from communication with the army of Lewenhaupt, which was hastening to join Charles in the Ukraine, at a distance of twelve days' march behind him. With this force was the whole of Charles's supply of provisions, upon which the Swedish host relied for its maintenance during the approaching winter. Peter, with whom was of course his faithful bear-hunter, in command of the Semenofski regiment, fell upon Lewenhaupt near the banks of the river Borysthenes. For three days a stubborn fight dragged on, and the brave Swedes strove to break through the opposing ranks of the equally valiant Russians; and when, at length, they cut their way through, and the general joined his master at the river Desna, he found himself at the head of but four thousand men—the rest of his army of twenty thousand fine troops being either dead on the battle-field or prisoners in the hands of the enemy, who had captured also all the guns and ammunition, and, worst of all, the invaluable convoy of supplies upon which the troops of Charles had relied.

This was a great day for the Tsar, and he celebrated his victory by a grand Te Deum in the cathedral at Moscow, leaving Charles and his famishing troops to winter as best they could in the Ukraine, in company with their perfidious ally Mazeppa, who, instead of fifty thousand lances, had provided but six thousand in all, the rest either preferring to remain loyal to Russia, or else joining Charles, but afterwards deserting. The Swedish army spent a wretched winter in the Ukraine, and Charles lost half his men by hunger and cold.

Before departing for Moscow, the Tsar demolished Mazeppa's castle at Batourin; and from that day to this, or until recent years, the name of Mazeppa has been solemnly cursed once a year in all the churches of Russia.

Mazeppa was safe with Charles, however, having discreetly fled before the Tsar appeared, carrying with him two barrels of gold, in which form he had consolidated the greater portion of his possessions.

The winter was spent by the Tsar, as well as by Boris, in busily preparing for the crisis of Russia's fate—a crisis which could not now be longer delayed, for the enemy was at the gates, and with the spring would commence to knock loudly for admittance. When the troops were collected and drilled into shape, Boris received a signal favour from the Tsar in the command of a contingent of these forces, which he was instructed to conduct southwards to Pultowa, a fortified city on the river Vorskla, which had the advantage of commanding the main road to Moscow as well as that of being close to the base of Charles's operations. Boris had charge of large quantities of provisions and ammunition for the use of the army during the coming season.

The trusty hunter safely reached his destination and took over the command of the garrison at Pultowa. And none too soon, as it turned out; for early in the spring Charles set out upon his march for Moscow, and as a first step towards attaining his end, invested the fortress of Pultowa, of which he expected to make short work. But Charles was not so intimately acquainted with the character of Commandant Boris as you, reader, and I; and all his efforts to bring the brave bear-hunter and his men to submission were unavailing. On the contrary, he found them perfectly ready and willing to meet him, in so far as fighting at close quarters was concerned, and many a time did the Russian troops sally out from behind their protecting walls and give battle to their assailants in the open. On one of these occasions, Boris had the honour of crossing swords a second time with his Swedish Majesty. The two men met at the head of their respective parties, Charles being, as usual, on horseback, the hunter afoot. Charles recognized his former adversary immediately. "Ha!" he cried, "Mr. Russian, we are old friends surely? There was a matter we left unfinished; come, lay on now. I am on horseback; you shall have the first blow!"

Boris did not wait for a second invitation, but aimed one of his bravest slashes at the king's head, which the king neatly turned aside, aiming a furious blow at Boris in return, which went near to lopping off one of the hunter's ears. Then the pair had a cut-and-thrust match, each laying on at his best, until something startled the horse of Charles and it swerved aside, just as the sword of Boris descended from a vicious sweep at Sweden's most precious crest. Most unfortunately for Charles, the sharp blade caught his foot in its descent and inflicted a painful wound, while at the same moment the horse bolted and the duel came to an indecisive termination.

On this occasion, as always, the sortie did no more than vex the besiegers, and the enterprising party of Russians were soon driven back. But Boris found that his men liked these sorties, as a change from the dulness of the siege, and he was not the man to refuse them their pleasure from prudential motives.

But the crisis was now at hand. In June, the Tsar, fearing for the safety of Pultowa, hastened to the relief of the garrison with a force of nearly sixty thousand men. He crossed the Vorskla and established himself upon the same side of that river with the besiegers, arranging his lines so that if the army of Charles should attack him and be worsted in the fight they must be driven back to the angle formed by the junction of the Vorskla and the Borysthenes. Here he strengthened his position with redoubts mounted with heavy artillery, and awaited developments; which he could afford to do, for his troops were amply supplied with provisions and ammunition, whereas what was left of Charles's force—about twenty-five thousand men—were in a wretched condition by reason of the hardships they had endured for many months while roughing it in the Ukraine.

The proud Charles, hearing that Peter intended to attack him, immediately decided to take the initiative and be himself the assailant. Still suffering from his wounded foot, he was carried to battle in a litter, and, placing himself at the head of his troops, he advanced to attack the Russian redoubts.

It was scarcely a fair fight, for Peter's force outnumbered that of Charles by two to one, besides having the fortress of Pultowa with its garrison at their back. But so bravely did the Swedes fight that day, that at the first advance they reached and captured the first Russian line of defence, and were actually raising cries of victory when the Russians, encouraged by the Tsar himself, who fought all day at the head of his men, made a tremendous effort and put a new aspect upon the affair. Forth from the walls of Pultowa poured fresh masses of Russians, with Boris at their head; the Swedes, at the point of victory, wavered, but fought bravely on; the Russian guns redoubled their efforts and poured a rain of cannon-balls among the ranks of the assailants; Peter called upon his men to make their effort, and like one man the Russian host, singing their soldier songs as they went, advanced and drove the Swedes before them. In vain the gallant Charles was borne up and down the lines in his litter, shouting, fighting, encouraging; in vain Mazeppa and his Cossacks made charge upon charge—for, in spite of all his faults, it must be admitted that the hetman fought well this day and performed prodigies of valour. The Russians would take no denial, but marched steadily forward. And ever as they advanced they drove the Swedes before them; and ever as the Swedish hosts retired the star of Sweden fell lower and lower in the heavens, until, on the evening of Pultowa, it sank for ever in the waters of the Borysthenes.

Boris, as well as his master, fought like a lion on this Russia's greatest day. His great object during the fight was to come to close quarters with the traitor Mazeppa; but though he was able at one moment to arrive within speaking distance, he could not approach close enough to exchange blows.

"Ha, traitor and liar!" Boris had shouted, as Mazeppa dashed past at the head of his Cossacks, "is this your sworn love and devotion to the Tsar? Come and answer for your lies!"

"My dear man," said the courtly hetman, "the rats leave a falling house. Peter should have made a better fight last year. As for meeting you now, I should be delighted, but there is no time for pleasure to-day, I am too busy. *Au revoir!*"

Mazeppa certainly was busy, and it was no fault of his that his side failed to gain the day.

Soon the battle became a mere rout. The Swedes were driven steadily onward towards the angle of the two rivers; and here they were forced to surrender to their pursuers, though a few hundred men, among whom were Charles and Mazeppa, succeeded in crossing the waters of the Borysthenes. About ten thousand had fallen on the field or in the redoubts.

That night on the banks of the Borysthenes Peter pitched his tent in joy and gratitude such as no words can describe. Weary as he was with the tremendous exertion and excitement of the day, sleep would not visit the aching eyes or soothe the restless brain of the victorious Tsar, and he left his tent and strolled out in the quiet moonlight in order to breathe the cool air of night and enjoy the luxury of a little calm reflection upon the events of the day.

The July moon lay upon the face of the river, so lately crossed in hot haste by Charles and the traitor Mazeppa. What were they doing at this moment, thought Peter, and where were they, poor wretches?—hurrying on, probably, in terror for their lives, somewhere in the heart of yonder forest, their hopes turned to despair, their lives spoiled, the greatness of Sweden buried for ever in the reddened soil of Pultowa field; while he stood here and contemplated the same events from how widely different a standpoint! To them Pultowa meant ruin, complete and irretrievable; to him it told of a fatherland saved, of an empire whose foundations this day had been secured for ever, of the removal of an hereditary enemy whose existence as a first-class power in the north of Europe must for ever have hampered and prevented the expansion of Russia. And then, what a battle it had been! how his men had fought, and how Charles's soldiers had fought also, to do them justice!

As the conqueror thus mused and watched the moon's broad highway over the water, a man came up and disturbed the Tsar's reflections. It was Boris. He, too, was unable to sleep after this exciting day, and had wandered down to the river side to cool his heated brow in the fresh night air. Peter grasped his old friend's hand solemnly and without a word and wrung it until the bones crunched together; then he took the hunter's arm and walked up and down by the river's bank in silence.

"Bear-eater," said the Tsar at length, "God has been very good to us this day. The Neva is safe; we shall have the Baltic for our own. You have served me well, my Boris, both this day and for many a day—ask what you will of me!"

But Boris laughed, and said that he had all he desired and there was nothing to ask.

"That is well," said Peter; "the wisest man is he who is the most contented."

After a while the Tsar spoke again. "My Bear-eater," he said, "I am so happy to-night that I even feel glad poor Charles escaped; but not Mazeppa—not Mazeppa! Ha! if I had come within reach of the traitor!" Peter burst out laughing. "Poor fellow," he said, "poor fellow! he thought Charles was our master, my Boris—poor Charles the Twelfth—the new Alexander—who is wandering among the wolves and the pine trees, tired and cold and hungry, in yonder forest—poor fellow!" Then after a pause, "Can you sleep to-night, Boris?" he asked.

Boris could not sleep, he said; he was too much affected by the excitement and wild joy of the battle.

"Neither can I," said Peter. "Sit you down here and tell me a stirring wolf tale or two, or a bear story—something which will take us both from the events of the day. This will ease our brains, and we shall sleep after it."

So the pair settled themselves upon the bank of the Dnieper and watched the moonlight weld its silver ladder over the broad stream, and Boris told many tales of adventure—of Nancy's bear, and of his little Katie carried off by the wolves, and many others.

And when he had done, and glanced at his companion, lo! Peter—like that other monarch whom Byron describes as listening on this very night to Mazeppa's tale in the sanctuary of yonder dark forest —Peter, tired out with the joys and exertions of this great day, "had been an hour asleep."

CHAPTER XXXI.

PEACE AT LAST.

The return to Moscow was a joyous procession. Never had the Tsar been so merry, so indulgent to all ranks, and so absolutely free of all traces of his evil temper. Charles had escaped into Turkish territory, indeed; but what cared Peter for that? he was harmless enough now. As for Mazeppa, it was a pity he had escaped; but perhaps the Sultan would hang him, or if he failed to perform this service, likely enough the wretched man would save others the trouble by doing it himself! In any case he was out of mischief's way.

Peter offered up thanks for Pultowa at every shrine and church and monastery on the route to the capital. Further, he gave way to no excessive service of Bacchus during this time, but passed his evenings with Boris and others of his intimates in song and laughter and tale-telling, using the vodka in moderation.

Boris became quite an expert spinner of yarns, most of them about his adventures with bears, as befitted his title of the bear-hunter; but the Tsar himself occasionally treated his hearers to one of his own reminiscences, many of which were of stirring interest. He told, among others, of an adventure in the forest, when, having lost his way, he overtook a soldier, by whom he was not recognized. With this man he had sought shelter in a lonely hut in mid-forest, which had turned out to be the headquarters of a gang of murderous thieves. Here, overcome with weariness, he had fallen asleep in an outhouse, where he had sought repose in company with his new friend. The soldier, however, suspicious of the good faith of his hosts, had preferred to remain awake and watch. During the night, this brave fellow had protected his sleeping companion from the attack of five ruffians, who ascended the ladder one by one and were in turn despatched by the soldier as soon as their heads appeared within the garret window. The Tsar added that the man's conduct when he found out whom he had rescued from assassination was more ridiculous than words can describe, as was his delight when he received his promotion to the rank of corporal, together with one thousand roubles in cash.

Right glorious was the entry into Moscow of the victorious Pultowa heroes. The church and cathedral bells clanged; flower-decked triumphal arches had been reared in every street; gorgeously robed priests and bishops met the troops and chanted litanies of praise, and sprinkled the ranks with holy water; while the wives and children of the returning soldiers marched alongside, singing and laughing and dancing for joy. Nancy was there with her little ones, and Boris took both the tiny wolf-maiden and her brother upon the saddle before him; for the hunter was now a general of brigade and rode a fine black charger whose long tail swept the ground. The children chattered in English as they rode and told their father all the news—that Katie had caught a young fox at Karapselka, and mother had given little Boris a new pony from England which had run away with him into the forest and upset him into a morass, spraining his ankle, but he was all right now; with other information of a like nature.

Those were happy days, and there were happy years to follow. There was war, indeed, for Charles by dint of much perseverance persuaded the Turk to enter the lists against Peter and fight his battles for him; and adventurous war too, for the troops of the Tsar suffered defeat on more than one occasion in the disastrous campaign of the Pruth, where both the Tsar and Boris himself were once well-nigh captured by the Mussulman enemy, and Peter was obliged to surrender the fortress of Azof, the capture of which had been the first exploit of Russian arms under his flag. But in spite of all this, and of the fact that the Tsar was still unable, as the years went on, to conclude a satisfactory peace with Sweden, there was more peace than war during the five or six years which followed Pultowa, and the building of St. Petersburg was the work that occupied most of the sovereign's attention. The greater portion of his time was spent there, superintending the erection of fortress and city, and there he collected a large fleet of both British-made and home-built vessels of war.

Boris lived in the new city with Peter, his house being one of the very first to be erected. Nancy and her children joined him on the Neva banks, and soon became as ardent sailors as the Tsar could desire his subjects to be.

As for Boris himself, he had plenty of congenial occupation in endeavouring to thin the numbers of the wolves which infested the forests around, and even swarmed into the streets of the half-built city. Even as late as 1713, about ten years after the first pile of the new capital had been driven, wolves still occasionally entered the town and carried away children and women during the severe weather, when starvation made them bold; and many were the exciting chases which Boris enjoyed after such depredators, and many were the lives he saved of those who had been seized and carried off by the midnight robbers.

Little Katie, now aged twelve years, and her brother, had an exciting adventure at this time. They had been for a sail in the boat which the Tsar had given them; but the wind having failed them while still in the gulf, they were somewhat late in returning, and landed at the farther end of the city in order to avoid the necessity of rowing home against the current.

It was dusk of a September evening, and the streets through which they had to pass were unfinished and unpopulated; the open country, with the forest but a short distance away, stretching straight from the road on their right, while the river flowed swiftly towards the gulf on their left. Of a sudden they became aware of two gray wolves standing in the midst of the muddy road, blocking their passage. Neither child was afraid of wolves or of any other wild animal that breathes; but they were unarmed, save for the knife which little Boris, like a true son of his father, invariably carried at his side. The children stopped to consult: should they move on, in the hope that the brutes would give way and allow them to pass; or would it be wiser to retire towards the boat and row homewards, in spite of the current? The wolves, however, decided the question for them by opening their savage mouths, showing their business-like teeth, and themselves advancing, in order to carry the war into the enemy's country.

"Get behind me, Katie," said little Boris, "I've got my long knife; I'll take care they shan't touch you!"

But this was not Katie's way. She remained at her brother's side, catching up a thick piece of wood, one of many with which the ground was covered preliminary to road-making.

And now occurred a most unaccountable incident. The foremost wolf made a rush at Katie, stopped, sniffed at her dress, and slunk aside. The other brute behaved very differently. It sprang towards young Boris, who stood up to it and smote bravely at it with his knife, inflicting more than one gash upon nose and head and shoulder. Each time it was struck the wolf whined but came on again, until at length, having had enough of little Boris and his sharp knife, it too slunk away and joined its companion, and the two trotted off towards the forest.

Nancy declared, amid sobs and kisses, as the children related their story, that Katie could never be hurt by a wolf, for every wolf would know by some mysterious instinct of the relationship which her darling little wolf-maiden bore to his kind, and would not touch her. But that rude man, her husband, laughed loud and long at the very idea of such a thing, as I daresay my reader will also; and yet I am half inclined to believe in Nancy's pretty theory, for want of a better.

While at St. Petersburg, Boris took part, for the first time in his life, in a naval engagement. His rank in the navy was now lieutenant, and in this capacity Boris sailed out with the Tsar one fine morning in the flagship of "Rear-Admiral Peter Alexeyevitch" as the Tsar loved to style himself, this being his rank in the navy at that time. A Swedish fleet had been reported in the gulf, and the Russian vessels were now sallying forth to sight the enemy, and if possible to offer them battle. The Tsar-admiral not only came upon the enemy, but engaged and overthrew him also, capturing the Swedish admiral in person, together with a number of his ships. With his prizes in tow, Peter sailed proudly up the Neva and landed at the senate steps, where he was met and requested to attend and present to the authorities a report of his engagement with the enemy. After hearing this report, the senate unanimously decided that, in consideration of his services, Rear-Admiral Peter Alexeyevitch be promoted then and there to the rank of vice-admiral. Thereupon the Tsar immediately hurried back to his ship and hoisted the flag of a vice-admiral. Nothing in the world could have made Peter happier than such recognition of his services as a sailor apart from his position as Tsar.

Boris lived to take the chief part in many adventures both by sea and land. He slew many bears and wolves in all parts of the country, and went through more terrible dangers and sufferings during an ill-omened expedition despatched by his master against Khiva and India, than any which I have narrated in the foregoing pages; but the limits of this volume forbid me to enter into any of these, much as I should like to introduce my readers to the ambitions of Peter in the Indies, and the misfortunes which overtook his arms in those distant parts of the world. Perhaps, if the fates will it, I may find occasion to treat of these thrilling matters another day; but the moment has now arrived when I must describe the closing scene in this present tale of the Tsar's triumphs and his faithful hunter's adventures.

For many years Peter laboured his utmost to make such terms of peace with Sweden as should secure to him those solid advantages which his victories and his perseverance warranted him in demanding. But ardently as he laboured for peace, Sweden, beaten and subdued though she was, still held out for war.

At last, when the eighteenth century was already a score of years old, negotiations were entered into at Nystad which promised to bring forward a satisfactory result. In feverish anxiety the Tsar sailed daily in his yacht about the placid waters of the Gulf of Finland, on the look-out for that longed-for messenger-boat which should bring him the news that peace was signed. One afternoon, the Tsar, with Boris and one or two others, cruised thus close to Cronstadt, when a small vessel was observed sailing with all speed towards St. Petersburg, now the capital city of Russia. It was the messenger-boat, and on board was that treaty of peace for which the Tsar had fought and negotiated and waited for upwards of twenty years. With this priceless document on board, Peter's little yacht fled through the waters; and as it approached the mouth of the Neva it fired first one gun and then many, in token of the glorious news it brought. As the yacht raced up the river, banging its guns and flying every inch of bunting it carried, every gun in the metropolis responded, and every house mounted its flag and sent out its cheering contribution to the thronged streets of the city; for all understood the meaning of the Tsar's noisy little vessel flitting up the Neva in this way. It meant that war was over, and that Russia had leave to grow and prosper and develop. Oxen were roasted whole in the large square in front of the senate, and the Tsar himself carved and dispensed the meat to all who came.

In the evening a display of fireworks was given, and here again Peter, in his capacity of all things to all men, personally superintended the fun and himself fired off the rockets. The senators assembled and proclaimed new titles for their adored sovereign, the maker of Russia: he should be known henceforth as "Emperor," in place of Tsar, and to all time he should be called "The Great," and "Father of his People." That evening there were banquets throughout the city, and the joy of the populace was shown in every way in which a happy people can demonstrate their delight; for all were weary of war and bloodshed, and longed for peace as ardently as their sovereign himself.

Lastly, there was a grand procession to the cathedral of St. Isaac —or rather, this came first though I mention it last; a procession of a fervent, thankful population. The crowds in the streets all joined in as it approached them, and the Tsar walked with the priests and sang and chanted with them as one of themselves. When the procession reached the steps of the cathedral, and the tall Tsar stood upon the highest and faced the multitude, a great shout of joy and praise rang out, such as had not been heard in all Russia before that day; and when, the shouting being ended, the Tsar raised his hand and would speak to the multitude, all were silent to listen. Then Peter the Great raised both arms high over his head,—

"*Sursum corda! sursum corda!*" cried the Emperor. "Lift up your hearts, O my people!"

And all the people with one voice made answer,—

"We lift them up unto the Lord!"

THE END.

Frederick James Whishaw

Frederick James Whishaw (14 March 1854 – 8 July 1934) was a Russian-born British novelist, historian, poet and musician. A popular author of children's fiction at the turn of the 20th century, he published over forty volumes of his work between 1884 and 1914.

He was a prolific historical novelist, many of his books being set in Czarist Russia, and his "schoolboy" and adventure serials appeared in many boys' magazines of the era. Several of these were published as full length novels, such as Gubbins Minor and Some Other Fellows (1897), The Boys of Brierley Grange (1906) and The Competitors: A Tale of Upton House School (1906). Other stories, such as The White Witch of the Matabele (1897) or The Three Scouts: A Story of the Boer War (1900), depicted colonial Africa.

Whishaw was also one of the first translators of Fyodor Dostoevsky, the first in the English language. He had several of the Russian author's novels published between 1886 and 1888.

Frederick James Whishaw was born in St. Petersburg, Russia, to English-born parents, Bernard Whishaw of Cheltenham and Isabel Maria Cattley, on 14 March 1854; he was one of eight children. His family had been in Russia since the 18th century. Eight weeks after his birth, his parents moved the family back to Great Britain and settled in Paignton, Devon where Whishaw would spend much of his childhood. He was educated at Leamington College and then at Uppingham where became an accomplished sportsman and tenor. He was also popular among his classmates for the food hampers he often received from Russia.

At age 16, Whishaw left school and returned to St. Petersburg to work for an office firm. He spent much of his recreational time running and rowing. He also had a collection of verses, Loves of the Flowers, published in 1878. Unhappy with his occupation, Whishaw left Hills & Whishaw and eventually emigrated to England after his marriage to Ethel Charlotte Moberly on 30 March 1880. Their first and only child, Gwendolen, was born on 13 January 1884. Returning to his childhood home of Paignton, he began a career as a musician and soon became a well-known and successful tenor.

During this time, he also began translating the work of Fyodor Dostoevsky which was published by Henry Vizetelly between 1886 and 1888. His efforts eventually resulted in many of Dostoevsky's novels being made available for English-language readers in Victorian Britain for the first time.

Whishaw was soon inspired to try his hand at writing and had his semi-autobiography, Out of Doors in Tsarland: A Record of the Seeings and Doings of a Wanderer in Russia, published in 1893. A year later, he wrote his first children's novel, ***Boris the Bear-Hunter***, followed by ten more novels between 1895 and 1898, including his first collection of English "schoolboy" stories, Gubbins Minor and Some Other Fellows. These and other stories were published as popular serials in many boys' adventure magazines throughout his career.

His schoolboy stories were a mix of gentle humor and more serious themes of public school life such as theft, house matches, and other common behavior of the time. It was his Russian-themed children's adventure stories and historical novels for which he was best known. Several of these stories took place in other parts of the world, such as colonial Africa, as seen in The White Witch of the Matabele (1897), and focused on then-current events like The Three Scouts: A Story of the Boer War (1900). Whishaw also wrote several books on Russian history, most notably the well-received Moscow: A Story of the French Invasion of 1812 in 1905. He wrote his final novel, A Bespoken

Bride, in 1914 though many of his earlier stories continued to be reprinted for years afterwards. Whishaw died at his home in Slapton, Devon on 8 July 1934.

CPSIA information can be obtained at www.ICGtesting.com
Printed in the USA
BVOW04s0528120215

387449BV00017B/175/P